For Chris

THE GUILTY WIFE

NINA MANNING

Boldwood

First published in Great Britain in 2020 by Boldwood Books Ltd.

I

Copyright © Nina Manning, 2020

Cover Design by Nick Castle Design

Cover Photography: Shutterstock

A CIP catalogue record for this book is available from the British Library.

Paperback ISBN: 978-1-80048-135-0

Ebook ISBN: 978-1-83889-192-3

Kindle ISBN: 978-1-83889-193-0

Audio CD ISBN: 978-1-83889-248-7

Digital audio download ISBN: 978-1-83889-190-9

Large Print ISBN: 978-1-83889-716-1

Boldwood Books Ltd.

23 Bowerdean Street, London, SW6 3TN

www.boldwoodbooks.com

PROLOGUE

I stood at the top of the stairs and held my breath as my anxiety spiked and my heart pounded in my throat. But I could no longer hear the noise that had drawn me there. As I stood, my foot perched ready to take the first step, I wondered if perhaps my mind was playing tricks on me. Maybe the events of the last few days had finally caught up with me. But faces were hovering in front of me. Those people I had trusted. And those who I had hurt.

All those years ago I was trying so hard to make a difference in any way I could. But I was young. And I was foolish. I knew the past would never be able to bury itself, and I had not been able to rest for twenty years because the horrors of that day would stay with me until I took my final breath.

But now it was time to face the past head on. I tightened my grip on my weapon and began the descent to the kitchen. I knew I was now in grave danger. I knew that I had to protect my children and face the person who had found their way into my home.

1

I slumped in the corner of the pub as the Barenaked Ladies' 'One Week' pounded out of the speaker right above me. I leaned my head against the wall. The landlord had rung for last orders twenty minutes ago and had cruelly put the house lights on. The pub was still rammed full of punters, all soaking up the last precious minutes of the atmosphere, knowing there was nowhere better to be than here, right now.

I looked round at the motley crew of faces that surrounded me; friends I had known for a few years and who were my whole world. We were an odd bunch, brought together by the same sense of humour and the same hopeful outlook on life. The local pub, the Chambers, was where we all began to frequent when the park just didn't offer the same appeal anymore. The landlord and bouncer turned a blind eye to our age and we became part of the furniture. But we weren't lager louts. On the whole, we had always behaved ourselves.

I was just sixteen. I was liked by everyone, especially by all the lads – Minty, Dave, and of course my brother, Kiefer, who always had one eye on me, always checking. He was nearly four years older than me, just passed his driving test that summer. His responsibility for me was by choice; the lack of interest our parents paid to us created some innate paternal protection on his part, meaning I was always in the back of his mind. Is Frankie okay? Who's with Frankie? Is Frankie getting home okay? I always felt an aura of protection around me that I took for granted; my brother, the protector.

I had nudged myself right up against the corner of the booth, ready to fall asleep but too tired to make a move to walk the ten minutes home by myself, knowing Kiefer would be spending the night at Reese's folks' place.

'Alright, Francesca' came a voice. There was only one person who had taken to calling me by my full name recently. I looked up and suddenly the room, which had been stark and bright, became rosier and hazier round the edges. A smile exploded across my face and I felt every part inside my body light up as well. I sat up and focused on the familiar sight of Todd in front of me. He had been on the other side of the pub most of the night. He was older than me, like most of the crew here. He was even older than Kiefer by a couple of years and I really liked the feeling that a bloke who wasn't my brother took an interest in me. I knew him as Martha's older brother, a girl I knew from the pub, and he had always known me as Kiefer's little sister. But since I had turned sixteen, I had been placed in a different light as the lads had started looking at me with a glint in their eye. As if only now I had something extra to offer.

Todd pulled out a bag of tobacco and rizla papers.

I knew he would roll one for me.

Todd had long messy straw-like hair, and a fuzzy beard. It suited him, and I liked it. He wore green army combat trousers and Timberland boots. His skin was permanently tanned from the snowboarding trips his parents took him on over the winter. Last year me and my best mate, Nancy, were really into making friendship bracelets and I noticed how he still wore the three, which were now grubby and frayed, that I had given him, making my heart swell every time I saw them.

I knew that Todd had just got back from Glastonbury, where they had managed to jump the gates. I was quietly envious as I had listened to him at the bar casually boasting about seeing the Chemical Brothers and Blur and how he bumped into Robbie Williams. He had turned to me and quietly said: 'He was dressed like a chav and was acting like a right wanker.' And I had smiled, privileged to be the only receiver of that information.

'You'll have to come with me next year to a few big festivals, reckon you're old enough,' he said now with a small smile as his tongue slipped out under his hairy top lip and licked the top of the rizla paper.

I nodded in agreement, even though I wasn't sure how I felt about being alone with Todd away from the others. How would he feel if he just saw the rawness of me away from the safety net of our group?

The barmaid came over and collected the empty glasses from the table, clinking four in one hand at once.

'One more for the road!' shouted Martha, who had just arrived and had somehow sneaked herself in past last orders and was now chucking money at the juke box. She chose Mousse T., 'Horny', and the song blared through the speakers. Martha started dropping some choice moves and I watched with amusement as she moved around the pool table, causing a ripple of interest from the lads. I looked across the pub and saw that the bar staff had started dancing as they cleared and washed glasses. I even noticed Todd's foot tapping under the table and I felt a wave of affection for him.

I could see Kiefer stood on the corner of the bar with Reese and her friends; every now and then he would shoot me a glance. Dave, Minty, Nancy and a lad I didn't know were deep into a game of doubles at the pool table. Occasionally I would hear Nancy whoop with joy as she or Minty hit a pocket.

Even with the stark lights of the pub revealing the cracks in the walls and those punters who had had one too many and were looking the worse for wear, it was the only place I wanted to be. Our group was the best. The peak of Cool Britannia, Labour in power, everything felt right and good.

But little did I know that I should have appreciated those times more because in just a few months' time our lives would be completely altered forever.

2

NOW

I could feel a dull buzz in my head, and my mouth was a little dry. I had been feeling a bit stressed about the interview last night, so at least I had that excuse, this time, for another night of drinking alone. I didn't let on to Damian in the morning, though. He had gone to bed early, having fallen asleep reading to Pixie.

The last bottle of wine kept creeping into my mind and threatening to ruin the morning. But I wasn't going to let it. I was made of sterner stuff and I had been through worse.

I had entered the office suite on the fifth floor where Bliss was situated. It was an opulent building in the city centre and I entered with the firm intention of getting the job I was about to be interviewed for. But I had arrived feeling jittery and I was struggling to shake off the sensation. I could have put it down to nervous energy, because I was about to meet Mason Valentine, one of the most renowned businessmen in town. But it felt like more than that. I kept thinking about the corner of Bridgewater Way which I passed to get here. I had tried not to look but I had rubber-necked the whole way and I couldn't deny I was hoping to see a glimpse of the

person from my past. The memories were flooding in fast and I
needed to focus on my interview.

* * *

I looked out of the window and saw the sun was already falling low
in the sky. It was only just after 3 p.m. and in a few weeks' time it
would be starting to get dark at this time. Then the hardest day of
the year would be upon me once more. Only this year it would be
even worse, signifying twenty years of loss. He would have been
forty this year. I blinked back the tears that seemed to appear from
nowhere and distracted myself by wandering over to the water
cooler and filling up a plastic cup. I took a long drink and sat back
down.

Thoughts of the journey here filtered through my mind and I
tried to push them away. I needed to focus on the impending interview. But flashes of a sturdy figure kept entering my mind's eye. The
face of the person I had never been able to truly forget about. He
was a part of my past. Yet here he was, in my present, hiding in the
shadows; pulling me back to that fateful night. I had known he was
residing close to the Bliss offices. I had always avoided the area
when I could. Until now. I wanted this job more than anything, but
to take the job would mean facing the past. And maybe facing him.

I stole a glance at the receptionist. She was typing at a steady
pace and every time the phone rang, with a tone that was set to an
almost inaudible level, she answered in a low monotone voice.

I had checked in with her fifteen minutes ago and now I tried to
catch her eye to gauge if I might be going in soon. As she finished
the last call she looked up and gave me a sympathetic smile. I
wondered what she thought of me. Did she see a woman in her late
thirties trying hard to hold it together? I played with a stray piece of
cotton on the edge of my suit jacket; already I was regretting
wearing something that now seemed more fitting for a funeral as I

looked at the receptionist in her tiny Zara jumpsuit and gold stage jewellery. She looked every inch the twenty-two year old woman I would love to model myself on for a Saturday night out in town. If I ever went out on a Saturday night. I couldn't remember the last time I had a good night out, the sort of night where I wanted to cry with happiness because I was purely living in the moment. Instead, I just let the alcohol find its way into the home and I would often find myself drinking alone long after Damian had gone to bed.

There was a time when I loved my life. When I felt untouchable, invincible. I didn't care about what I did. I would get drunk, pass out somewhere and not care about my safety. Now I was scared of everything; of buses coming too close to the path where I walked with my kids, scared of the amount of unreadable ingredients in a shop-bought loaf of bread, scared of using deodorant for fear of inviting cancer into my pores. But most of all I feared losing touch with who I was. Which was why I was here today and allowing myself to feel judged by a receptionist who was born when I was nursing my first hangover.

* * *

I took a subtle look in my compact mirror. I had tied my dark brown hair back into a severe ponytail, and now, as the time was ticking on, I regretted doing it. I wanted to let it down, to feel the protection of it round my face.

I threw the compact back into my bag and began to play with my wedding ring, a rose gold band with sapphire green stones. It never seemed to sit straight, it always slid off to the left. As I sat, anxiously waiting, I twisted it back to the middle of my finger and wondered if the ring that never did quite fit was a representation of what Damian and I had become. I thought again about the person in the shadows and how they had once fitted so perfectly into my life.

* * *

'Mrs Keegan, you can go in now. It's Room Three, just round to the left there,' the receptionist said and I smoothed down my suit and threw my bag over my shoulder.

'Thanks.' I glided past the oversized desk she was cocooned in and where an elaborate display of white and pink lilies was situated just to her right. They were usually my favourite flower but suddenly the scent of them in my nostrils was too overpowering and I felt my gut tighten with nerves.

I walked around the corner, stood outside the boardroom, and gave a firm knock on the heavy wooden door.

'Come in.'

And I heard for the first time that deep modulated disembodied voice.

Him. The man who would change everything from that moment on.

* * *

28 October 1998

You didn't cry out; it was so sudden. That I must be thankful for, they say.

It would have been quick, they say. But all I have thought about, since it happened, is those last moments we spent together. How as I lay trapped, we were so close, close enough that we could have been tiny foetuses encased inside a womb. Safe and warm. Close enough that I could feel your breath on my face as your body emptied itself of oxygen. I lay there. I held your hand as you took your last breath.

I hope you know that I held your hand.

3

NOW

After finding out there and then that I had been offered the job I went straight out into town and bought myself a whole new work wardrobe. To hell with the cost. I had just received a huge pay rise so I would give myself the dignity of looking decent when I turned up for my first day. I bypassed my usual favoured clothes shop and stepped into a boutique store just off the high street. I had walked past it a thousand times or more, always curious to know what it felt like to walk out with a bag full of clothes.

Half an hour later, as I strode out of the store laden with three square paper bags, I knew what that feeling was. Guilt. Peppered with a tiny amount of excitement to have new smart dresses, skirts and shirts hanging in my wardrobe.

I can't say if it was him, Mason Valentine, who had spurred me on to want to dress differently. Perhaps it was the modern offices with relaxation pods in the common area or the subsidised lunches of organic quinoa and bang bang chicken. I can't imagine that it would have anything to do with the ocean-blue eyes or that olive skin with just enough wrinkles to suggest he'd lived an interesting and fulfilling life so far. An older man? And one fifteen years my senior. That sort of thing had never done it for me.

* * *

This was my third job in as many years. I had stumbled into marketing a while ago and spent the past few years hopping from one job to another between having the children, always looking for that perfect opportunity. My last job allowed zero flexibility for things such as watching the kids in a nativity or seeing them off on their first school trip, so I had taken up the job hunting again.

I knew who Mason Valentine was, of course. I knew he was fifty-two and that he had singlehandedly built his own empire of several successful businesses and social enterprises. He was the sort of person people always knew, even if they hadn't met him. I found it all extremely inspiring and a few months ago I had, without real-ising it, begun to align myself with him. I started by following his Instagram and Twitter accounts. I had no idea if he ran them personally or someone managed them for him. Then I began researching Bliss and the several charities he was a patron of. So it didn't come as a surprise when the job spec for a New Product Developer came to me via an email from a local recruitment company.

I knew I didn't have the exact experience, but it turns out Mason Valentine saw plenty of potential in me.

* * *

I shocked myself at how much I was taken aback when I first laid eyes on him in the flesh. I had seen him so many times posing next to other businesspeople on the back of a local magazine or on a social media site, or even sitting on his boat on his Instagram account, that it almost felt like meeting a celebrity.

I had entered the large conference-style office upon his command and was welcomed by the warmest of smiles as he sat at the head of the table.

If he knew that he had gained substantial status in this town, he neglected to show it. Instead he was charming and unaware, it seemed, of his own mystique and striking features. He was tall and slim, immaculately dressed in a grey suit that looked so soft that I felt an overwhelming desire to reach out and stroke it. Underneath he wore a white shirt with the collar unbuttoned. He had a smattering of salt and pepper stubble. His eyebrows cast down towards the middle and his forehead wrinkled; he rubbed his hand across his cheek as he looked down at my CV. It was a completely unconscious act that felt more intimate than it should have done under the circumstances. Then he looked up and shot me a smile that seem to come more through those ocean-blue eyes than anywhere else.

'You've some great experience, Frankie.'

He ran his finger across the stubble on his top lip, leant his chin in his hand and looked at me; his head was tilted and a small smile crept across his lips. I felt an exquisite rush of excitement shoot through my belly.

But the most unexpected element of the interview was when I told Mason about losing my brother. I barely even spoke of it to my own husband. No one had been able to extract that sort of private information from me so quickly. Mason looked at me and said, 'I can sense you have lost someone special.' I felt my arms and shoulders erupt into goose bumps. I had unconsciously allowed more of myself to come out than I had intended. But I felt perfectly calm. Mason knew I had lost Kiefer and that was okay. What I didn't tell him was that it was more complicated than that. That more lives had been taken and ruined that night, and it was all because of me.

I dumped the heavy shopping bags on the floor. Within seconds my arms were full again with a little body, his limbs wrapped round my waist and draping off my neck as my knees hit the floor.

'Mummy.' Maddox snuffled into my neck and then untangled himself from the grip that I hadn't even realised I'd enforced upon him. 'Come. And. See. What. I. Have. Built,' Maddox said with the intensity of a wild-eyed three year old. I picked up the supermarket carrier bags and followed my son through into the kitchen.

Before I had even entered the room, I could sense what was seconds away, the dreaded after school chaos. My eyes fell upon the usual scene. Damian sat at the table with his iPad open and scrolling; toys, jumpers and school bags were strewn around the kitchen.

Pixie sat on the stool at the kitchen island, furiously writing on a large piece of card. Pens, coloured pencils and shavings adorned the space around her.

'Mummy, I'm going to do a concert, I mean, um, I have been practicing with my guitar for weeks now and Daddy said I could, so can we do it?'

I shook my head with bewilderment, my mind suddenly in disarray as I took in the mess and tried to listen to Pixie at the same time. I placed the carrier bags down in the middle of the island. The sound brought Damian to and back into the room.

'Hey.' He gave me a tired smile that suggested he had found the last few hours of the day pretty hard. The familiar edgy feeling was creeping its way back into my system. The feeling that had been absent for the past few hours when I had been away from the house and from Damian. How, after so many years together, had I forgotten how to be around him?

'A concert?' I raised my eyes at my husband. He laid the iPad flat and clicked the screen to blank.

'Apparently,' he said, standing up, scraping the chair hard against the floor. I winced at the sound. Without noticing, he walked over to the kettle.

'Tea?'

'I bought this,' I said, as I retrieved an expensive bottle of red wine from the top of the carrier bag.

'Ah, celebrating or commiserating?' he said flatly, pausing with one hand on the tap.

'Depends how you look at it,' I felt a wave of apprehension fall over me.

I knew either way it was never going to be great news for Damian. He was officially a computer technician but hadn't worked for an actual company for years. He had managed to slowly retreat from the workforce, so subtly at first I barely noticed he had stopped taking on as much freelance work. Now he was the stay at home parent and had been since Pixie was little.

'I got the job.' I rushed out the words without any hint of emotion. It was the first time I had been offered a job on the spot.

I was constantly torn between the need and desire to be at home with my kids and my career. But I had got used to being away from them, and now the latter felt more natural. I knew feeling this way was wrong. But to be offered a new job with a bigger pay packet, more responsibilities and another step on the career ladder gave me the opportunity to smash through that glass ceiling, which most women at thirty-seven would kill for.

'Wow.' Damian looked at me, his eyes wide.

Was that excitement he was feigning? For the kids' sake?

'That's great,' he added.

I ignored his awkwardness at congratulating me. We both knew it was the most practical option while Damian decided what it was *he* needed to be doing, and the longer I stayed out of the house and at work, the better it was for all of us. In so many ways.

'Better open the wine, then.' Damian took the bottle and lifted two glasses out from the cupboard.

'Did you get the job, Mummy?' Pixie said with the high-pitched enthusiasm she had for most things in life.

'Yes, darling, I did.'

Pixie jumped down from the stool and wrapped her arms around my waist. 'That's great, Mummy, well done. Let's have a toast.' She laughed at her own attempt to sound grown up and took a wine glass and filled it with apple juice from the fridge. Damian handed me a glass filled with the wine that I had deliberated over for twenty minutes in the supermarket.

'Cheers.' Pixie led the toast and Damian and I followed suit, allowing our eight year old daughter to smooth over one of the many cracks within our relationship.

'Well done, Mummy,' Damian chanted.

I waited to see if he would address me, give me that look that he charmed me with fifteen years ago; call me Frankie instead of Mummy. I gave it a few extra seconds before raising my own glass and extracted my best smile, mainly at Pixie who stood so eagerly with her glass poised.

'Thank you, darling,' I said, clinking her glass, and she giggled in that endearing awkward way before sipping her juice like she thought a proper grown up lady might. I looked over to Damian, my glass still raised, but his iPad was already on and his head was bent. The familiar look of intent back on his face. I looked around the kitchen with a heavy heart and took a large gulp of wine.

5

NOW

I played that memory of Mason over and over as I sat in the kitchen with just Maddox on a bleak Saturday afternoon, ready to start my new job on the Monday morning. It had been over two weeks since I had last seen him, and I was feeling that familiar fizzing in my stomach at the prospect of a new beginning. I needed it now more than anything. The darkness had already begun to seep into the shorter autumnal days. I could feel the weight of its presence growing closer every day. As the clocks would make their way back an hour, so would the darkness coat the afternoons an inky black. Then I would be thrust back to that time when I lost Kiefer.

The prospect of a new job was a welcome distraction. I had just over a week's holiday left at my old job, so the manager had agreed on me finishing before the full month was out. I figured they were as keen to get rid of me as I was to leave.

But now I was trying to decide how to entertain a hyperactive three year old boy on a Saturday afternoon. Pixie was on a playdate down the road with her friend and Damian had 'popped out'. One of his many talents, to disappear at the weekend when there was family life to deal with. He dropped Pixie at the playdate, so I figured he felt this was his contribution to the day.

I heard the post land with a thud on the mat.

'Maddox, go and grab the post for Mummy, please,' I said. I didn't have to wait for him to jump up and scurry into the hallway, his keenness to appease his mama still spilled out of him. He was back moments later, envelopes of all shapes and sizes falling out of his awkwardly bent arms.

'There go, Mummy.' He opened his arms and the envelopes scattered around my legs where I was sat next to a pile of LEGO. I felt a sudden surge of love for my son, which started in my belly and ended in my chest. I puckered up for a kiss and he planted his own tiny lips on mine.

'Thank you, my baby boy,' I said and scooped them up and took them to the kitchen island. 'Can you build me a super big tower whilst I look through all these boring bills?'

I placed the bills aside and attended to a large white envelope which had caught my eye. It was what I thought it would be: my contract for my new job. On top of the three sheets of contract was a thick compliments slip with the name of the business – Bliss – in large gold embossed letters and then underneath:

Really looking forward to working with you, Frankie. M x

I looked at the sentence for a long time, possibly longer than any sentence I had read before, and considered the handwriting. It was long and sloped and suggested it had been written quickly, yet it hinted that there was some consideration in those words. I traced my finger over the ink, felt the rough texture of the paper. I looked at the one kiss, an x. Just a letter, but the very thing I added to the end of a text to my friends, even Damian, when I was caught off guard and I had momentarily forgotten his aloofness. Yet here was the same mark I left as a sign of endearment, posted at the end of a short note from a man who was about to become my employer. Then I was thrust back to the room where I had been with Mason just a few weeks ago. A room that was so large, with a central mahogany table, that it could easily seat twenty, yet he insisted I take the seat to the right of his. At one point I had felt comfortable enough to stretch my legs out and I felt my shoe meet his. He acted as though he hadn't noticed. But I felt something shift in the atmosphere and I sensed he had too.

* * *

I was just about to start flicking through the contract when I heard a loud clatter coming from the direction of the front door. I put the pages down on the island counter.

'Stay here, poppet,' I said to Maddox and headed cautiously for the front door. I peered through the peep hole and couldn't see anyone there. I was curious to see what had caused the ruckus, but I could feel my skin prickling, and my heart rate had increased. I pulled the door back slowly, trying to brace myself for what I could only presume would be danger. Over the years I had surprised myself with just how many eventualities I could envisage happening to me or my family. Some might say it comes with the stress and responsibility of becoming a parent. I knew my insecurities stemmed from expecting tragedy to strike at any moment. I was still learning how to adapt.

I inched the door open, hoping a reflex action allowing me to slam the door closed at any moment wouldn't fail me, but then my eyes struggled to take in several things in front of me. To my right, one of a pair of metre high potted bay trees was now a smashed mess on the floor. The pot was broken, and the soil was scattered around it. The sturdy tree still looked intact. Then my gaze settled on the object that was right in the centre of the top step, almost at my feet. I hadn't noticed it at first because of the fallen potted tree. I could see it was a toy car of some sort. My first thought was that Maddox had dropped it outside our gate and a passer by had brought it to the step. It didn't explain their haste and clumsiness in doing so. But as I crouched down, bringing myself closer to it, I could see that it wasn't one of Maddox's toy cars. A cold sweat swept over my body and a retch erupted in my throat. I would recognise that car anywhere. It was an old green vintage 1969 Mini. The exact same model of car that my brother Kiefer drove. And the very car we were both in the night he died.

6

JULY 1998

It had been a particularly hot summer already. I would be starting a business communications course at my local college after the holidays, but right now there were six long weeks ahead of me.

We had all gathered in the local gardens near the bandstand, where a small summer music festival was to take place. It was barely lunchtime, but we had a bag of cold beers, and someone was passing a spliff around. Nancy was lying down, her head in my lap. Her blonde curly bobbed hair was accessorised with a yellow daisy clip on either side of her head and I could smell the coconut from her conditioner mingling with the warm afternoon breeze. There was a CD Walkman on the grass next to us; we each had an earphone and were listening to Bob Marley's, 'Three Little Birds'. We were free from the shackles of school, education and exams.

A few more people joined us. Minty arrived in his trademark black Diesel baseball cap and white t-shirt with combat shorts. He was mocking Dave's curly blond locks. Dave was far too pretty to be hanging around with us lot. He was the only one who had gone to a private school and would probably go on to do something spectacular and leave us all by the wayside.

As Minty got settled next to Nancy, taking over my turn with the second earphone, and Dave started skinning up, Reese and Kiefer arrived. Reese had been dating my brother for about six months. You could see how madly in love they were but it didn't take any of his attention away from me. I could still sense his attentiveness when the spliff came my way; he subtly watched to see how much I was taking and the effect it had on me, without ever allowing anyone else to see what he was doing.

A band began warming up; the twanging bassline came through a small sound system and I felt the tingling effects of the spliff mixed with a few swigs of beer. Everyone was lying on the grass soaking up the mid-July sun and not really thinking of anything beyond this summer.

Suddenly Todd was next to me, flopped down on his side, the familiar scent of soap as the undertone to a smattering of aftershave lingered in the sweet heat of the summer afternoon.

'Francesca,' he said quietly, so only I heard. My stomach did a small flip. I felt Kiefer's eyes on me, and I looked up to catch his mouth open and jaw tensely locked. I looked over at Nancy in her crop top and tight three-quarter length jeans showing off a newly pierced belly button, wondering if Todd would take some interest in her, but I barely saw him look at her the way the other boys did. Todd skinned up and passed me another beer. I could feel the looks from Kiefer growing stronger but I tried to ignore him. As I watched Todd rolling the joint I began to think about how he and I might be if we were together as a couple. The feeling was so novel that I found myself watching him more intently, the way his fingers worked the rizla paper as he lay perched on one elbow. I felt a flutter in my stomach when I saw how close he was to me compared to anyone else, and I allowed myself to bask in Todd's attention, despite Kiefer's disapproving glare.

After another beer and a spliff, Todd leant over and whispered, 'I've got to go, I'll see you soon.' The way he looked at me directly afterwards, a momentary glance which held so much promise. I felt a rush of desire, and I didn't want him to go. As I watched him stand and brush the grass from his trousers and say his departing words to the others, accompanied by a few brotherly handshakes, I wished he would turn around to look at me again. Most of all I wanted him to kiss me. But he didn't turn back and I had to watch, every inch of my body aching, as he walked away.

In Todd's absence the afternoon no longer bore the same promise. The air felt a little cooler and I found I could no longer immerse myself in the conversations I had been having with Nancy and Minty before Todd's arrival.

As I sat with my head tilted to the sun, which now felt a little cooler, I heard Kiefer's voice next to me.

'Just don't get too cosy with him, Frank, that's all. He isn't all sweetness.'

I dropped my head down to my brother's level. His almost twenty years to my sixteen years made him seem like the respected elder, and usually I absorbed his protectiveness. I would have done anything he suggested or asked.

But my interest was piqued by Todd, and there were so many things I was starting to love about him: the way his hair was on the verge of turning into dreadlocks and how he wore his clothes, layered and loose. I loved to watch him toke on a spliff. He always offered it to me before anyone else, so I got to feel the slightly damp residue from his lips on mine through the rizla paper. I had begun to recognise his distinctive walk from a mile away and my stomach would tie itself in knots as I anticipated his arrival. And so it was all of these things I was feeling and discovering that made me hear the words from Kiefer and then immediately push them from my mind.

NOW

Later that afternoon, after I had read and digested my new work contract and built endless LEGO spaceships, I settled Maddox in front of a film and found myself staring at the Mini car. It was coming up for Kiefer's fortieth birthday, and then after that the twentieth anniversary of the crash. Occasionally I would still see some of the old crew but most of them had moved abroad or to different towns. I still had Nancy close by. But there was only one person I thought about still, who haunted me from the shadows of the buildings at the top end of town. Thoughts of him peppered my mind daily. Even after twenty years, he was the one I thought about the most. It was a relationship cut short before its time, so I was left with a bitter longing, as though I had forgotten to do something twenty years ago and still couldn't remember what it was.

All I could think of was, why now? Why would someone wish to remind me of what happened all those years ago? My past was with me daily like an unwelcome travel companion. I was used to reliving the mistakes and feeling the regret; what was alarming was that someone now wanted me to know they were also thinking about it.

I tucked the car into a nook in the kitchen, ordered a new plant pot online and tried to push the nagging thoughts away. I found the enthusiasm to suggest a date night with Damian as a distraction. I texted him later that afternoon, proposing a meal out; my treat to celebrate the new job. I ended the text with a small lowercase x.

His response was brief.

Sure. You called the babysitter?

No kiss.

I called the girl who lived four doors down, Aimee. She was only sixteen, studying for her exams, but she had a certificate in first aid and religiously checked on the children every thirty minutes, even though we left the monitor on for Maddox. It was a total blessing she was so close and always available. And she seemed to relish the time away from her home.

Aimee answered in a breathless manner as though she had run to pick up.

'Hi Aimee, it's Frankie,' I said in my happiest singsong voice.

'Hi Frankie. What time do you need me?' Aimee said in a mocking tone that didn't seem quite right for her tender years.

'And how do you know I wasn't just ringing to say hi?' I mocked back.

Aimee let out a small giggle.

'Okay, you got me. Damian and I are going to go out for a bite to eat tonight, could you sit from seven?'

'Yes, that's fine. I have no plans.'

I felt a wrench of despair for Aimee, who by now should have a busy social life; God knows I was up to all sorts at her age.

My best friend Nancy was always offering to babysit. She now lived on the outskirts of town, in a huge detached house, with Harry, a divorcee with three boys. Nancy never had any children of her own. I always thought she would end up marrying Minty but he took off to France and still lives there running a snowboarding school.

But Damian never seemed to show much enthusiasm when I spoke of her. I found myself turning down her childcare offers because of this. To be honest, with Nancy you were never quite sure what might happen. It was like watching a clunky TV personality present live TV – there was always a sense that something awkward and embarrassing might happen. It usually did.

'No decorum,' I heard Damian mutter once when she catapulted herself into a slow moving taxi head first through the window on a rare night out together, whilst I stood on the pavement doubled over with laughter.

By the next day Nancy was a different woman, all: 'Oh my God, I didn't do that, surely?' Nancy was an extrovert who sucked the life out of introverts like Damian.

* * *

Damian finally arrived home just after 6 p.m.. I was grappling with thoughts of the toy Mini Cooper car that had appeared on the doorstep and whether I should mention it to him.

'Good afternoon?' I asked, not able to keep the sarcasm from seeping through.

'Yep. I went to that café on the high street, the juice place.'

I knew which one he meant. It was all organic fresh ingredients. Expensive. I knew I would check our joint account later to see exactly how much he had spent and then spend time weighing up his role against his frivolous spending of our surplus income.

'Did you get much work done?' I asked with a vagueness to my tone.

'Yeah. Yeah, I guess,' he said distractedly as he looked in the fridge. I could see that faraway distant look in his eyes was back, the one that suggested he hadn't been thinking about work. I decided now was not the time to bother him about a silly toy car.

Damian had an idea for an app. He began working on it a few months ago. I had a feeling he had lost momentum, the way he had done on many an occasion before. I valued Damian's role, staying at home with the kids, but I wasn't sure if I would prefer him out working and then have to leave Maddox with a child carer when he wasn't at preschool. Deep down I knew financially it made better sense for only me to be working until next year when Maddox started school properly, otherwise anything Damian earned would go straight back into childcare costs.

Staying at home with the kids, although he wouldn't like to admit it, was easier for Damian than trying to decipher what exactly it was he wanted to do.

I would often think back to when we met and how different things were. I was not long out of uni and had taken up a job working as a barmaid. Damian came in most nights with his friends, and after my seventh or eighth shift he asked me if I'd go out on a date with him. I was shocked into silence initially. His boyish good looks had caught my eye. Yet even though I'd had plenty of relationships at university, never once had I been asked if I would like to go out with someone. It was the kind of chivalry I was unaccustomed to. Up until that point, blokes had just presumed I would go out with them. He had a job as an IT technician in a high school, and not long after we met I began working in the bakery, so our days finished around five and we would both have the rest of the evening to ourselves. No playdates or after school activities, no separate meal to be cooked for kids, no clearing up all day after a pre-schooler and a tweenager. Just endless empty units to fill with activities of our choosing at the end of a working day and the week-end. We didn't know what we had then. All that time and no responsibility.

Damian was so full of aspiration back then. His was a bright light that burned out so slowly, I only noticed once the kids were here. Now there was no time to think about what Damian needed. I had my hands full.

* * *

That night we had headed to the restaurant in near silence. Damian drove. A strange system we'd adopted when travelling together. I fiddled with the radio for the few short miles, only just finding a song I liked as Damian was parking up. It was one we knew together pre-kids and I joined in with the lyrics quietly as Damian switched off the engine. I swung my head to look at him.

'Sorry, were you listening to that?' he said with bewilderment.

Damian, in our other life, would have sat and let the song play out, rested his head against the seat and looked over at me as we shared the appreciation.

'Not any more,' I mumbled to myself as I opened the door and stepped out into the cool damp night. I was savouring these last few weeks until the clocks went back and we lost the light in the evenings.

The drawing in of the nights brought with it memories far more painful than losing a few hours of daylight. And as each day it came nearer the weight of my past would hang heavier than at any other time of year.

* * *

Damian walked behind me by one step. From the corner of my eye I could see his face illuminated by the glow of his phone. I had started racking up the ways he had annoyed me so far. He was going to need to pull out a whole lot of charm over dinner to compensate for his ignorance.

* * *

We perused the menu probably longer than needed. I feigned interest in the specials board even though I knew I was going for the low-fat pizza and salad option.

'So,' I said as I laid my oversized menu on the table. 'How's the app going?' I had no idea what I was going to say to him when I began the sentence. Asking him about his project seemed to be the most appropriate way to start a conversation over dinner.

'It's really hard. I've been looking at funding options. It seems people are interested but they want a bit of investment from me.'

'Well, yes, it makes sense that people would want a little bit of financial commitment from you – it shows you believe in the product.' I adjusted the knife next to me so it was in alignment with the fork and napkin. 'Do you believe in the product?' I asked quietly.

A moment's pause and then I watched as Damian swallowed; an action normally so effortless suddenly appeared laboured.

'Yes, of course. I thought of it.'

A waiter swaggered past us and I raised my hand to attract his attention. He flicked his floppy hair to one side with one swift jerk of his head.

'You guys ready to order?'

Damian began reeling off his food order complete with sides and a beer. He continued staring at his menu as I gave my order with specific instructions for a Negroni just the way I liked it. The waiter gave a thin smile and flounced off to the till.

I looked at a painting on the wall, swirls of Mediterranean colours merged into a surreal impression of a sea scene. I could just make out a sailing boat, all twisted and contorted. I began to wonder what the artist was thinking when he painted the fury of reds and dark greens.

'Frankie.'

Damian's voice penetrated through my thoughts.

'Mmmm?' I looked away from the painting. The waiter had arrived at Damian's side and was placing our drinks on the table.

'You still love those pink drinks,' Damian said without a question as he took a swig of his beer straight from the bottle. My mind jumped to a story I had heard somewhere about the amount of germs around the rim of a glass bottle. That sort of information would have passed me by before.

'Why don't you use your glass?' I motioned to the heavily frosted tumbler.

'It will be *too* cold. Plus I like drinking from a bottle. It feels... nice.' Damian examined his bottle as though it were the most important thing in the room.

'Fine, enjoy the germs.' I picked up my Negroni and swirled it around in the glass. 'It's such a rich vibrant colour, you just don't see drinks this colour.'

'So you like the drink. It makes you feel "wow".' Damian put up his hands in a jazz hands style and I narrowed my eyes at his mocking tone.

I took a long drink and looked round the restaurant at anything other than him.

Eventually we began small talk about the children, Pixie's Egyptian project which needed to be made by next week and hadn't been started.

'She has one parent at home full time, there's no reason why her project can't be up there with some of the crafty mums' award winning masterpieces,' I said with exasperation.

'Oh, so just because I'm at home with the kids means I'm Mr Bloody Maker does it?'

'Well, no, Damian, I know you're not, but you have the time to experiment with a few things, get it wrong a couple of times, look at Pinterest with her after school. I don't want to have to start crafting a project when I get back from working a long week. This is your field.'

'I didn't realise we were on separate fields.' Damian swigged his beer.

'We are when I'm at work all day and you're sat at home,' I said, and I watched as Damian squinted his eyes at me.

I couldn't help but say it. I was rarely able to express my feelings on our setup. I usually refrained from speaking my mind. His look stopped me in my tracks and told me not to say any more. We both knew how it would end, not in a fight, but in Damian walking out of the restaurant and leaving me sat alone. And that was worse.

'And so, to me.' I raised my glass towards Damian who then lifted his beer bottle and gave my glass the lightest of clinks whilst we held eye contact for a second.

I took a moment to take him in. My eyes had become so accustomed to seeing him every day that when I stopped and really looked at him it was like looking at a total stranger. He had dark brown hair that he always kept fairly short and he styled it into a ruffled look. I often thought it was to make him seem younger than his thirty-nine years. He was usually clean shaven with maybe a smattering of stubble from time to time and religiously wore long sleeved sweatshirts of various neutral colours with low slung blue jeans. He had never gained any weight in all the years I had known him. Occasionally I would allow myself to search his face for that carefree boyish charm I fell for once upon a time. Some might look at his overall appearance now and consider him dependable. I supposed there was something to be said for knowing where you were with someone, even if things weren't perfect.

I took a long drink of my Negroni, then found the drive to praise Damian too. 'And to you, who holds the fort, does the dishes, keeps the kids alive when I'm not there.' It didn't matter how I worded it, it still sounded lame. I wondered if it would still sound as lame if someone was describing me staying at home and looking after the kids whilst Damian worked? I couldn't help but feel a flutter of relief that it wasn't me, that I wasn't left all day to construct more elaborate LEGO buildings, wipe sticky jam hands and walk down to the school and back in the pouring rain. I loved my kids with everything I had, but I was drawn to the organisation of a working environment over the chaos of the kids.

I was really looking forward to starting my job, but I didn't feel I could tell Damian that.

In the same way I hadn't ever told him everything about that night twenty years ago.

I had managed fifteen years with Damian and he never knew more than he needed to know. He saw I was fragile, but if he knew how much of that was a manifestation of my deep-seated regret, maybe he would see me differently. I wondered again about the toy Mini and who would have decided to remind me of it all again. Someone who was affected deeply by Kiefer's death? I thought of the one person who loved Kiefer as much as I did and how I was responsible for tearing that relationship apart.

* * *

Our food arrived and we ate in silence. At one point I checked in with Damian that his pizza was okay. He grunted his response back. There were never any complaints from Damian when it came to food. But then these days I rarely heard any complaints about anything. I knew that alone should worry me more.

The bill arrived and before I looked at the total, I noticed the date looming out at me in bold print. Time was a seamless event, never stopping for anyone, and these dates came round and held me hostage every year. I was never going to escape. I was still as trapped as I was that day.

* * *

30 October 1998

I find it hard to write every day but I do because I know it makes sense to. Although some days it is hard to do anything except crawl into a bed and block the world out. A kind lady from a charity gave me these books at the hospital and told me to write in them every day, or whenever I felt as though my feelings were starting to control my behaviour.

I have a few of them. All different colours. I have vowed to fill them all up.

I saw the therapist today for an hour. She reminded me of the importance of letting it all out. It's only been a few weeks since it happened, and I don't know what people expect of me. You were my life. You were all I had. It was always going to be us against the world. Ever since we were little kids, people expected to see us together all the time. And we were, often enough. Your friends were my friends.

I keep thinking back to how things were a few months ago and I can't believe so much has changed so quickly. We didn't have much, did we? But we made the most of what we did have. Friendships. We forged a unit. We would huddle together in a rugby scrum singing along to Oasis in a pub we were too young to be in.

It was the beginning. A year that started out with so much hope, but then you were snatched away in a heartbeat. And now my heart beats alone.

8

NOW

I arrived at the Bliss offices on my first day ignoring the buzzing in my head. It wasn't a good idea to drink the night before my first day in my new job.

It was agreed that my working hours would be eight until four so I would have some time to spend with the kids. But on my first day Mason had insisted I come in for 9 a.m.

I approached the receptionist, who eyed me for a second, then a flush of recognition flooded her face. Her lips were a deep red and the intensity of the colour unnerved me. I was suddenly thrust back to the final drink I had after Damian went to bed. I had felt such a warm sensation last night as the silky golden liquid slipped down my throat, yet this morning there was a violent pain raging inside my head, which felt as fragile as an eggshell that could break at any moment.

'Oh hiiiiiii!' She sang out the word 'hi' as though it had ten syllables and I winced and half closed one eye. 'I've got a few bits here.' She reached under the desk. 'Right, for you. ID card, lunch tokens.' She placed each item on the counter one at a time, her long manicured nails and chunky jewellery hitting the surface.

'What's your name?'

'Carys.' She smiled. 'Mason is waiting for you,' she added as I took the ID card and lunch tokens and put them in my handbag.

'Thanks.' I felt a sudden flutter of nerves as I walked around the curved reception desk to the corridor where Mason's office was. His door was closed so I knocked twice, loud and firm.

'Come in,' he said immediately.

The anticipation was building, and despite the threat of a hangover I wished more than anything that I had a drink in my hand. Before I was even through the door Mason was up from his desk, which was tucked in the corner away from the huge conference table, and was striding across the room to greet me. His easy manner eased my anxieties.

'Frankie.' He reached his hand out and I felt the warm softness of his skin on my hand as he shook it firmly. He looked at me and smiled, and I felt the pull from those piercing blue eyes. 'How are you, Frankie?'

I wanted to tell him I was hungover to hell, that I drank excessively from time to time and had done for twenty years and it was especially bad at this time of year when there was the threat of the memory surfacing.

'I'm good.' I laughed a silly laugh. I cleared my throat, 'Sorry, first day nerves.'

'Of course. How are the kids?' he asked.

'The kids?' I questioned. 'They're fine.' It felt strange to hear Mason, who had never met my kids, ask after them and to do so with a genuine deliverance.

'Good, good.' We walked next to one another along the corridor. Mason towered a full three inches above me. 'Has Carys given you all your bits? And lunch, you know, just take an hour when you want. Walk, read.'

We stopped outside the door to the main offices and I looked up at Mason. For a moment I forgot that my skull was pulsating like one giant nerve and I felt a rush of emotions tugging, terror and nervous energy, as he smiled down at me.

'Do you have kids?' I found the courage to ask.

'No. Never the right time,' he said with self-assurance and pulled the door revealing the open plan office. Immediately all eyes fell upon me. Some people waved and greeted Mason. I heard a few murmurs of 'Alright, boss' as we picked our way through the maze of furniture. My desk was situated near the back. A vast white counter with a large Mac and phone. Behind that was a relaxation area with soft furnishings and a coffee machine.

'I'm going to put you in the capable hands of Penelope today, Frankie, okay?' and as though he had called her telepathically, a skinny, austere woman of about five feet tall, with sleek straight black shoulder length hair, arrived next to Mason. She was wearing a plain white blouse buttoned to her neck and a black pencil skirt. She wore a lot of foundation and I could see mottled skin under the streaks of makeup. I ran a warm hand down my high waisted bell-bottomed trousers, then I reached it out to greet Penelope. Her hands were cold, and her grip was surprisingly strong.

'Hi,' she said in a meek voice. I couldn't gauge her age – her older face didn't match her tiny childlike frame.

'She's my right-hand woman, this girl. Been with me for years. I couldn't manage without her.'

Penelope looked fondly at Mason as he spoke.

'I'll leave you to it.' Mason turned to me. 'Frankie. My door is always open.'

'Thank you.' I held his gaze for an extra second. Then he turned and I watched him stride confidently across the room.

He stopped and bent down to say something to a pretty blonde woman seated near the front. I heard her giggle resonate through the room and I felt my gut twist as I eyed her with something that felt like envy.

I heard Penelope clear her throat behind me and turned back to her. She gave me a tight smile accompanied by wide eyes.

'Right then, let's get you set up.'

* * *

At lunchtime, Penelope and I sat opposite each other in the cafeteria. Penelope picked at a green salad and a strip of pita. I tried not to look at her, although so many questions were hanging off my tongue. She had a strange calmness about her that hinted more towards drug-induced than earthly serenity. I stole intermittent glances at her as I ate a cous cous salad. She had said very little, but the information I was able to extract from her was that she had worked for Mason at various companies for fifteen years, she was effectively his PA and the office manager, and knew her way around every system in the company with her eyes closed. I naturally felt inclined to ask Penelope about her home life, her hobbies and generally what it was that made her tick. She didn't have a boyfriend and had no children. Despite her childlike physique she was forty-two years old. She didn't seem to have any hobbies except online bingo. It appeared to me that Penelope led a very solitary and lonely life, and perhaps it wasn't what she had hoped for herself but she was making the best of what she had.

As we sat in the cafeteria, I felt a chill in the air. I looked up and noticed that the aircon unit was directly above me.

'Can we turn that thing down?' I said, pointing at the unit. Without replying, she reached to take the remote from the wall, and as she did I saw a smattering of healed cuts, ten or so, all different sizes and lengths, on her arm. I could tell they were old cuts, but the scars remained, dark and prominent. I looked at Penelope and thought about her life and suddenly I felt sad. I had seen the same cuts on the arms of Todd's sister, Martha, when things started to go wrong for her. And I knew that was how women like Penelope and

Martha dealt with the hurt and pain in their lives. Whilst I turned to the drink, others would cut until the pain bled from them.

* * *

As we sat finishing our lunch, a few people I had seen making eyes at me earlier made their way over and stood in front of us.

'You going to introduce us to your new mate?' said a girl with blonde curly hair. She said it with a smile, and when she did it revealed a full set of braces. She couldn't have been much older than twenty-five. Next to her stood a guy in a sky-blue shirt, immaculately pressed, his dark hair intensely styled to one side. I could see his muscles bulging through his shirt. He was eyeing me with intrigue.

'This is Lil.' Penelope pointed to the girl, 'And this is Fish.' She made the introduction with barely any enthusiasm, then returned to her picking.

Fish was straight in there, 'Hi.' He shook my hand firmly.

'That's quite a grip you've got there... Fish,' I said, experimenting with his name. 'Did your parents not like you?'

A flash of confusion swept over his face then he let out a laugh. 'My name? It's short for Fishwick. That's my surname. My actual name is Graham, but no one's called me that for years.'

'Yeah, under no circumstances must you call him Graham. Unless he's been really naughty,' Lil said, and reached her leg out to give Fish the faintest of kicks.

Oh, I thought, I get it. These two.

'Hi, I'm Lilian.' Lil reached out her hand. 'You can call me Lil or Lilian. I don't mind,' she laughed then quickly closed her mouth and smiled self-consciously.

'So, you're our New Product Developer then?' Fish said, making my job title sound far more glamorous than we both knew it actually was.

'Sure am,' I said with a wide-eyed smile.

'So exciting.' Lil gave a little shimmy. 'How is your first day going and is brainy box here showing you everything you need to know?' She gestured towards Penelope.

'I've been through all the software. We're just about to look at Trello,' Penelope said drolly, with a slow blink. Her laid back approach was still fascinating me and strangely refreshing next to these two who were like a pair of eager school kids desperate to be friends with the new girl. But I wasn't going to give away too much about myself. I didn't need to make friends here.

'Well, we'll let you get on. We do drinks after work on Friday.' Fish said 'Office shuts at four. I mean, you don't have to or anything, if you have kids or whatever, it's just a nice thing Mason does, he puts a few quid behind the local bar on the corner, the Chambers. Do you know it?'

I felt my gut tighten. Of course I knew it. It was where I had my first proper drink, where I had spent so many years laughing, dancing. That bar had given me so many memories, some I was still unsure how to process.

'Yes, I know it,' I said through a dry gulp.

'Great, hopefully see you there,' Fish said.

'Well, anyway, it's good to meet you,' Lil said in a singsong voice.

'Yeah, great to meet you,' Fish said and I was sure he winked at me.

As soon as they had gone, I looked up and there was a girl standing in front of me. She had vibrant red hair that hung loose and wavy all around her face. She looked like she was in a hair advert. She had strong features, big green eyes, a defined jaw line and a ring through her nose.

'Thought I'd better come and rescue you. I'll show you where we smoke.' She gave a small nod of acknowledgement to Penelope, then she flicked her head to one side to indicate that I follow. Which I did.

Outside she pulled out two cigarettes and handed me one. I thought for a heartbeat, then took it. I hadn't smoked properly for years, save for the odd one on a night out. I took the first drag as I handed her back her lighter and the memories came flooding back. All those long lazy days smoking in the park with nowhere to go, no need to be anywhere. No responsibilities. No one to think about.

'So, what's your story? What brings you to Mason Valentine HQ?' She blew her smoke out in one long trail and leaned against the wall. I still didn't know her name.

'I hated my other job, and there was no flexibility. I have kids. You need to be flexible when you have kids.' I felt as though I needed to reiterate that to this young woman who seemed so bohemian and free. The way I was once. I took a drag. I felt the head rush and then my body flooded with adrenaline, followed by dizziness.

'Stella.' She stretched her fag free hand over and I took it in mine.

'Frankie.'

'Short for Francesca?'

'Yes,' I said, feeling a warm glow at the memory of the one and only person who had ever called me that. 'I just need to stretch my wings a bit.'

'Yep, there's room for that here. Can't fault the room for growth. If you don't mind the noise. I mean, that office is like a soap opera on acid sometimes. The raging hormones, the sex scandals. You'll get used to it.' She looked at me. 'Although you look like you've been around. Not like that, in a good way. Like you've lived a life. I can see it in your eyes.'

I had to admire her perceptiveness.

And, of course, she was right. I had lived.

And I had died.

* * *

3 November 1998

I knew you were trying to go, so I pleaded with you. I think I actually said, 'Don't go.' But you didn't reply. Next to you in the car, we were so close, yet for a fleeting second I imagined a world without you. Now I know, by daring to imagine a world without you, it was me who put that in motion. Every moment we lay there was a moment you were leaving me. And I just had to wait. Wait for help to come. Why did it take so long? Why did no one come?

You went way too early. Before it had even begun. Is this the punishment, is this what we deserved?

I wasn't ready to give up, so why did you?

I came through the door, exhausted. I needed to either go to bed and crash or get myself a hair of the dog. I was just beginning to side with the idea that an early night might be in order when my phone buzzed with a text from Nancy.

How was it?

I quickly texted back:

A great day I'll fill you in later

Great I'll be over at 8

Nancy was notoriously reliable, and as much as an early night was calling, so too was a catch up with my oldest friend. I shook my head and chucked my phone in my bag.

It was eerily quiet. Where were they? I hadn't heard from Damian all day except for two words, 'good luck', in a text that morning.

I automatically called out to the kids first.

'Pixie, Maddox.' There was no sign of them in the kitchen except the usual post-apocalyptic scene. Discarded bits of toast and jam and empty juice cartons, bags sprawled on the floor with their contents spilling out.

Then I heard the cheerful whoop of Maddox, followed by Pixie shouting something to Damian, and I looked out of the kitchen window into the back garden. The sun was just beginning to go down and there they all were, playing contentedly on the grass. I took a second to watch them and take it all in. I allowed myself a moment of what felt like gratitude. Gratitude for my babies, for their health. I loved them with a furious love that I couldn't put into words. It was easy to forget they came from me, that they were part of me, sometimes. Well, more than sometimes. There was my family, living and breathing and I watched it through the window like I was watching a TV series, and from there I felt safe. From there I felt as though I could cope. If I could watch it like this all the time, instead of being swept up in the madness of it, it would be so much easier.

Then Pixie swung round as though she could feel the weight of my stare and before I knew it she was through the back door, followed shortly by Damian and then Maddox. I was no longer a spectator. Time for reality.

'Mummy, how was your first day in your new job?'

'Alright?' Damian walked over and gave me a half hug with one arm. He went to the fridge and took out a beer. 'Kids have eaten.'

I looked at the discarded toast on the counter, knowing I would be pulling out fruit and yoghurts within the hour to fill them up. I watched Damian open his beer and take a long slow gulp of it, and I wanted to delve into the bottle of white wine I had put in the fridge this morning so that I could celebrate my first day. But I knew I would have to wait another few hours until the kids were in bed.

'Was it a good day, then?' Damian followed up on Pixie's question.

'Yes, yes, it was great.'

'Did you make any friends, Mummy?' Pixie asked. Maddox was winding his leg around mine and hanging on to my arm, so I bent down and scooped him up. I walked over to Pixie and bent down to kiss her.

'Yes, sweetheart, I think I did.' I couldn't help but laugh. Being an adult and working was no different to being a kid at school. We still sought affirmation. But the thought of making real friendships at that office didn't sit comfortably with me. I wasn't ready to expose my vulnerability to any of them.

'It's good to have friends.' Damian said, half to me, half to Pixie, and I wasn't sure of the connotations of that statement.

* * *

That evening, Nancy arrived wearing her best smile and carrying a bottle of champagne under her arm. She was wearing tight blue trousers that were cropped above her ankles, a blue and white stripy body suit with ample view of her full bosom and white canvas wedge heels. She hadn't changed her style since she was sixteen. Her blonde curls hung around her face and I felt a sudden fondness for my best friend as I thought of all the years we had seen together. And here we still were, drinking and celebrating life.

'Don't worry, darling, Harry dropped me off and I have cash for a taxi so the night is ours!'

'It's a Monday night, Nance.' I protested as I popped the cork and Nancy whooped. Damian must have heard the commotion as he arrived in the kitchen shortly afterwards. His usual look of disdain on his face whenever Nancy was around.

'Hello, Damian,' Nancy sipped her champagne and gave me 'the eyes' that held mischief. She knew how Damian felt about her.

'Fancy a glass?' I said to Damian.

'No. Thanks. How are you, Nancy?'

'Oh, you know, Damian, hanging in there. Life's pretty good at the moment. Harry treats me like a queen so I can't complain. But it's this girl we're here for today, starting a job with the biggest business tycoon in town. So, Frankie, what's he like?' Nancy gave me the eyes again.

Damian went to the fridge and collected himself another beer. 'Have fun,' he said.

What a pointless statement. I couldn't remember the last time he was interested in whether I was having fun.

Nancy put her glass down and leaned forward on the island where she was propped up. 'So, what the hell is he like, Frank? I Googled him again, he is one hot mother f—'

'Shhh,' I put my finger to my mouth and whispered, 'The kids.' But the kids were fast asleep. It was Damian overhearing I was worried about. 'He's fine. Really nice. Friendly.' I said quietly.

'Friendly? What the... Did you not get a look at his crotch, what's his office like, oh, the thought of doing it in there with him.' Nancy rolled her head back and groaned. 'Come on, Frankie, I know you think he's hot too.'

I took a sip of champagne, knowing I was on my way to that better place where the jokes were funnier and life seemed much sweeter. 'Let's not get things out of perspective, I'm a married woman and Mason is my boss,' I said with a serious tone and a small smile.

'Ooooh, Mason! Well, he could boss me around any day. He's single, isn't he? I started following him on Insta. No kids?'

I shook my head and took a long gulp of champagne, feeling the bubbles hit my throat.

'Well, if you're not up for him,' Nancy said, and I couldn't tell if she was serious.

'Harry loves you very much.' I took the champagne and topped up my glass, for it was already empty.

'Sure, he does, I mean why wouldn't he?' Nancy gave her hair a pat and pushed her chest out. 'Don't panic, I'm not going to steal Mason off you, if that's what you think.'

'I am not bloody into Mason Valentine!' but even as I spoke those words, the image of his face flashed before me and something within me stirred.

I walked into work the next morning, my head feeling dense. Last night's hedonistic drinking was a distant memory, replaced by a splitting ache right in the centre of my forehead.

The office was empty and quiet except for Alan, the finance manager. Alan lifted his hand in acknowledgement from the far end of the office, and I waved back. I dumped my bag at my desk and headed straight to make coffee. I hit the latte button and listened to the comforting sound of the brewing and pouring out into a mug. There was a selection of pastries on a silver foil platter covered in cling film. My empty stomach gurgled as I peeled back the film and picked one out, grabbed my coffee and returned to my desk. I slid into my chair and took in my surroundings, trying to enjoy the peace and quiet and to will away the sensation that someone had opened up my head, removed my brain and replaced it with an iron dumbbell.

I was just taking a sip of coffee when I saw Mason striding across the room towards my desk. I did a surreptitious wipe of my mouth in case of stray milk froth and pastry crumbs.

'Morning, Alan,' Mason called over to the other side of the

office as he arrived at my desk. I sat up straight and hoped my drab skin didn't give away how I felt inside.

'Morning, Frankie. I see you've joined the early bird club with Alan over there.' He raised his eyebrows up and down once. It seemed cheeky and boyish and my stomach gave a small flip. The hangover I was nursing like a true professional suddenly seemed less intense for a second.

'Yes, good old Alan,' I said, aware of my own voice, which sounded a little shaky.

'How are you settling in, Frankie?' Mason swiftly pulled up a chair from the desk opposite me and sat down, confidently crossing one silver trouser leg over the other.

I paused for a heartbeat as Mason sat watching me and waiting. I felt my heartrate go up and sweat began to prickle under my arms. What did he see when he looked at me? I was able to hold it together enough in the interview to impress him, but could I keep getting through each day without breaking? I was struggling to cope with things and felt regret at opening the bottle of prosecco with Nancy after we had finished the champagne.

'I...' I suddenly lost my train of thought and struggled to unscramble my brain enough to speak a coherent sentence. 'There's a lot to learn.'

Mason smiled. He was so damn sure of himself. I was usually able to cover up my raging insecurities but somehow it was as though he were looking into my soul and I didn't have the power to stop him.

'Well,' he said after a pause, 'It will take you a few weeks to settle. But take it at your own pace. I'm here for you, Frankie, I can completely hold your hand through these first weeks.'

I felt my cheeks flush at the thought of Mason's hand on mine and I took a long sip of coffee to hide my face.

'I mean, everyone here is pretty helpful, have you found?' Mason tilted his head to one side.

'Oh yeah, yeah, absolutely. Penelope, she couldn't have been more helpful, I mean that girl knows her stuff.'

'I struck gold when I found her. I have a knack for sourcing the gems though.' Mason smiled. 'Listen, I'll let you get on and find your feet this week and maybe we can have a bit of a meeting on Friday to discuss this new hot sauce I want to start on. We need a really good name for it and a launch date.'

'Absolutely,' I said.

Mason stood to leave.

'This is going to be great, Frankie. I'm really looking forward to getting to know you.' He gave me a dazzling smile, showing me his perfectly white teeth, and he turned to walk away. I grabbed my coffee for protection and held it against my chest.

'Friday!' Mason turned as he was walking and pointed his finger at me.

'Friday,' I said with a salute.

* * *

The first week flew by in a flash and suddenly Friday arrived. There was a buzz in the office as everyone was getting geared up for the weekend. I would hear snippets of conversations and I thought about the stark weekend I had ahead.

So I immersed myself in the sounds of everyone else's plans and imagined myself in a world where Damian and I would come together on Sunday for a big lunch out somewhere with a forest walk, both the kids would behave and Damian and I would hold hands and argue over which Netflix series we were watching that night.

'Penny for 'em?' came the cheeky voice of Fish. I had felt Lil's looks all week as her boyfriend fluttered around the new girl.

I looked up from my screen and smiled at Fish.

'You ready for the weekend?' I asked him so I could swiftly swing the focus back on to him.

'Always,' he announced in the trademark overconfident manner that he adopted for almost all interactions from accepting a cup of coffee to conversations with clients on the phone. 'You coming for drinks in the Chambers?'

'Absolutely,' I said, feigning enthusiasm. Really, I wanted to go home, have a long bath, drink a bottle of wine and go to bed. The thought of being in that pub again after so many years was causing a dull ache in my stomach. But I had to make the effort, to mix a little of my personal self with the professional. I knew that was how I would win affection and respect. But I also knew where to draw the line.

'You'll need a drink, meeting with the big boss today isn't it?'

'Oh yeah,' I said casually as though I hadn't been thinking about it every second since Tuesday.

'You'll be fine.'

'I know,' I said a little too curtly.

'Coffee?' Fish was oblivious to the stress in my tone.

'I just had one. I'm a wreck if I have more than one in the morning.'

'Save the acting like a wreck act for tonight. I bet you're a bloody brilliant drunk.' His enthusiasm for life was admirable.

I laughed. 'Yeah.'

Although I wished more than anything that were true.

* * *

I'd arranged my meeting with Mason for 3 p.m., meaning as soon as we were done the office would be closed and I could head straight to the pub. I had texted Damian, told him I was doing the obligatory after drinks at the end of my first week, so he should feed himself and the kids. I thought about adding, 'I won't be late,' but I wasn't one for making false promises. I wasn't overly keen on drinking with complete strangers, let alone thrusting myself back into my past by heading to the place I drank as a teenager, but I knew after one drink I would be pretty relaxed.

Damian texted:

Remember you have that thing with Pixie in the morning

I resisted the urge to text back a smart-arse reply, but all I could think about was how he referred to it as 'that thing'. Pixie had her trial dance class tomorrow. But the fact was I could manage most things on a hangover. I was used to it; I had been doing it for long enough.

* * *

Mason's office was cooler than the main office and this time I was thankful for the change in temperature as I felt the nerves take hold of me. I had been subtly prepping all week, a few stolen moments throughout the day and each night after work, cradling a glass of wine.

I stood in front of Mason, my laptop grasped awkwardly under one arm.

'Hi,' he said.

'Hi,' I said.

'So...'

'I...'

We both laughed.

'You go first,' Mason gestured with his hand.

'I... I was only going to say, you know, thanks and everything, for this opportunity.' I shifted the weight from one foot to another.

'You're welcome, I want you to feel you can grow here.' Mason pulled out a chair. 'Please, do sit.'

'Thanks.' I slid into the seat and placed my laptop on the table. Mason took the seat right next to me. I turned to him and smiled. He smiled warmly back. Then he rubbed his hands together.

'Shall we get cracking? I don't want to keep you on a Friday. I appreciate you coming up with these thoughts this early on.'

I cleared my throat. 'Great.'

He looked at me thoughtfully. 'So, what have you got for me? I'm intrigued.'

* * *

Fifteen minutes later I closed the laptop and Mason sat shaking his head in disbelief.

'It's brilliant, Frankie, I can't believe you put so much work into it.'

I flashed a smile and breathed out a sigh of relief. My mind was now firmly on having a drink at the bar.

'Well done. It's like you went into my mind and read all my thoughts.'

Mason left the words hanging between us and I couldn't speak for a moment. I fiddled with my wedding ring, twisting it back to the centre of my finger.

'I can see a real passion for food in that presentation, do you like to eat out a lot?' Mason turned his chair inwards, so he was now facing me.

I found myself another hour later still talking with Mason about our past jobs, countries we'd travelled to. Our favourite foods and flavour combinations. He hadn't pushed for any more information on my brother, which I was thankful for. I had never spoken properly about that night to anyone. Not even Damian.

I was vaguely aware of the staff slowly filtering out of the building past the large windows of Mason's office suite, but I was engrossed in conversation with this man whose brain I was slowly beginning to love.

'You know, it is officially knock off time,' Mason said and gestured with his eyes towards a small fridge with a glass door. 'I'm going to have a small one, if you fancy one before you head off? I presume you're joining the others at the pub?'

'Well, yes, I thought I needed to show them how it was done, you know, as it's my first week and all,' I said, laughing. The presentation was behind me and I could now relax.

Mason laughed. 'Right, in that case, you'd better have something to get you ahead.'

Mason walked over to the fridge and opened a bottle of prosecco. He poured two glasses and brought them to the table. It was chilled and the first glass went down so quickly I barely noticed that he had topped my glass up a second time.

When I next picked it up, I was shocked to find it empty.

'Ahh, and there I was trying to be so refined.'

'It's okay, Frankie. You've had a successful first week. You should be proud.'

I cleared my throat. 'Well, anyway, I should get going.' I didn't want Mason to see beneath the veneer, to find that so many years of guilt and grief had seeped into my DNA so that I was barely the person I once was. I felt as though everything about me now was merely a projection of who I wanted to be.

I looked down at my phone. Everyone would have left the office by now. I went to stand and instantly wobbled. I realised I hadn't eaten anything for lunch as I was so nervous about the presentation. Mason was on his feet in an instant and grabbed my elbow.

'Whoa there. Okay?' he asked, leaning his face towards mine.

I laughed it off. 'Yes, yes, just sat down for too long. I'm probably due a snack or something.'

'Yes, got to keep those blood sugar levels steady.' Mason let go of my elbow and pushed his hands into his pockets.

I picked up the laptop.

'I should get going then, let you get off. Any plans for the weekend?' I asked as I swung my handbag over my shoulder.

'I have a few engagements, nothing spectacular.' He shrugged.

I contemplated Mason's bachelor lifestyle for a moment. I imagined him with a faceless woman on a Saturday night, an arrangement that was 'convenient' for both of them. He didn't ask anything about my plans or home life.

'Enjoy drinks with the gang. Say "hello" for me.'

'I will, and thanks.' I wanted to add, 'for putting the money behind the bar,' but I guessed someone like Mason wouldn't want me drawing attention to such generosity.

I headed to the door with my laptop under my arm.

'Thanks, Frankie. Well done this week. I have really good feelings about this.'

'Thanks.' I lifted my hand in a small wave. 'Have a good weekend.'

I stole a glance back at him as I walked out of the door. Mason was stood with one hand in his pocket, his other was rubbing the stubble on the side of his face. He appeared lost, as though he wasn't ready for me to leave.

* * *

I cautiously strode into the bar at 4.30. Lil, Fish, Stella and even Penelope, were all huddled around a large round table. A few of the other staff were there too but I was yet to get fully acquainted with them.

Fish and Lil let out a loud roar as I walked in.

'Here she is,' Fish said in his loud confident voice.

I waved at them all and headed to the bar. I took a moment to take in my surroundings. The place had changed a lot since I had last come in, which was almost twenty years ago. They had refurbished it to a really high standard with tanned leather sofas, an extensive dining area and barrel chairs in deep shades of green positioned next to coffee tables and well-stacked bookcases.

I swung a look to my right and saw that the pool table was still there. I could tell it wasn't the original but still, for a second, I saw us all huddled around it, lining our coins up on the edge of the table and waiting for our turn.

'Long meeting with the boss,' Stella appeared at my side and startled me.

'Oh, hi.' I swung round to my left. 'Yes, we just ended up chatting about the new product, didn't realise the time.' I didn't know why I felt the need to justify my lateness, but I did anyway. 'That lot half cut already?' I motioned to Lil and Fish.

'Getting there. What's your poison?'

'Do you think they know how to mix a Negroni?'

'Nice.' Stella pulled an impressed expression. 'You can always ask.'

The barman appeared; a fresh-faced lad of about twenty with zero stubble and blonde hair slicked to one side. I gave him my order. He had a word with an older guy who was obviously the manager, then returned with the information he needed to make the drink.

A few minutes later I squeezed into a chair next to Lil, who had an arm draped theatrically over Fish.

Penelope sat quietly in her chair sipping a pint of lager. I smiled and she nodded back and continued sipping slowly whilst staring into the distance. She looked almost childlike cradling such a large drink.

'You made it then, Keegan!' Fish called across the table. 'Boss let you go, did he?'

Fish had taken to calling me by my surname, which made me feel like an inmate.

'Yep, it was tricky but he finally dragged himself away from me.'

Joining in with the banter was easier with Fish. I found him mildly endearing.

'Oh, yeah, I getcha!' Fish laughed a deep loud laugh and turned back to Lil. I caught Lil's gaze and I was sure I saw her narrow her eyes. I took a swift drink. It had been a long week.

'Well done for a first week at work,' Stella said loudly over the noise.

'Yes, you did really well, Frankie. It's a lot to pick up. Well done.' Penelope continued to stare into the distance. I watched her with interest.

'She's fucking weird,' Stella said out of the side of her mouth and I noticed for the first time she had a slightly soft Irish accent. I shot a glance over at Penelope, who hadn't heard what Stella said.

'You're Irish,' I said.

'Only when I have a drink.' She laughed.

'Right. A woman of many sides.' I said.

Stella raised her eyes at me. 'As if there's one side to you,' she scoffed.

I tensed up. How the hell could she see. I was trying to keep everything in and yet here˙ was this complete stranger who appeared to have sussed me right out.

I finished my Negroni in a couple of gulps. I began to relax after that and began receiving drink after drink from Fish, Lil and Stella until we had finished up Mason's weekly gift. Then we all opened our wallets and purses and then, well, I didn't remember much after that.

* * *

1 December 1998

Grief counselling. The very words cut through me. Why the hell was I having grief counselling? I shouldn't be grieving for anyone. I'm not

*married, I don't have any kids, my parents are still alive. I've been encour-
aged to keep writing in these books, to write this stupid bloody diary, to
get all my feelings out onto paper. Then I can keep them or burn them.
That's what Sharon said. She's the 'grief counsellor'. I wanted her to be a
complete arsehole so I could walk the hell out of that poky little room with
magnolia walls and an overwhelming scent of pine pumping from a
plugin air freshener. But Sharon is a small petite blonde lady with a soft
calming voice. She wore a rusty orange coloured roll neck jumper. I
wanted to hate her, so that I could leave after the first session and never
come back, but I found myself watching her and taking her in. I liked her
jeans and knee high brown boots and I imagined how I would like to copy
the style and reinvent myself. I never really knew how to dress. Fashion
was never my thing. I like to check other people out and see if I can
emulate their style.*

I barely spoke in the session. My mind was on so many other things.

*Everyone is scared and timid when they approach me, like I might
break if they say anything about you or how I am feeling. Then Sharon
quietly asked something I had never heard from anyone before.*

*She looked at me and asked: how am I going to celebrate my love
for you?*

It's only then that I broke down.

*Because you were my lifeblood and I couldn't go on without you. It
was as simple as that. Now you're gone, I realise I loved you more than I
loved myself.*

11

NOW

I opened one eye, but the pain seared through my skull like a knife. My eyesight was hazy. I could barely see. Then the panic set in. I was not in my house. It had happened again. As if things weren't bad enough between me and Damian, I had slept in a stranger's house. I couldn't remember how I got home, or how much I had to drink. I had a vague image in my head of being thrown around in the back of a taxi. I tried to sit up so I could get some perspective on my surroundings.

A small voice broke through my manic thoughts. I looked up and saw Pixie.

I said a million prayers of thanks to the universe in the space of three seconds. I was at home and in my bed.

'Darling,' I croaked as she threw herself on to the bed next to me. I pulled myself to sitting.

I didn't know how I got in a taxi, how much it cost or how I got through the front door. I looked down under the covers. I was still fully dressed.

'Mummy, you went to bed with your clothes on!' Pixie looked

highly amused as she tried to pull back the covers to get a better look.

'Yes, darling, I was so tired last night after work I fell straight to sleep.'

I heard a loud snort coming from our en suite and I could just picture Damian's face.

'You worked very late,' she said with a hint of interest.

I looked at the clock next to my bed, which read 8.06 a.m.. Still over an hour to go until Pixie needed to be at her dance class.

I heard my phone beep a text message and I looked around the room until I spotted it on the floor.

'Pixie, be a doll and grab Mummy's phone.' Pixie obediently jumped off the bed and retrieved it from the floor. She handed it to me then planted a huge kiss on my head, complete with sound effects. I felt like the worst mother. I wanted to just grab Pixie and wrap her into the bed clothes with me and stay there all day.

'Are you ready to go, sweetheart?' I said as I navigated my way into my text message.

My mouth went dry. My heart rate sped up. My mind was going into overdrive trying to fathom out the meaning of the words I was seeing and why I didn't have the number saved.

'Mum!' Pixie's exasperated voice filtered through, but I still couldn't tear my eyes away from the message.

'You won't get much out of your mum today, she has a poorly head.' Damian emerged from the en suite, dripping, wrapped in a towel.

'Yes, sweetie,' I said, finally looking up from the screen but still seeing the words in front of my eyes.

'My black leotard, you said you'd buy one.'

My heart pounded hard. Did I buy the damn leotard? Then relief. Sheer relief. Yes, I did. 'It's in my car, sweetie, in the boot.' I had raced out and bought it on my lunch break yesterday.

'And where is your car, Frank?' Damian said with an air of superiority.

Shit. Damn. The car was in the staff car park behind the Bliss offices.

'Pixie, darling.' Pixie looked obviously forlorn. 'I'm so sorry, sweetie. I'll make it up to you later. I'll take you to that café you like and you can get one of those ridiculous milkshakes with cakes on them.' I tried desperately not to return to my phone and study the cryptic message that was plaguing my mind.

I hated winning with sugar, but it was the only hand I had to play.

'Go and pop your vest and leggings on then and that will have to do for today. I'm sure the teacher won't mind for the first lesson.'

Pixie dutifully hopped off the bed and trotted out of the door.

I could feel the weight of Damian's disappointment.

'Good night was it last night, then? Worth waking the whole house up at 3 a.m.?'

'What?' I snapped. I knew this was nonsense because Pixie would have mentioned it. If she is woken by anything in the night we are put through a long description of it the next morning. Even if she has a vivid dream, we get to hear the full theatrical version.

'That's rubbish and you know it,' I said, still itching to get back to my phone. 'I presume I lost my keys and you had to let me in.'

'No, Frankie, it was far more dramatic than that,' Damian said, pulling on jeans and a t-shirt.

I could feel myself burning up with fury. He was enjoying this too much.

'I was woken up by the doorbell, yes, but it wasn't you. No, it was a very nice man who drives for the taxi firm. He asked me if I would come and remove the unconscious woman from the back of his car before he dropped you outside the local hospital.'

'Unconscious?' I stared at Damian. But I knew he was speaking the truth. Before the kids came along I would often wander off on a night out and he wouldn't see me until the next morning. The next day I would crawl into our flat looking like a waif and stray, feeling like hell with a mouth full of things I wanted to say but unable to release them. Then a few days later I would mumble a half apology. It had been years since the last time. The horrific thing was I had no idea of anything after the free drinks had ended last night, and that would have been at around 9 p.m.. So, I had lost a whole six hours. But I didn't dare tell Damian that.

'I was just tired, Damian. I had finished a week in a brand new job that's *bloody* hard. I passed out in the taxi. Big deal.'

Damian ruffled his hair dry with a towel. 'You need to get help, Frankie. Not for the drink, the drink is just the cover up. For what's really going on inside. You need to talk to someone about Kiefer. And about the other person who died that night.'

'Don't you dare...' I shouted, but I couldn't even finish the sentence.

Damian dropped the towel by his side, pulled his lips together and looked at me solemnly.

'It's been twenty years, Frankie. Why do I feel as though there is so much you need to say yet you won't say it?'

I ignored Damian's attempt to dig into my past. He rarely asked about that night. Except when things like this happened and he began to doubt me all over again.

'I've done my therapy,' I said.

He stood the end of the bed and looked at me gravely. 'I'll take Maddox to the park for a bit while you take Pixie to her class.'

Damian pulled a sweater from his wardrobe and headed out of the bedroom.

I hadn't noticed the tears that were streaming down my face to start with and then my whole body was shaking with anger as I curled up into a ball under the covers.

Pixie waved at me from the middle of the room, looking self-conscious in her leggings and t-shirt. I cursed myself again for not having the leotard at home ready for her. I knew she was nervous. I gave her a wave back that was probably too enthusiastic but I wanted her to feel loved and that I had her back. Once I could see she had settled into a group with her teacher I took my phone out and brought up the message again. I hated being that mum who sat there with her phone, but I hadn't been able to stop looking at it since this morning. After I had finally dragged myself from under the covers to the bathroom, I had sat on the toilet seat and stared at the message before getting in the shower.

Hope you enjoyed yourself last night

That was it. No sign off or indication of who sent it. I had been thinking of how to reply all morning. Before I hesitated any longer, I typed out the words:

Sorry, did we meet last night?

I hit send. I didn't want to appear rude, as my memory of the evening was pretty shady as it was. If this was someone I met in the pub or after the pub then I need to know what I did and how they got my number.

Pixie came running over half an hour later for a drink from her rucksack.

'Well done, Pixie,' I told her. 'You're doing really well.'

She gave me a big grin and skipped back over to the floor where she immersed herself in a circle of girls roughly her age.

I was distracted once more by my phone. As I watched the seconds tick by with no reply I started to get fidgety. My hangover had come on thick and fast. The pint of water I drank before I left was not enough to shift the headache that was making my head feel fuzzy.

My phone pinged. I looked down and saw a message from Damian.

Hope her first lesson is going well. And that your head hurts

It was a sign that he had forgiven me, at least.

* * *

Pixie and I walked hand in hand to the café on the high street after her lesson, and I watched her indulge in a crazily high calorie treat. She offered me some and I gladly received it; the sugar would help my hangover.

The reply came just after I had taken a bite of the cake off the top of the freak shake.

You know me better than you think you do.

The cake in my mouth now felt too sickly sweet and I forced myself to swallow.

'I'm just going to get a glass of water, baby, want one?'

Pixie shook her head but I poured out two glasses of water from the jug at the counter and headed back to the table, all the time aware of my stomach growling. I hadn't eaten enough today and I felt sick.

My phone ringing startled me.

I looked down and saw 'Mum' on the screen. In a mixture of relief and anxiety at the prospect of answering I pressed the green button, wishing I could just feel one static emotion when it came to my family. I was always longing to be home, to be somewhere familiar, only to arrive and to feel angst fuelled with shame, and then a longing to be somewhere else, but I never knew exactly where.

'Hi, Mum,' I said, monotone.

'Hiya, love.' Mum spoke slowly and softly, the drugs that she has been on for years still slurring her speech.

'You ok?'

'Yep, everything is fine. I wondered if you were popping in today, your dad was asking after you.'

Mum couldn't say it herself, that she longed to see me, that she missed me. Instead, Dad, who had the onset of dementia, was used as a ploy to get me there. Just to check that she still had one child who was living and breathing.

'Yes Mum. I'll see you soon.'

* * *

Half an hour later Pixie and I arrived at the semi-detached house I had spent my childhood in and the nostalgia was palpable. I often questioned myself: after it all happened, why didn't I just pack up and move away? But I busied myself with finishing college and then the local university and before I knew it, I had met Damian. I often wondered what would have happened if I had left. How different my life would be now.

I walked through the door and looked at the faded red carpet my parents had had since the day we moved in when Kiefer was just tall enough to reach the door handles and I was still crawling about in nappies. I wiped my feet on the mat and walked along the brown runner in the hallway. Mum greeted me with her usual pat on my arm.

On the wall to my right was the photograph of Kiefer and I from our primary school days. We were all goofy, gappy teeth, starched white shirts and shiny blue blazers. My hair was pulled into tight neat plaits, Kiefer's was slicked to one side, our small round faces were pressed against one another. I stole a moment's glance as I always did, and felt my eyes well up with tears for a second at the sight of the two us. So innocent. So unaware.

We headed into the lounge. Pixie had run ahead and was already perched on Dad's knee. His face was illuminated with one of his golden smiles and my heart sank at the injustice of it all. I walked past Mum, who was fluffing up the already perfect cushions, and planted a firm kiss on Dad's cheek. He slowly turned his attention from Pixie to me.

'Here she is.' His smile didn't fade. It was strange how Dad's interest in me had piqued as his illness took over. He was never the sort of dad to show me much attention as a kid, but now, with the dementia slowly taking over his mind, he seemed to look at me with the joy and intrigue that one had for a baby.

'Hiya, Dad.' The sadness pressed against my chest. 'Have you had your lunch?' I motioned to an empty plate.

'Where's Kiefer then?' Dad looked at Mum with concern etched across his face.

'No, he had a flapjack. Do you want a flapjack, love?' Mum came up behind me. I noticed how she ignored Dad's question. It wouldn't matter if we sat and explained it all to him, he would be asking the same thing again tomorrow, she would say.

My mind was cast back to the sickly sweet 'freak shake' and the text messages on my phone from the unidentified number and I felt my stomach swirling. 'Er, no thanks, Mum.'

Mum turned to Pixie.

'And she can't have one either,' I said. 'Tell Nana and Grandad what you just had in the café.'

Pixie began describing the concoction and I sat down on the sofa opposite them and listened to her enthusiastic description coupled with Dad's cooing and ahhing.

'Is it nice out there today?' Mum looked absently towards the window.

'It's not too bad.' I sat back and stroked the fabric of the sofa.

'Going to start getting cold again soon, once the clocks go back,' Mum said with obvious deliberation. Her obsession with openly discussing this time of year far outweighed mine. I remained silent in the hope she would let the subject slip away, but I knew she wouldn't. She had that faraway look in her eye as though she were right there again. 'I still don't know why they have to change the clocks like that.' I wonder if she knew she was repeating herself, or if after twenty years it was inbuilt and there was nothing she could do but keep churning out the same words on a loop.

I wondered if she would ask me about my job that I'd been in for a week. Of course, I knew by now these conversations would never happen, but I waited for them all the same.

'My job's going well, Mum.'

'Well, you always were a clever girl. Cleverer than me,' Mum said dreamily, and I thought about the antidepressants and how much they had changed her.

I didn't have the patience to wish for more from her. I could feel the hangover shaping into something impenetrable and the only thing that would see it off was a bath and an early night.

Half an hour later I made our excuses and told Pixie it was time to go home.

I scooped up our coats and my bag, kissed Dad on the forehead and herded Pixie to the door.

'See you soon, Mum.' Mum followed us and I embraced her for a second.

'Yes, love. See you again. Take care. You'll have to tell me all about your new job next time. Don't work too hard.'

'Yes, Mum.'

I walked down the path to the car and felt the usual chasm of sadness open up within me.

* * *

9 December 1998

I feel most inclined to write this journal when I have had my counselling. It's the only time the feelings surface enough for me to need to write anything. It's as though the counsellor has got a stick and stirred it about in a pond and dredged up all the muck and debris from the bottom, I could wait until it settles again or I can pick it all out and put it in this journal. To wait until it settles takes too long, sometimes days, and I walk around in a fuzzy haze with a film of anger and resentment, so I've started writing things down straight away. Because this therapy is the thing that everyone has told me I must have or I couldn't possibly get over the fact that you died within an inch of my face. I will forever carry the grief that I was in the car when we crashed, trapped with you for over half an hour until the fire service could get to us. I guess the therapy is working. I couldn't speak those words before, let alone write them down.

I can begin to talk about it but it doesn't make me feel less angry. It doesn't stop the hurt or the fact that I'm here but you're not.

13

Damian had made dinner. It unnerved me at first, I couldn't remember the last time he cooked anything. My hangover had reached peak state. He looked sheepishly at me when I arrived in the kitchen, as though it was he who had behaved outrageously last night. It had been a while since we had been here, him creating something to smooth over the mess from the night before. I remembered when I would do crazy stuff when we first got together. I would sidle off somewhere for an afternoon beer with some of the gang who still knocked around, trying desperately to keep alive something that died the night Kiefer did. I would roll in at 3 a.m., a whole fourteen hours later. Perhaps Damian thought we were in danger of sliding down that slippery path again.

Food was the unspoken message; a home cooked meal in return for some stability from me.

'Smells good,' I said as I approached Damian's side at the hob.

Maddox was stretched out on the sofa in the kitchen watching something on the iPad. 'Thought you might need some carbs to soak up all that alcohol.'

'I'm fine,' I lied, knowing that all I wanted to do was collapse upstairs in a dark room. But I couldn't let my family see what last night had done to me. I was struggling to remember and that was the scary thing. I got too drunk, too drunk to remember the second part of the night and how I got home. And, most alarmingly, whom I had given my number to.

'It was just a few drinks after work, to celebrate my first week in the job.'

'Well, a spot of spag bol will sort you out.' Damian stirred and I watched him as he did, the smell of the sauce mingled with the scent of fresh linen coming off his clothes. I could see he was wearing a clean t-shirt, not the one he had been wearing that morning. I wondered if he had changed for me or if Maddox had spilt something on him.

'How's Maddox?' I motioned over to the stationary body on the sofa fully absorbed in the screen.

'Yep. All good. He went over to Cody's house this afternoon for a couple of hours.'

'Oh, right,' I said, alarmed by the news even though Cody only lived two doors down.

'Yes, I had to get this proposal together, Craig has found me a manufacturer interested in designing the app, without me putting in any capital. I would earn back on a rising scale, as the app makes money.'

'Oh, wow.'

'Yep, pretty good, isn't it.'

'So, you stayed here to do that?'

'Yep. We were just coming back from the park and saw Harriet. She asked if Maddox wanted to come over and so I thought great, gives me a bit of time to prepare for the meeting and make some dinner. So, grab a pew, it's ready in ten.'

Everything about the situation was ringing alarm bells. Damian's clean appearance, the smell of a fresh meal cooking on the stove, and Damian talking about his project so animatedly whilst rushing through the information about Maddox's play date.

But then I felt my head start to pound and I stopped over-thinking.

I sat myself down at the island in the kitchen. Damian produced a bottle of red wine and placed it near to me. He took out two glasses.

'Don't suppose you'll be wanting one of these, or is time for a hair of the dog?'

I couldn't decide if I detected a hint of malice in Damian's tone.

'Kids!' Damian shouted without waiting for my response. He put my bowl of spaghetti in front of me and nudged a bowl of grated parmesan my way.

The kids gathered round without needing a second or third call, and I really started to feel as though I was in a trippy dream.

Damian poured out half a glass of red wine and handed it to me,

'Here's to your first successful week at work. One can't hurt, can it, Frank?' Damian held my gaze as he raised his own glass to me. It was something we always did, always eye contact when we toasted with a drink. I held his gaze for as long as it took for our glasses to clink then I busied myself with cutting up Maddox's spaghetti. I was acutely aware that Damian's eyes were on me and that his overall demeanour had shifted, as though there was some sort of power trip going on.

In three gulps, my wine was gone.

* * *

After dinner, as the kids watched TV in the snug, I helped Damian load the dishwasher.

'I think I'll go for a bath,' I said to Damian, once the final plate was cleared.

'Okay. Thought we could take the kids to that new adventure playground tomorrow?'

'Okay, if you think it will be warm enough.'

'Yeah, it will be fine. Still got a few more days of light afternoons left.'

And on those words the conversation was hung. Was it the wine, the hangover, I didn't know, but I had a sudden urge to throw the bottle of wine at Damian's head. His words sounded callous and empty, the very use of them, as though he didn't know their significance after fifteen years together, ten of them married. At that moment I felt as though he were toying with me.

In just over a week's time, the clocks would go back and once again my life would be thrust into darkness and the thought of it made me want to run far away and find a safe place to hide until it was all over.

There was a rave happening next weekend. Everyone was going, including Todd. Nancy and I had already begun planning our outfits, even though it was over a week away. Then there was the question of drugs.

'Are you going to take anything?' Nancy asked as she paraded around in my multi-coloured halter neck top.

'I don't know. I'm planning to wear that top though, so can you get your sweaty pits off it.'

This was our first proper rave. Everyone would be on something.

I had yet to join them on that journey, but I felt as though next weekend was the time.

I pulled the A5 flyer out of my shorts pocket to look at it again. It was fluorescent green with a cartoon cat's head in the middle with really wide eyes, surrounded by the words, 'If you go down to the woods today.'

We all knew Brian, who was organising it. He was well into his forties and had been doing these events for years. He owned a clothes shop in town selling all the urban cool stuff I saw Todd dressed in. Todd dealt in a bit of weed which was how he made his money. He was the only dealer in our area and we were all his customers – he seemed to do pretty well and he could afford the clothes in Brian's shop, where t-shirts cost what I earned in an entire evening as a weekend waitress.

I held the flyer in my hand, knowing that it was Kiefer who had designed it on Reese's parents' computer. But he would never tell anyone. He had more talent than he allowed himself credit for. He seemed to do okay working in a warehouse. He and Reese were saving up for a flat. I was quietly envious of his studious nature which never really got noted at school but instead was overlooked by most of the teachers. Hence why he was skulking round designing flyers.

Reese lived in one of the bigger three storey houses at the top end of town. Her mother owned her own temporary workers' agency and drove a Toyota Celica GT. They never judged Kiefer or me for where we lived or the fact that Dad now claimed disability allowance for his depression and Mum had never really worked. In the end it came down to politics. We all wanted nothing but fairness and equality for all.

I folded the flyer and whilst Nancy was distracted, sifting through my wardrobe, I placed it in my bedside table drawer. I felt a connection to something that Kiefer had help create, even it was just a silly old flyer.

* * *

I knew Kiefer had seen something between me and Todd, but even I couldn't say what it was yet. Todd hadn't asked me to start seeing him, but there was something there, slowly unfurling like a fern in spring. It felt like it could be the beginning of something wonderful, and every time I thought about what that wonderful could be, I couldn't control the spontaneous fizzing in my stomach. I wondered if we would get a moment alone together next weekend, and maybe then something would finally happen between us.

Whilst Nancy continued rifling through my clothes, I had already made my mind up.

Even though I could hear my brother's protests ringing in my ears, I chose to wear the top Todd had commented on the last time I had worn it at a house party.

Todd said it accentuated my best features.

More than anything, I wanted him to see me in it again.

As I walked into work on Monday I heard my phone ping a text alert and I ignored it as I made my way to my desk. I felt shivers of mortification and the remnants of Saturday's hangover. A little while later, as the office filled up, I tried to catch everyone's eye to read what they thought of me. I had wanted to set a precedent for my colleagues to see me as someone to aspire to. So far I had failed colossally.

I couldn't remember anything anyone said in the Chambers, or for that matter what *I* said, which was more worrying.

Finally, with a coffee in hand, I pulled my phone out and clicked into messages.

Hope you're not feeling too hungover today

It was the same unrecognised number. My heart sped up as I realised that whoever it was had not given up.

Penelope arrived in the office after everyone else. She put her bag on her desk then came over to mine. She looked even more emaciated than she had the last time I saw her. I saw her flash her eyes up and down me. Even though I felt like hell I had managed to pull off a good look today and I was impressed that Penelope had obviously noticed.

I shoved the phone back in my coat pocket.

'Morning,' I said.

Penelope stared at me absently as though she couldn't remember why she was here, then looked at my computer screen.

'Thought I'd run through some more of the client lists with you, so they're not totally alien when we talk about them.' Penelope pulled out a rice cracker from her handbag and pecked at it, bird-like. I observed her as she ate, feeling nauseous. My hunger pangs turned to sickness pangs.

Her aloofness perturbed me. 'How was your weekend, Penny?' I tried to lighten the mood.

'Penelope,' she said monotonously.

'Right. Sorry. I just presumed...'

'Never liked Penny.' Penelope looked thoughtful for a second. 'I was called it by someone once. But never since.'

'Oh.' I was about to ask who, but I let the moment pass.

'Hey, here's a funny thing, you didn't happen to see if I was talking to anyone weird on Friday night?' I said instead.

'Apart from Fish?' Penelope made a sound like a snorting pig.

'Mmm. Yep. Apart from Fish.' I said, narrowing my eyes.

'You were pretty hammered,' she said, and I thought I heard something spiteful in her voice. It was too soon for me to have let my guard down like that. Penelope seemed like the type of girl to hold a grudge, and my behaviour on Friday night had obviously not sat comfortably with her.

'Yeah, right, I didn't really eat much that day. I had that presentation with Mason. I guess I was a little stressed.'

'Hmm.' Penelope seemed disinterested in my excuse and busied herself with bringing up the system we would be working through today.

'So, no weirdos circulating the area?' I said breezily.

'You really don't remember, were you that drunk?' There was an accusation in her tone.

'I... I guess I was a little.'

'There was this guy,' she said quickly.

'Really?' I felt my heart pounding fiercely in my chest.

'Uh huh.'

'So can you remember what he looked like?

'Tall. Blond. Gangly.'

'Gangly?'

'Yeah, like he was going to get his head stuck in the ceiling or something. Long coat. Messy hair.'

I felt my palms go sweaty and my mouth went dry. I thought back to the text message I had just read and then I thought about Penelope's accurate description of someone I had been avoiding for so long who resided in close proximity to the Bliss offices. We were living our lives a mere few metres apart.

I pulled in closer to Penelope.

'And you actually saw him. Did I talk to him for long?'

'Sorry, I couldn't say, I wasn't surveying you all night. I do have a life, you know.'

I laughed nervously. 'Of course. Don't worry about it. Thanks anyway.'

But I couldn't bring myself to think about training. I had an image stuck in my head. Of him. What did he want after all these years? Perhaps it was the same thing I needed but had refused to officially acknowledge. Closure.

'I'm going to get a coffee.' I stood up and headed for the coffee machine and Penelope gave me a sour sort of smile. I stood by the machine, lost in thoughts about what I needed to do and how I had been avoiding the situation for so long. Then suddenly I could smell him before I could see him. Aromas of sandalwood and citrus drifted my way. I felt the atmosphere physically shift.

I turned, and as I did he seemed to look me up and down in one swift movement, then his face turned to a look of approval.

'Morning, Frankie, how are you today?' Mason said.

'Yeah, good.'

'Can I get you something? A coffee?'

'Um, yes,' I said taking a step to the side, and letting Mason take over. 'I'll take a latte if there's one going.' Mason flicked his eyebrows up in a quick movement and his lips twitched into a semi-smile. Then he turned his concentration to the coffee machine and delivered my latte. I took the glass mug from him carefully so the transaction of passing the coffee took several seconds, and all the while Mason was close enough for me to hear him breathing.

'Can I get you a pastry with that?' His hands were back at the coffee station as though nothing happened.

'Erm, I... No, I shouldn't. I've got a banana in my bag.'

What did I just say? I felt the heat rising in my cheeks. A banana in my bag? Why would I tell anyone that, let alone Mason flipping Valentine?

'Thanks for the coffee though.' I raised my coffee cup to a 'cheers' and turned and went to walk away. I blew out an exhausted breath.

'Oh, Frankie?' Mason called and I turned back round to face him. He had one hand in his pocket and the other lifting the coffee cup.

'I thought we could go over your proposal again this week, nip and tuck it, fine tune a few pieces and try and get it to moving to the next stage of development?'

I shook my head in disbelief. I'd been here a week and already a product of mine was going to market?

'Shall we say Wednesday?'

I nodded, 'Yes, sounds good.'

He leant in closer and his aftershave was surrounding me. 'Let's do lunch, out. I'll book somewhere.' He whispered those last words as though they were just for me, and something roused inside me. I held on to it, but I also knew those words were already drenched in danger.

* * *

I arrived home to find the house empty, which was a surprise because Damian was never usually one for making plans after school with the kids.

I checked my phone to see if he had called or texted, but there was nothing. I walked round the house for a little while and then out into the garden and breathed in the chilly autumn evening air. I tried to live in these moments. In a few days' time everything would be steeped in darkness from late afternoon onwards, and when the world around you was that dark for so many hours, it was hard to keep living for the light.

* * *

I stood in the garden and tried not to see the amount of work that needed doing out there, the things that I knew Damian could be doing while I was at work.

Then I heard a shriek and instantly recognised Maddox's voice. I stood and listened harder. Then I heard a woman's laugh, and Damian's deep voice. I found a large terracotta plant pot, turned it upside down, and stood on it to peer over the fence. I could see Damian two doors down, standing in Harriet's garden. Harriet was all about the vintage. Today she was wearing a long ditsy print dress in a chic forties shape with delicate cap sleeves and a pinched waistline, which highlighted her petite figure. Her jet black hair was scooped up on either side, meeting in the middle to make a quiff. I found myself wondering just how long it took her to get ready in the morning. I knew she only had Cody, and that she was a single mum.

Looking over at them, what I found most alarming about the situation was how relaxed Damian looked, so different to how I had seen him in a long time. The blank look had gone from his face and in its place that boyish charming smile was back as he kicked at the leaves in her garden. His hands hung loosely in his pockets. He said something and she laughed again. He followed her into the kitchen. Maddox and Cody were running on the grass and I hoped that Pixie was somewhere in the house. I watched the boys for a little while longer, unsure if anyone was keeping an eye on them from the house. A few minutes later Harriet and Damian came outside again, both holding a glass of red wine. Harriet was laughing again. When the hell did Damian become so funny?

I stepped down from the plant pot and headed back into the house to sort out dinner.

I unloaded the dishwasher, put the sausages in the oven, began the onion gravy and was about to text Damian when I heard a commotion behind me as they all fell through the back door.

'Oh, hi, you're back?' Damian said with an air of bemusement.

'Yes, I do live here,' I said sharply.

'Yes, we know that,' Damian said, matching my sarcasm.

'Where have you all been?' I feigned ignorance, wondering if Damian would tell the truth but knowing Maddox would rat him out in a second.

'Cody and Maddox were having a little play date.'

'And were you on this playdate?' I sliced the onions and my eyes began to water.

'Yes, Harriet invited us all over.'

'Harriet?'

'Yes, Cody's mum.'

'Oh, yes, that's right, I always forget.'

'She's nice, isn't she, Maddox,' Damian said, ruffling his son's hair and I felt a stab in my gut. 'Come on, son, let's go and watch some TV,' Damian said to Maddox and I heard them both leave the kitchen.

I put down the knife and went to the worktop counter where there was some kitchen roll. I took a sheet and dabbed at my eyes and then blew my nose.

'Mummy, you're crying?' Pixie said and touched my arm.

'Oh, no, sweetheart, it's just those silly onions.' I shrugged off Pixie's words of concern and went back to the chopping.

The words Damian and I weren't saying had become an invisible barrier between us and I could feel their weight pressing down on me. I wanted to bust through it, shouting all the things I needed to say. Things I should have told him about the past when we first met, and how watching him laughing with Harriet made me feel like a small percentage of what I wanted to feel as a wife and a mother. I was trying so hard to do the right thing for both of us by going to work. But then there I was at Bliss not knowing what to do with this feeling that lingered whenever Mason and I were in the same room, and maybe it was something Damian and I needed to both acknowledge. Then deal with it. Or not.

What a mess everything had become.

My shoulders shuddered slightly as the real tears came.

* * *

13 December 1998

We didn't always get on brilliantly, there were days when I hated you, because you always thought you were right. I hadn't been respecting your opinions recently either but then why should I have lived my life according to your values? People expected to see us together so often but I was beginning to feel sick of it and wanted to break free, become my own person. I didn't feel as though you wanted me to do that. I never asked you why. Looking back, I didn't need to. You saw us as one and I suppose we were.

I never gave you the time to tell me, to explain why you felt you needed to keep protecting me so much.

I'm sorry I made you sad. I'm sorry I didn't give you that time that you needed to talk. I'm sorry I never stopped and listened.

Rest in peace, my darling.

16

NOW

On Wednesday I found myself on the top floor of the biggest hotel in town, looking out past the terrace and across the skyline. I had browsed outfits in my wardrobe at any opportunity, considering what I would wear for today. After I saw Damian chatting like a silly lovesick teenager with Harriet, I knew he was slipping away from me, so I wanted Mason to see me in the same way that Damian saw Harriet. I wanted him to see me as someone who was stylish, sophisticated and cool, the way that Damian no longer did. Perhaps I even wanted to feel attractive. I couldn't remember the last time I felt attractive.

Mason was coming straight from another meeting so I was able to arrive at the restaurant before him. I couldn't bear the thought of walking in with him watching me.

I looked around at turquoise heavy velvet chairs, dark grey wooden tables, heavily starched white linen napkins and a small blue piece of card with just a few choices of exquisite lunch delights. I decided on my meal so that when Mason arrived, I could say my selection without pressure. The waiter came over, and although I desperately needed a real drink to calm my nerves, I ordered a still mineral water.

I saw him arrive at the front of the restaurant. A waiter was next to him in a flash so he didn't have to do any of that awkward standing around that I had to do. I wondered if Mason Valentine was ever left in limbo, or did people like him attract so much attention that they never experienced an awkward moment?

I sipped my water and looked out of the window until I heard him.

'Hello, Frankie.' His tone was deep and soft.

'I didn't see you sneak in,' I lied.

Mason took the seat opposite me and smiled unassumingly. The waiter hovered for a drinks order. Mason ordered whisky on the rocks and a large bottle of sparkling mineral water.

'Thanks for meeting me,' Mason said. 'How are you?' He asked with the sort of sincerity I haven't heard in a long time, but I still avoided what he was really asking.

'I'm good, thanks. I'm loving the job—'

'I mean, how are you?' Mason said quietly but with a small amount of authority.

'I'm...' I twisted my wedding ring back to the centre of my finger. 'I'm okay.'

Mason adjusted his cutlery. He bobbed his head slowly from side to side and lifted his palms upwards. 'We all say we're fine, even when we're not. Why is that?'

The waiter arrived back and placed the whisky next to Mason, then swiftly opened the water bottle and poured it into two glasses. He placed the bottle down and left. I could sense Mason didn't want the momentum to waver.

'You're an enigma. There's something else you don't let out. I'm intrigued.' Mason sipped his whisky, the ice cubes clinked clumsily together as he set the large tumbler back on the table, half the contents gone. 'You intrigue me, Frankie Keegan,' he said again, and laughed so I felt I could finally smile back.

'So, what is it about you, Frankie, that intrigues me so? I can't put my finger on it,' Mason said.

'I didn't realise I gave off such a mysterious aura,' I scoffed.

'It's not so much mysterious. I don't know...' Mason shook his head and looked at me, his hand placed slightly over his mouth as he leant his elbow on the table.

His look lingered for another beat, then he cleared his throat and quickly picked up the menu.

I gazed at the menu. I could feel my heart thumping against my chest. I let my eyes cascade downwards.

'I think the chicken terrine looks good,' I said, trying to control my voice. 'And the seabass with samphire and spinach beurre blanc.'

Mason kept his eyes on his menu but raised his eyebrows at the speed of my decision.

'Great. Times two.' He laid the menu on the table. 'I'm going to trust you on this one.'

He leant back and did a nervous half stretch half yawn and I couldn't help but smile and let out a small laugh.

'What?' Mason rubbed his chin and for a moment he looked coy and I felt a rush of all the feelings I had forgotten about that had been lying dormant for too many years.

'Nothing. It's just nice. To be here, I mean. This place is great. Do you come here a lot?'

'Do I come here often?' Mason laughed. 'Now, there's a chat up line you don't hear any more.' He took in a big breath. 'I came here once last month with a friend.'

I felt myself almost deflate at the prospect of Mason with a friend who was at the moment in my mind absolutely female.

The waiter arrived to take our order and Mason accurately reeled off what I had suggested, along with a bottle of wine.

The lunch passed in a blur of wine with our food. When we finished Mason ordered coffees.

'There's a trip coming up.' Mason said. 'Belgium. Liège. I have a supplier friend over there. I didn't expect to have to ask you so soon into starting the job but I'd really like you to come, to see how it all works.' Mason looked at me. 'And to see how drunk I can get you on the super strength beer.' He laughed wholesomely. Then he shook his head. 'I'm joking.'

I felt a tingle of excitement at the prospect of time away. 'I've never been to Belgium.'

'Oh, you'll love it. The city is beautiful. We can do some sight-seeing. There will be plenty of time for that as well as the meetings. Do you think your family could spare you for a couple of days?'

'Are you sure I'm the one you want to take?'

'You're my product developer. And you understand the products so well already.'

An image of Damian flashed into my mind and then my body felt as though it were seizing up when I thought about all the unspoken words that had taken our relationship hostage. 'Of course I can be spared. I would love to come.'

Mason's eyes glistened as his whole face beamed a smile.

'That's great, Frankie. That's really great.'

* * *

We talked of everything and nothing. Mason was careful not to tread too close to the edges of my personal life, testing the water occasionally with a broad question to see how much I was willing to reveal about myself.

At the end of the meal, he laid his visa card out on the plate after glancing at the bill and we walked the short distance back to the office together. My head felt a little woozy from the wine as I got back behind my desk. It was only then I realised that at no point had we discussed the new product.

17

On Friday morning I padded downstairs and headed for the kitchen, and even through blurry morning eyes I could see there was a large blue envelope lying on the floor. I tentatively approached the mat and my mouth was suddenly filled with saliva, and I felt sick.

I picked up the envelope. My address was typed and not hand-written.

I went into the kitchen and laid it on the counter. It was still early; the kids wouldn't be up for another hour. But I had woken to a noise, now I knew it had been the letter box. I inspected the envelope more closely. There was no post mark. It was far too early for the postman. It had been hand delivered.

I tore at the paper.

The words 'Happy 40th Birthday' were staring at me. It was a very simple design with just the words in blue on a white card. I looked inside.

'Happy 40th Kiefer' was scrawled in big black capital letters, almost childlike, but perhaps because someone was trying to disguise their handwriting. My hands were shaking as I clumsily stuffed the card back into the envelope and slid it behind a row of cookery books in the nook of the kitchen counter. I felt the anger rising in my chest, then suddenly tears were prickling in my eyes. I rubbed my fingers across my face to try to stop myself from crying but all I could see was Kiefer that night, the last time I saw him. I was so angry at the injustice of it all, yet I knew how much blame I carried with me daily. But I had my life and Kiefer had lost his. I couldn't feel sorry for myself. Only for Kiefer, who would have been celebrating a landmark birthday today. We probably would have had a party. Everyone would have been there.

* * *

A few hours later, as I headed out of the front door and reached the gate, I heard Damian call after me.

'Frankie,' he said from the doorway.

I swung round.

'I have a thing tonight, a meeting, so don't be late back. Please.' I eyed him, waiting for something along the lines of, 'Sorry it's Kiefer's birthday today, sorry you can't celebrate a milestone birthday with your big brother.'

'Meeting thing?'

'Yep.' No hesitation. No further explanation.

'Sure.' I turned back and headed down towards the bridges which would lead me towards the centre of town. To a place and a distraction I needed more than anything.

* * *

As I walked past Mason's office, I could see him standing talking on his mobile. He waved when he saw me and I waved back. I watched him for a second as I cruised past the window. He put one hand in his trouser pocket and looked down at his feet as he continued talking enthusiastically to whoever the person on the other end was. As though he felt my gaze he looked up and our eyes locked; I was about to look away when he gave me a lopsided smile and I flashed him another one back.

'You look rather jolly to be in this early,' Penelope said as she stood next to my desk. I realised I was still wearing the smile I had just given Mason, but it quickly faded. Penelope was in early. Even earlier than me it seemed. I had taken these working hours to spend extra time with my kids. There was no need for Penelope to be here. Was this now her fight for the best employee award by trying to compete with me?

'Penelope.' I greeted her with an edge to my voice as I sat down.

Was that alcohol I could smell? The sweet stale stench of a heavy night's drinking seeping through her pores? I wrinkled my nose. She didn't greet me back but gave me an absent smile and then seemed to glance for a second longer than necessary at the paraphernalia I had around my desk. Her stare seemed to linger longest on the photos of my kids.

I looked up towards the office entrance and I saw Mason walking past the open double doors. I paused for a heartbeat as I watched him, willing him to come through, but he carried on past. Penelope was now at her own desk opposite mine.

My phone beeped and my attention was then on my calendar reminder, which told me I was having drinks with Nancy tonight. Of course I was. I would have booked that in weeks ago as a distraction from Kiefer's birthday.

I pressed the speed dial to Aimee's number on my mobile.

As usual, Aimee picked up within three rings.

In less than thirty seconds I had arranged for her to sit the kids tonight so Damian could have his 'thing' and I could be far away from the house and get to have a drink or two with my friend.

An hour later, as the office filled up, Fish cruised past my desk.

'Friday drinks tonight, Keegan?' he said in a suave manner with a few flicks of his eyebrows.

I looked up apologetically.

'I'm sorry, Fish. I have plans tonight.'

He pulled his mouth down and shrugged his shoulders. 'Fair enough. More for the rest of us then!' he said laughing as he walked away.

I looked back at my screen but all I could see in my mind's eye was an image of Kiefer and what he might look like now at forty. My brother wasn't here to celebrate, but I would be raising a glass to him tonight.

* * *

'Darling.' Nancy greeted me at her front door later that evening. 'Now you're a sight for sore eyes. Come and let out all your sorrow. This is a safe space.' Nancy opened her arms and pulled me into a hug and all the day's anxiety and stress was finally released as I fell into my best friend's embrace.

Nancy took me straight through to the snug where I was greeted by the warmth of a log fire. There was some champagne in an ice bucket on the coffee table and a few small white ramekins filled with nibbles. I sank into the soft grey sofa and Nancy poured us a glass of the champagne.

'Here's to Kiefer.' Nancy got straight to the reason for my visit and raised her glass. 'I'm sorry Kiefer isn't here to celebrate this day. I know he would have been really proud of you and what you have achieved these last few years. Damian is a great husband and father and your kids are gorgeous. Now you have your fantastic job with Mason Valentine and you have so much more to look forward to.'

I had been watching Nancy through watery eyes, trying not to break the seal and let the tears wash over my face. But suddenly my raw emotions hardened as I heard her praise Damian in that way.

She knew how difficult things were between us at the moment and also how I constantly berated Damian for his lack of effort. Did she honestly see him in that way? I guessed that without children of her own Nancy would never truly be able to see things from my perspective or understand the enormity of trying to be a mother and hold down a full time job.

I picked up my glass and clinked it against hers.

'Thanks, Nance,' I whispered.

* * *

I arrived back from Nancy's later that night. It was coming up for midnight and I felt a little guilty. Perhaps the guilt would have been greater had I not been fuelled by my share of two bottles of Nancy's favourite champagne. I rooted in my handbag and cursed myself for forgetting my door key. I let out a loud sigh and navigated my way unsteadily through the darkness to the side gate and into the back garden. I realised I was more drunk than I had initially thought as I lost my balance pulling at the patio door, which to my relief was unlocked. I let myself in and clumsily kicked off my shoes.

The house was deadly quiet. The kitchen was spotless; I could see Aimee had cleared up. Damian couldn't have been back as Aimee's laptop was open on the kitchen island, but she wasn't in the room. I paused for a moment to listen, it was so quiet I could hear blood pumping through my head as I swayed to the beat of my own heart. I edged closer to the laptop and I could see it was open on Facebook. I approached the screen and leant in closer. My eyesight was a little blurry from the night's drinking, but I could see she had scrolled to a recent photo I posted just over a week ago of me and Damian in the restaurant celebrating my new job. I remembered that after a few drinks I had thrown my arm around him and asked the waiter to take a photo of us. Damian had a wry smile and my eyes were half closed.

I took a step back and realised that it wasn't just my blurry eyesight but that the image was extra pixelated because Aimee had zoomed in on the photo.

I heard the toilet flush, so I stepped back and rushed to the fridge as Aimee arrived back into the kitchen.

'Hey, Aimee.' I popped my head round the fridge door as though I had been there the whole time.

'Oh, Frankie, hi, I... didn't know you were back. I didn't hear the door?' Aimee pulled her cardigan around herself and pushed her glasses up the ridge of her nose.

'I forgot my key, popped in the back. Can I get you anything?' I said as I rooted around unnecessarily. I felt embarrassed for Aimee for what I had seen. God knows I had zoomed in on enough photographs before.

She walked straight round to the laptop and casually flipped the lid shut.

'Did you have a good night?' she asked, and I heard an edge to her voice that I had never heard before. I reminded myself she was still only sixteen, full of hormones and curiosity.

'It was just lovely, thanks, Aimee. How are the kids?' I pulled out a bottle of sparkling water.

'Pixie had a nightmare, but I don't think she really did because she had only been asleep for about ten minutes, I just think she didn't want to be alone. Which is perfectly normal, kids tend to not want to sleep alone at night and so will come up with all kinds of excuses. When we lived in caves children who were left alone were more likely to be eaten by a sabre-toothed tiger.' Aimee was rambling.

I sat down at the island with the water and drank it straight from the bottle, not caring that I now probably appeared drunker than I thought I was. Aimee looked at me with slight disgust but again I couldn't say if I was imagining it. I was pretty sure I was swaying. I wiped my mouth with my hand.

'So you're telling me my kids mess me about at night because they don't want to be eaten by a sabre-toothed tiger?'

Aimee bit the side of her lip, pushed her glasses up her nose and shifted the weight on her foot. 'Yes. Basically, if you believe in the evolutionary side of things.'

I nodded in agreement. 'I had no idea, you are a fountain of knowledge. Are you enjoying studying psychology? All that studying of humans.' I felt as though I no longer had any control over my own words, which were coming out a little slurred.

'Er, yeah. I love it, actually. People are... fascinating.'

I looked at Aimee for second. 'Yes, they are,' I said.

I clumsily pulled a few notes out of my handbag and placed them between us. I shoved them towards Aimee.

'Erm, thanks,' she said when she realised there was more there than I would normally give her, but she was savvier than she looked and she quickly pocketed the cash and picked up her laptop and her shoulder bag.

'Thanks, Frankie. I'll see you later.'

'Yes, Aimee, see you later.'

Aimee slipped out of the back door.

I looked at the time on the cooker and saw it had gone midnight. I felt a pang of guilt at staying out so late and leaving Aimee for so long. And, of course, tomorrow I would suffer. I stood up and walked through the house towards the lounge then I heard the familiar sound of Damian's shoes walking up the path approaching the front door. I heard the jangling of his keys and the high tone of his voice as he greeted Aimee as she was leaving. I quickened my pace to get up the stairs so I didn't have to see him.

I quickly used the loo, stripped down to my underwear and fell into bed. I didn't bother taking my makeup off. I already knew I was going to feel hideous when I woke up, but at least it was the weekend. I still had another week to get through until the worst day of the year was upon me.

It was Saturday, the first day of August and the heat of the summer showed no sign of relenting. I had worked six straight shifts in the hotel restaurant, and I was wiped out, but with a wad of cash in my back pocket. I was buzzing. I suddenly loved the feeling of earning money and I had started to toy with the idea of not going to college in September. I mentioned it in the kitchen when Kiefer had got back from working a night shift at the factory, smelling of oil and metal. He listened to me talking and showing him the wad of cash.

He stopped chewing on his cheese and crisp sandwich, swallowed and said, 'Now listen to me, Frank. You go back to school, do you hear me? You need to be the one to get the education. Mum and Dad...' Kiefer lowered his voice for this bit, even though the TV was on full blast in the other room. We heard the familiar sound of the *Friends* theme tune start up. Mum's howls of laughter floated through from the lounge into the kitchen.

'It's not their fault. They never had the education. What I am saying, Frank, is it's got to be you. Look at me! I'll be lucky to get promotion and then that will be me, stuck in manual labour jobs for life. I am never going to do better than that. Reese knows that and she loves me for it anyway, so I guess I'm luckier than I think. But you, you have prospects. Don't flunk out. Go to college. Just for two years. Get the diploma. Get a good job. Please,' Kiefer said earnestly as he locked his eyes on mine. He picked up his sandwich and finished it in two bites then washed it down with milk that he drank straight from the bottle.

Kiefer was right, but the idea of having money now, every day, rather than going to college and only being able to work the weekends, was really enticing. I picked up the notes and looked at them again. Right then I knew what I was going to do with them.

I walked into town and headed straight into Brian's shop. I looked at the silver halter neck dress I had been eyeing up in the window for weeks and handed over almost half of my wages. The top I thought Todd would want to see me in was nothing in comparison to this beauty.

Brian looked intrigued. 'You wearing that tonight, doll? You'll be the belle of the ball.'

I smiled all the way home, clutching the brown paper bag with the dress in it, and thinking of Todd's face when he saw me in it.

I didn't receive any strange text messages over the weekend and so by Monday, with Kiefer's birthday done and dusted, I hoped things would start to simmer down.

But lying in bed at 6 a.m. on Monday, when I heard my phone ping, I felt my gut tighten.

So many lives ruined

I read the words and felt the weight of them.

I resisted sending back a response and considered whether I should block the number. So far there was no malice in the messages.

My mind started to wander, and I began to piece together the details of the events leading up to receiving the first text message. There had been a lingering feeling since that first message that read:

Hope you enjoyed yourself last night

Along with Penelope's description of the man I was talking to in the Chambers and the location of the Bliss offices it was glaringly obvious to me who the sender was. But I had been distracting myself and trying not to consider why he would want to contact me after so long. I knew there was unfinished business. I had been holding onto the emotions from 1998 for two decades, unable to file them away under 'history' or 'completed' because they weren't. That night so many lives changed but there hadn't been any closure. I didn't get to say goodbye. And I had carried that feeling with me all this time, like a letter I kept forgetting to post; it loitered around me every day.

* * *

Damian began to stir beside me. I put my phone on to charge and got up and went to the shower. When I arrived back in the room he was gone. I could hear the sound of the kids making their usual morning racket, protests about which cereal they wanted and who was going to sit where. I felt a huge wave of relief that Damian was downstairs dealing with it and all I had to do was get dressed and walk to work.

I could not face any breakfast this early. I had been drinking last night and now the clouds were moving in across my cranium and would stay there until later when I could have another drink or sleep it off. I already knew I wouldn't be doing the latter.

* * *

I walked through into the kitchen to grab my work bag and my stomach gurgled at the sight of the empty cereal bowls and toast crusts all over the island. I looked at Damian, who was deep into something on his phone. He was dressed in running gear.

'Why are you wearing that?' I asked him.

Damian raised his head from his phone and looked down at himself.

'I'm going running, Frank, it's what people do.'

'People, yes. Not you.'

'You don't know what I do any more.' Damian put his phone in a small pocket on his gym top, turned and walked past me; as he did his arm brushed against mine in what felt like an aggressive manner.

'Well,' I turned to the kids. 'Everyone have a wonderful day,' I said in my sunniest voice. It felt painful to be so enthusiastic.

'Bye, Mummy,' Pixie said, giving me a cuddle, and I took a moment to let my daughter melt into my arms as I inhaled the scent of her hair.

'Mummy.' Maddox tried to cling on to me for too long and I could feel my outfit crumpling.

'Okay, that's enough, sticky fingers. Mummy loves you. See you tonight.'

* * *

I rounded the end of our road and thought back to when this area was a lot more run down. We would rush around as kids and not care how it looked. Every road, path and patch of grass was our playground.

It now housed a lot of families who, like Damian and I, even though we were surviving on one income, weren't as stressed as we could have been had we not bagged a bargain ten years ago.

I turned the corner which would take me over the bridge and into town. The Bliss offices were located at the top end of Bridgewater Way. I had been avoiding this end for many years. I knew what I would find there, and from a distance it was visible, so I always took the route straight up Mill Road and headed round. I knew I needed to face it soon. And I would. Just as soon as I could find the confidence to go back twenty years and face the past.

On this particular morning, I took my usual route up Mill Road by all the main clothes shops and coffee houses. As I headed past the small hotel where I worked as a kid, I practically bumped into a woman coming out of one of the doors. She didn't see me because she was fumbling for something in her handbag as she raced out of the door and straight into me. When she looked up, her hand still poised in her handbag, our eyes locked for a second and recognition flashed across her face. It was apparent it was too late to look away, to pretend she hadn't seen me the way she had been doing for twenty years. There was a moment between us when we could have both said something, but neither of us did. It was over before it started as she pushed her way past me and down the street. I turned to watch her leave. I noticed how she was dressed: soft linen trousers with flat ballet shoes, her dark hair tied up in a messy bun that looked as though it took hours to perfect. The pangs of guilt and grief that resonated around my body were painful. I wanted to reach out and touch her, the way we used to do so effortlessly. I had always admired her and looked up to her like a big sister or motherly figure. Because back then, without my parents' effort in any part of our upbringing, Reese was the one I would turn to; her advice, along with Kiefer's, was what I had listened to the most.

* * *

I was aching with nostalgia that was so painful, for the loss of what could have been. For all the stupid mistakes I made that affected so many lives, Reese's, my parents', Kiefer's. So when I stumbled through the door of Bliss and found myself face to face with Mason, I was lost for words, my mind jumbled up with the morning's incident and all the things I wished I had said but hadn't.

'Frankie?' Mason spoke softly and I felt his hand on my shoulder. 'Is everything okay?' He ushered me into the doorway of his office.

'I, yes, it's fine. I just need to get some coffee.' I couldn't look at Mason, my mind was racing with so many thoughts.

'Sit, I'll make you one.' He walked into his office. I followed shakily, closed the door and fell into the nearest seat on the end of his conference table. He brought me coffee. Then he sat down in the chair next to me.

'Thanks,' I mumbled, already feeling ridiculous for causing such a fuss when I should just get to my desk and get on with my work.

'You can't start the day like that. Take a moment, drink the coffee. Hopefully you'll feel better.'

Mason sat back in his chair and put his hands behind his head.

I didn't open up to Mason, even though I had an overwhelming desire to fall into his arms and for him to hold me and whisper into my hair that everything was going to be okay.

Instead I just said. 'I bumped into someone from my past this morning. Literally bumped into her. We haven't spoken for twenty years. It's really complicated, and it just set me back a bit, that's all.'

'I understand. Well, not fully, obviously, but I know how it feels when you see someone you can't speak to or haven't spoken to for so long, yet there are all these words forming in your mouth waiting to be said, going stale, going to waste.'

I looked up at Mason over my coffee and he was looking past me as he spoke, and I realised he was off somewhere else entirely, thinking of the stories of his own life.

'I'll be fine. It was just a shock. This coffee is helping, though,' I said, already feeling better.

'Okay. Well, try not to mull it over too much. Sometimes we just need to be able to let go of the past.'

I looked at Mason, waiting to see if he would offer something else. He had told me he knew there was more to me than I was offering. Should I open up? Maybe he was the one who could help take away the pain and anxiety.

'So, this trip away?' Mason said quickly. 'Did you get a chance to think about it?'

I felt a sense of loss that we hadn't been able to talk about the things I really needed to say. Perhaps there would be an opportunity in Belgium.

'Yes, yes, absolutely,' I said. I knew that time away from one another was exactly what Damian and I needed.

'Have you been able to clear it with your husband? A few days away with the boss!' Mason said jovially.

I thought about Damian this morning and his lack of love, the way he insinuated I didn't know him at all.

'Absolutely,' I smiled.

* * *

I had heard my phone ping on the way to my desk, and when I sat down I opened my text messages.

Enjoying your job?

It was the same number again.
I texted back an impulse text.

Who the hell are you and stop sending cryptic texts? I can block you in an instant

Thirty seconds passed before the reply came in.

That's exactly your style isn't it? You think you can just make the problem go away?

I tried to put the face to the texts. The face of the person I had been avoiding for so long who was the only person I could think of right now who must be responsible for the messages. Surely they were just as angry and confused as I was. I had been harbouring the guilt for so long. If only I had listened to Kiefer that day, everything could have been so different.

'You want to go away for three days with a man you have only just met?'

I had just arrived home and decided to broach the subject straight away with Damian. Then I watched as his face turned a light beetroot colour.

'He's not just some man, though, is he, Damian, he is my employer and I have to go for work.'

'Oh, right, you just have to swan off to Belgium for three days for work reasons whilst I stay here looking after the kids.'

'Well, yeah? They are eight and nearly four. They can't really look after themselves, can they?'

'Glad you find it funny, Frank.'

'So, are you saying I can't go, Damian?' I asked facetiously.

'I'm just wondering why it suddenly came about and why silver fox man – yep, don't worry, I Googled him – has suddenly decided he needs to sweep you off to Belgium for three days?'

I looked at Damian with wide eyes.

'You Googled him?'

'Yes, Frank, it's a thing. People do it.'

'Okaaay. Well, I'm going to Belgium because Mason believes I have proved myself to be a worthy asset and he wants me to be in on the buying.'

'A worthy asset, and what about your assets around here, like ummm, oh yeah, your kids? Maybe you should consider being here for them more instead of running out of the house at the crack of dawn.' Damian ran his hands through his hair frantically.

I took a deep breath and instead of exhaling all the venom I had wished to dump all over Damian I simply blew it away and turned to leave.

I felt Damian's hand reach down to grab mine. He squeezed it tightly. I felt shocked by his touch; it had been so long since we had touched one another through love or anger.

'What's going on, Frank?' he whispered, as the kids were in the snug watching TV. He moved his head closer to mine. Damian and I both looked at his hand on mine at the same time just as he released his grip and took a step back.

'I know it's the time of year, Frankie. I know it's a big anniversary this weekend. Why are you acting like this? When are you going to have some proper therapy?'

'When were you going to mention Kiefer's birthday?'

'I can't remember every little detail, can I? Besides, it's all one isn't it, his birthday, the crash?'

'Yes, he died a few days after his birthday. What do you mean, it's all one? They are two separate events, which I like to have time to think about individually. And besides, Damian, I have had my therapy,' I said through gritted teeth.

'Writing in those poxy diaries wasn't therapy, Frankie.'

'I did more than write in poxy diaries, Damian, and you know it. Have you ever looked in my diaries?'

'No, of course not, what do you take me for? How would I be able to anyway when they are locked up in Fort bleeding Knox.'

I thought of the safe I kept in the walk-in wardrobe in our room, where the diaries sat, untouched, unlooked at for nearly twenty years. I was suddenly drawn to them, an unhealthy desire to go back and reread the words of a messed-up teenager. But I wasn't sure I could.

'I need an early night,' I said, and walked away up the stairs.

I arrived in our bedroom and instantly, as though Damian had instigated the urge, I felt a pull towards the wardrobe. It had been so long; I felt I needed to remind myself that I had come so far. I was a mess back then. A total mess. I still cowered at siren sounds and I watched Damian like a hawk when he drove. I got my car checked over every three months at the garage. I wasn't any good in a plane either these days. I didn't take my first flight until I was twenty-four. Damian and I flew to Ibiza but as soon as I got inside that plane my throat seized up and my arms went weak and floppy.

The grim metal outer casing of the safe glared at me. After I had finished writing in the final diary I locked them up in the safe that had belonged to my dad and they had remained there ever since. When Damian and I finally moved in together, I had to explain what was in there and that I had no intention of opening it again, yet I needed to keep them close to me.

The code to the safe was a number that had been engraved on my brain since that night. For years, whenever I went anywhere, I would see portions of that number together, the first three digits or the last ones, it was freaky and bothered me for ages as though it was some weird sort of sign. I moved towards the safe and reached out. I turned the dial, a nudge to the left, a nudge to the right, until I heard the safe click open. Twenty years ago, I locked those diaries up, and I hadn't seen them since. I wondered if they were even in there, whether Damian had worked out the combination, perhaps I shouted it out in my dreams. He'd probably seen every crazy thing I ever wrote in them.

I pulled the handle just an inch and as I did so I got a flash of the contents; my heart leapt into my chest as I slammed the door. I moved away from the safe and sat on the end of the bed with my head bent, hands clutching the side of the mattress. Why couldn't I bear to look at those diaries? Why couldn't I find the strength to face the past?

Damian was so very right about everything. I was far from well, and in a few days' time, when the darkness came, I would be as ill-prepared as I was every single year.

* * *

The next morning I made an effort to get up early and be ready by 7 a.m. to go into the kids' rooms and wake them. Damian's words had cut me last night and I wanted to make an effort, I needed them all to see that I was trying and that I was a good mother.

I laid out pancakes and smoothies and I got the good maple syrup out of the cupboard. Pixie sat up, bleary eyed, and Maddox stayed in his pyjamas as he didn't have preschool. They both looked like startled sparrows initially, sharing a conspicuous look with each other which I found endearing; they were a true brother and sister team and my heart pounded for the love they had for one another. Eventually, when they had got over the shock of Mummy cooking them breakfast on a school morning, they tucked in hungrily and Pixie started to chat away animatedly about what she had planned at school today. I listened intently, and nodded in all the right places, peppering her chitter with relevant questions.

'Does this mean you can play with me today, Mummy? I want you to play with me, not Daddy.' Maddox looked up at me with his beautiful brown eyes.

'I'd love to, sweetie, but I have to go to work and so Daddy will play with you now and I will play with you when I come home from work, how about that?'

'Okay.' Maddox looked down at his pancake.

Damian walked in, greeted the kids and tried to steal a bit of

Pixie's pancake. She squealed and laughed at his audacity then he walked over to the stove and helped himself, pouring what I considered to be an indecent amount of maple syrup over three pancakes.

'This is a novelty, having Mummy here for breakfast,' Damian said and shimmied onto his stool by the island.

'What's a novelty?' sang Pixie.

'A novelty is something that is brand new that we haven't experienced before,' Damian addressed Pixie, 'But it also means we like it,' he said and looked at me. For a second something passed between us, something familiar, a look that was heavily laden with meaning and more than that, hope. Damian was pleading with me to continue this. But I already knew I would let everyone down again by the end of the day.

* * *

I arrived at work at quarter to eight. As I reached my desk my phone let out its familiar ping. By now I was becoming accustomed to the messages which were coming in regularly.

I sat down at my desk. There was no one in the office, not even Alan today and Carys the receptionist didn't start until 8.30, and I hadn't seen Mason in his office when I walked past. I sat down in my chair. Only some of the main lights were on, which meant half of the office was in partial darkness. The whole place felt eerily barren and I looked round at the vastness of the room and the large imposing desks and furniture, wondering if indeed I was alone.

I cautiously opened my messages, keeping one eye on my surroundings.

Not long to go now. How will you cope? How do you cope every day knowing what you did?

A sound reverberated around the office; it sounded like something large and metallic had been dropped on a concrete floor and I jumped so much I dropped my phone. I fell to my knees and groped under my desk while my heart raced, and eventually my hand clasped around the soft outer casing.

I sat back down in my seat, glanced round the office and let out a loud breath.

I was about to get up and investigate when one of the cleaners appeared in the doorway clutching a mop and bucket. They were late leaving today.

'Morning,' I said with a wobble in my voice. The woman cleaner smiled as she walked past me to the cleaning cupboard and locked up the mop.

I blew out a long breath.

Once the cleaner had left the office, I felt the anger bubble up at the injustice of it all. How so many lives were ruined and how all that love, all that beautiful young raw love that had been building and growing into something spectacular, had evaporated overnight.

I stood in the kitchen in the silver baby doll dress with the halter neck. I surveyed myself a hundred times and then Reese came over. Kiefer was upstairs having a shower and hadn't seen me yet.

'Will he like it?' I asked Reese.

'It's not up to your brother, is it, Frankie. For the record, you look amazing. Really grown up. I like that eye shadow. It matches the dress. What bag are you taking?' She pushed a stray strand of hair behind my ear.

I showed her the white patent tiny rucksack that had just enough space for my wallet, keys, a packet of fags and small bottle of vodka. I intended to drink the vodka with some Diet Coke in the pub before the party. After I that I imagined myself buying Todd a drink with the tips I earned that week from the hotel.

'It's cute. Shoes?'

I went into the hallway and came back carrying white knee high canvas boots.

'Sweet. You've got it sorted, girl. I'll be taking some styling tips off you.' Reese high fived me.

I coloured a little. I looked at Reese. Today she was wearing her long hair loose, the natural dark curls cascaded down her back. She wore a white crop top, blue hipster jeans that revealed her pierced belly button and canvas wedge platform shoes. Her toe nails were bright pink.

Just then, Kiefer came into the kitchen with a towel wrapped around his waist. He looked me up and down and then walked to the fridge and opened it. Reese shot me a look.

'You wearing that tonight?' he spoke into the fridge.

'Yep,' I replied nonchalantly.

Kiefer backed up out of the fridge with a few slices of wafer thin ham in his hand. He shoved them all in his mouth and then sidled up to Reese, slipping his thick arm around her tiny tanned waist.

'So, babes, what do we think about my baby sister heading out in this outfit tonight?'

Reese folded her arms and tilted her head to one side as if she were assessing me for the first time.

'I think she looks fantastic.' Reese grinned at me and I grinned back.

Kiefer nodded. 'Uh huh.'

He went back to the fridge and looked inside.

'She is sixteen now, Kief.'

'I know, I know,' came the muffled voice of my brother. He spun round, shut the fridge and emerged clutching a stubby beer. 'Right, what time are we off to the pub then?'

Reese and I exchanged a sly smile.

* * *

In the pub Nancy and I ordered lager and limes to start ourselves off.

We settled in our favourite spot by the window near the pool table and juke box. I sent Nancy over with coins and she put on our favourite Jamiroquai song and sashayed her way back to me.

We sipped our lager and I stole surreptitious looks out of the window.

'Waiting for lover boy?' Nancy sniggered into her pint.

I pulled my mouth down. 'Don't know what you're talking about.'

'He isn't going to come any quicker with you rubber necking at the window all night.'

My dress had ridden halfway up my legs and I could feel a slight breeze as people came in and out of the door. The bouncer, Gary, greeted everyone with his usual charm and turned a blind eye to those who were clearly under the legal drinking age.

Once we'd finished our pints, I headed to the bar to buy Cokes for me and Nancy and then we put them on the floor and poured our respective spirits into them. I took a sip and winced at the strength of the alcohol that sat at the top of the glass. I whisked it with my finger and took a sneaky look round the pub now I knew that Nancy was onto me. I felt the anticipation for the night building as the vodka hit my bloodstream, and I wanted more than anything to see Todd.

More of the group joined us. Kiefer was milling around, socialising, Reese was there with all her girlfriends, Minty arrived and the level of banter shot up. He and Nancy started talking about the evening's proceedings, who was coming, how we were getting there. There was talk of going in several cars as the rave was ten miles away in a disused barn. The time was ticking by and it was almost ten. I could see our clan finishing drinks, a few people started to disappear outside to organise taxis or lifts.

Kiefer came over with Dave.

'I'm driving, so you can hop in with us.' I looked out of the window and saw Kiefer's green Mini Cooper parked there.

'What about Reese?' I said, hoping that I could get left behind and wait a little longer to see if Todd showed. I downed the last of my vodka and Coke.

'She's going with Kaz and them lot. You comin', Mints?'

'You betcha. I'm totally psyched for tonight. I'm gonna get twiiii-isted!' Minty started body popping.

Nancy hung off his arm, laughing at everything he said, and I was intrigued at how her interest in him had suddenly been piqued.

As everyone started filtering out of the pub, I couldn't think of any more excuses to stay put. I had used the toilet three times, and my glass sat empty on the table in front of me. Kiefer stood next to me.

'You coming, then?'

I did a final scan of the pub then grabbed my rucksack and followed Kiefer out to the car.

* * *

The drive to the barn where the rave was took twenty minutes. Minty rabbited on about God knows what, he'd properly come up on whatever he had taken. I clutched my bag. Nancy had her head on my shoulder, her eyes were closed. I knew she wasn't asleep because every now and then I felt her shoulders shuffle as she giggled at something else Minty had said.

Kiefer pulled into the drive and I could feel the bass pumping through the car. Nancy sat up and did a loud stretch. Minty got out of the car and held the door open, bowing his head like a butler for Nancy who climbed out his side, laughing at his chivalry. I felt a pang of jealousy that Nancy and Minty might become an item tonight and Todd was nowhere to be seen.

I pulled my bag onto my shoulder and started to walk, my head bent down, trying to let the beat from the house music get inside me so I could relax and enjoy the night. But the thought of Todd not being there had already marred my mood and I just couldn't shake it off.

'You alright, sis?' Kiefer put an arm around me as we walked in tandem towards the barn. I could see the flashing strobe light and it sounded as though there was an MC on the mic. I looked up and gave a reassuring smile to Kiefer.

'Babe!' I looked up as Reese tore herself away from the other girls she had arrived with. One was wearing huge Elton John glasses, a pink feather boa with multi-coloured leggings and white stilettoes. For a few seconds I was so mesmerised by her that I almost didn't see him.

As the group of girls passed and dispersed, leaving only Kiefer and Reese locked in an embrace as though they hadn't seen each other for weeks, he was there, as though he had been all the time.

He headed straight for me, took my hand and without saying anything he pulled me towards the music. I could feel the bass filling my insides and the electricity from the touch of Todd's hand and suddenly my world had lit up with a million volts.

Devoted to the moment as I was, I still couldn't help but steal a final glance backwards, where I saw Reese still firmly attached to Kiefer, but instead of looking at her, his eyes were locked firmly on mine and his jaw set in a way that displayed his disappointment.

* * *

24 December 1998

How is it possible that I can still feel you here? In bed at night I can hear the front door opening and your familiar footsteps walking through the hallway and into the kitchen. You were always the night owl of the two of us. Even though we spent so much time together, were always seen together, I preferred to be at home. I loved the sanctuary of it, of my bedroom, the one we shared together as little kids but you needed your space and freedom sooner than I did. Mum would come in and find us nestled into one another. I wish I had felt those moments more instead of trying to move away from you. Yet I never stopped feeling your gaze, the vibrations of your love found their way back to me, it was inevitable, we were closer than anyone we knew. I just presumed we would always be that way, even though I had begun to seek my independence, I thought I could come back to you like a boomerang at any point.

I always sought more, like any young girl does, thinking that my life was worthless, that I needed material goods to make me feel more than I did, that I needed to have friends that weren't you. But of course, we don't need anything other than what we are given in the beginning. The true binding love of siblings is a rare thing and we were so lucky. We never knew how lucky. I wish I had been able to show you in more ways that I cared for you, instead I felt I let you down too many times. I would look over and see that familiar look of distaste spread across your face, more so towards the end.

This therapy that I have only seems to make me miss you more. The gaping hole that is now my life without you doesn't feel worthy of living without walking behind you in your footsteps. I realised I looked up to you so much. Now I only look down.

And the darkness that will creep its way around every year to mark the day you died means I will never be free of the grief.

The most special time of the year is here and I can't imagine Christmas without you, but here I am planning how I will get through the first one. They say the firsts are the hardest. But I know every one will be hard.

Happy Christmas, my darling.

On Saturday morning, I woke with dread in the pit of my stomach. Today was the anniversary of Kiefer's death and I had been living this day over and over for twenty years.

Damian eyed me with curiosity when I arrived downstairs and took a seat at the island. What will happen, will I go off whistling like a boiled kettle or will I sink quietly into the background, not wishing to speak or be spoken to?

The kids would have been prepped. 'Be extra kind to Mummy today – she is feeling fragile.' Maddox would question what fragile means, as this is the first year he is old enough to understand that Mummy will be a little vacant for a while; before now Pixie was the only one Damian needed to explain the change in atmosphere to. I got up but I felt weightless, like an autumnal leaf, its threadbare exterior clinging to a thin central vein which could be crushed by pressing ever so gently and then disintegrate to nothing.

I wished today was happening on a work day so I could disappear and immerse myself in the glorious organised monotony of the daily tasks of my job.

Damian said very little and we allowed a whole day to pass with some card games in the snug, a simple lunch of jacket potatoes and salad, and by the end of the day he finally spoke to me with some sincerity.

'Well done for getting through today.' He poured me a glass of red wine. I noted it wasn't my favourite, which you would have to go to the main supermarket to pick up, but a cheaper version from the corner shop. I tried not to wince when I swallowed but I wasn't sure I succeeded as Damian looked at me with intent as though he were about to say something, but then he remembered himself and quietly retreated to the snug, patting me lightly on the back as he walked past. I heard Netflix fire up and I thought of all the places I would rather be than here.

I headed upstairs, checked in on Maddox first and then Pixie in their separate bedrooms, and began setting clothes aside for the trip away to Belgium which was happening in three days' time. It was a most welcome distraction.

Damian was wrong. I was Mason's New Product Developer. Penelope would be holding the fort in his absence and of course it was my job to be there.

I had texted my mum a few days ago to tell her I was going on a work trip. It had been weeks since I last saw her and Dad with Pixie. Only now did my phone ping through with a simple message:

Okay then, have a nice time

I wondered what had prevented her from replying straight away and then I stopped myself immediately from overthinking. Mum was on strong drugs that she had been on since Kiefer died. There was no rational explanation for her behaviour.

Damian always said I should be thankful I have parents. His divorced when he was five and his mother died of a heart attack five years ago. Now his dad lived and worked in Japan and had met Pixie twice and only met Maddox once when he was a baby.

So between us we considered ourselves unfortunate on the grandparent front, although my dad, through his illness, was probably the most endearing.

I put my phone aside and began to fold comfy trousers and t-shirts, some pyjamas and several sets of underwear. I glanced at my better underwear, the stuff I rarely wore any more. I grabbed the first matching set I could find.

I stared at it for a few seconds, then without further hesitation, I shoved it between a pair of black trousers and a polo neck sweater. I kept repeating to myself that that kind of underwear fitted better under the types of dresses I would be wearing for the evening meals and drinks with clients.

Then I sat on the end of the bed, and yet again I could feel the pull of the diaries from inside the safe. I thought of the number that kept them locked in there. It was going round and round in my head, and I would let it because I knew it would subside later. It was the repercussions of the day, the trauma and shock that reared itself every year. I would drown those feelings right now. I picked up a carrier bag, stuffed it with the inner card from the pairs of tights I had bought, and went downstairs. I looked at the recycling bin in the kitchen, which was full to bursting, so I picked it up and with the carrier bag, I walked barefoot down the side of the house where we kept our main bins. I paused in my tracks as I heard Damian's voice from the other side of the tall side gate which led to the front of the house, muffled as though he were purposely trying to speak quietly into his phone. He must have thought I had gone to bed because his voice was an audible whisper, but I heard him clearly.

'I know, I just don't know what to do any more. I'm running out of patience. This time of year is particularly bad but I feel as though she's getting worse.'

And although a part of me wanted to run through the side gate and demand to know from Damian who he was talking to, part of me wasn't surprised that something was going on with him. With the way things had been recently, it was likely Damian could be keeping things secret from me.

I walked back into the kitchen, opened the fridge and grabbed the first alcohol I could find, a Corona beer, and opened it. I took it back upstairs with me. As I walked back into the bedroom, I heard the echo of a text message notification. I took a long drink of the beer, placed it on the bedside table and opened my messages.

I saw the unrecognised number and the words:

Twenty years today

I stood at the door with my bag in hand, ready to leave the house for three days. Damian loitered in the hallway, neither wanting to bid me farewell nor wanting me to go. He hit me with a few quick questions.

'So, you'll be back when?' and 'You're getting a car to the airport, then business class? Alright for some!' and finally, 'Enjoy, then.'

I thought about the phone call I heard a few nights ago and I supposed it was inevitable that I would end up at this junction with this distance opening up between me and Damian, and me, standing in the doorway of our house, clutching a suitcase with sexy lingerie stuffed between jumpers and trousers.

'Ok, well, you know, take care and look after yourself.' Damian shifted from one foot to another and looked at the floor tiles. 'In *Belgium*,' Damian added for extra effect.

'So, I'll see you in a few days.' I had already said goodbye to the kids before Damian took them to school that morning. 'I'll be back Saturday.'

'I still don't get how if it's a business trip you need to come back on Saturday.' Damian said again, throwing us back to where we were days ago.

I shook my head. I had been through this so many times with Damian. Mason had booked a dinner on the Friday night with clients. A late night flight on Friday was completely out of the question.

'I'll see you Saturday,' I leant in and gave Damian a peck on the cheek. His skin smelt faintly of soap and beneath that, his familiar scent that was just him. I felt a pang of something familiar, something that Damian and I had between us, the thing that brought us together and held us together. I didn't often think about love, I was never one to try and analyse why that happened or this happened. But I read somewhere once that we are drawn to someone by their smell and if we continue to love the way they smell, and not be repulsed by it, then that in itself is enough. I tried to push away any yearning thoughts of absence making the heart grow fonder whilst I was away, and reverted my thoughts back to Damian and his vacant ways. Most of the time I was absent in body and mind. I didn't really feel anything. I just felt numb about us. I thought about all the feelings that had been stirred up recently every time I was with Mason. Suddenly, panic set in, and I wondered if, with what was going on between Damian and I, now was the best time to be hundreds of miles away with Mason.

A sleek black car pulled up outside the house, rendering my doubts futile. It was time to go to work.

I stepped outside and Damian went to take a few steps forward then appeared to change his mind.

'Ok, then, see you Saturday.' As he walked back into the house he turned back as though he was going to say something. I hovered for a split second, willing him to say something profound, to make it all better, to change the dynamics, the situation. Every awkward scenario and angry comment could be erased in a matter of seconds, with one or two words. I thought about the underwear in the suitcase; already I felt seedy, not knowing what it was I really wanted and if something Damian was or wasn't about to say could make any difference to anything right now.

He remained silent and stood looking at the car with a wounded expression. I was no longer able to decipher what he wanted.

* * *

I sat in the car and the smooth journey lulled me into a snooze. I had woken every hour last night, so many little things were bothering me. As I sat still, resting my eyes, I heard my phone ping and I remembered when Damian and I were dating, pre-kids, when we would text all the time and every message that came through was almost certainly going to be from him and if it wasn't then disappointment would take hold and linger until he finally came through. But something told me this wasn't a message from Damian, I felt the sensation that it was delivering something unsavoury.

I opened my handbag and pulled out my mobile, sighing as I did. The endless invasion of technology was wearing me down. I opened the cover and hit the text messages.

How does it feel after all this time, knowing what you did?

I slammed the phone cover shut. I wasn't going to play this game any more. After this trip I would be confronting them head on.

My phone beeped again and this time it *was* Damian. So soon after leaving the house, that was something he would have done years ago and not something he had done of late. His text simply read:

Safe journey

Damian knew I wasn't a great flyer. I could see there was some sort of innocence behind the message, but anyone who wished you a safe trip when you were about to get on a plane was not really thinking about what they were saying at all.

* * *

The car arrived at the airport and I thanked the driver profusely, realising that in all that time in the car I hadn't uttered a word to him. I rushed my way through check in and into the departures area and headed for the business class lounge where Mason had said to meet him. I realised I was sweating slightly and pulled in a deep breath before opening the door to the lounge. As I did, there was Mason, sat behind a newspaper stretched out in front of him, one leg casually crossed over the other. His silver trousers revealed the black socks underneath which clearly displayed a tiny white Gucci logo.

As he heard the door open, he hurriedly put his paper down and strode to the door to relieve me of my hand luggage, then took my arm and escorted me over to the bar.

'Come on, girl, let's get you a drink.'

I laughed in spite of myself. 'But it's only 11 a.m.'

'That, my dear, is no excuse.' Mason squeezed my arm. 'I reckon these guys could mix you something nice.'

'Erm, Negroni?' I asked tentatively.

Mason turned to the barman who had been waiting attentively, who then set to work quickly and efficiently.

'Nervous flyer?'

I looked around anxiously. 'Kind of.'

My gaze reached his and he gave me a kind smile.

'Anyway, look, here comes your drink. Get it down you, girl. You'll feel so much happier in a moment.'

* * *

The plane shook and shuddered as the mass of metal began to hurtle to top speed upon take off. I had hoped that the two Negronis I had drunk would have numbed the panic, but as I sat there and tried to control my breathing, I found I needed to look at my lap and visualise the kids there for extra distraction. Then I felt a hand rest on my arm and I looked up, startled, thinking it was the flight attendant. But it was Mason to my right. His calm face and soft touch made me feel instantly less stressed.

* * *

Once we were in flight, and the seat belt sound beeped, Mason simply removed his hand and took out his paper again.

A hostess arrived next to us with a bottle of champagne. Mason gave her his best smile. 'No, thank you,' he said. 'I'm saving myself for later.' The hostess tilted the bottle of champagne towards me.

'Madam?'

'What the hell, I'm on my holidays,' I said, relieved take off was over.

Mason looked up with wide eyes. 'Sort of, anyway,' I laughed as she filled the champagne glass and handed it to me. Mason handed me a bottle of mineral water.

'You will need to drink some of this too, or you'll know about it later.' Then he handed me a small file of A4 papers.

'This is the schedule for the next few days. You will see I have managed to squeeze in a tiny bit of sightseeing but other than that it's all work, I'm afraid.' He raised his glass of water at me.

'But don't worry, there will be a bit of down time, some nice food and more of those Negronis you're rather fond of.' And he winked in a really endearing way and through my slight intoxication, I sensed something else in that smile and that wink which brought with it an urge that I wasn't sure what to do with.

* * *

After touchdown we retrieved our bags from the carousel and took a cab to the hotel, twenty minutes from the centre of Liège.

'Why so far away?' I questioned Mason as we stepped out of another mode of transport. I felt so weary and the alcohol was wearing off. I needed to get to the bar, quickly.

'This hotel is the best,' Mason said frankly as he stood back to let the porter collect our luggage.

'Well, yes, it's gorgeous, but this is rather... remote. Are they woods?' I looked beyond the beautifully lit hotel as the sun was just beginning to sink below the horizon.

'Why? Fancy a hike later?' Mason said, raising his eyes as he handed over a wad of euros to the taxi driver.

'I didn't bring my hiking boots,' I said distractedly.

'Never mind, it's amazing what you can borrow here if you do fancy escaping. I find woods so enchanting, so full of mystery, don't you?' Mason stood looking towards the dense mass of trees and I stood next to him.

'Anyway, shall we check in?' He turned to me eagerly.

'Yes, let's,' I said and followed him and the porter towards the majestic front entrance.

I watched Mason do his thing at the reception desk and I allowed my eyes to cast past him to the stretch of woods beyond. The sunless sky was already starting to feel greyer as the day crept to an end and I felt myself shudder at the darkness that shrouded the trees.

'All set?' Mason appeared next to me.

I smiled weakly.

'Here's your key. Our rooms are fairly close to each other, so if you need me for anything...' As Mason handed me the card his finger grazed mine and the moment of intimacy shocked me, but I refused to look at him even though I could feel his eyes on me.

We headed for the lift, following a porter who carried our luggage.

The lift arrived on the second floor and we stepped out into another beautiful foyer with huge flower arrangements and exquisite ornaments.

The porter stopped outside a room and I did a double take at the number on the door.

'This is your room, madam,' the porter said with an accent I took to be French. I stared at the number on the door again, my feet were rooted to the spot.

'Room 2461, madam,' the porter said, looking at me.

'Frankie, are you ok? Do you need some help getting in?' Mason's voice filtered through.

'I...' I couldn't speak, my throat was closing up. I couldn't breathe.

I took a deep breath, swallowed and said, 'Why are the rooms in the thousands when there are only about 150 rooms in the hotel?'

The porter looked perturbed, so Mason began to speak in fluent French. The porter listened and then replied, Mason said something else in French and looked at me.

'This is a chain of three hotels and they are all on the same system, the rooms carry on in numerical order from hotel to hotel. Are you ok?'

I laughed nervously, 'Of course, I just thought it was a bit weird.'

Mason eyed me curiously.

'Okay. Shall I meet you back in the foyer in a couple of hours?' I said with all the enthusiasm I could muster, even though my mouth was so dry I could barely speak.

Mason assessed me for a second longer. 'Sure. I'll make dinner reservations. But meet me in the bar at six. Ok?'

'Great,' I said.

'Frankie?'

'Uh huh?' I was fiddling with my key, trying to get into the room.

'Just hold it against the door, like this.' Mason took hold of my wrist so the key was upright.

'Oh yeah, sorry, it's been a while since I used one of these things.' I held the key at the handle and the door made a loud click, indicating it had unlocked.

The porter had long gone but I was fine carrying my one small case and my handbag into the room.

I was barely able to acknowledge the space and simplistic luxury of the room. I dropped my handbag and case on the floor as the door clicked shut and fell onto the super king size bed, which completely cocooned my body as I lay there.

Thoughts flooded my mind. Was this some sort of joke, a weird coincidence? All I could see was that number over and over in my head. On the door of the room and also all those years ago.

24

There was no air tonight, the barn was packed full of bodies. At the back was metal sheeting acting as a protective wall; it had been spray painted with all sorts of images – flowers, smiley faces and a huge man with dreads, smoking a spliff that was almost half the size of the wall. There was a block of hay bales and a few people were gathered on them sitting, and a few were lying down. The decks were next to them and two speakers on either side so huge I could feel the bass vibrating in my chest.

Todd held my hand, there were lights rotating, blue, red, green – Todd's face was illuminated each time the light passed. I could feel the heat from his hand and every now and again he squeezed mine for no reason. The first time he did it I looked up and tried to ask him why over the music but he just smiled a hazy eyed smile. I knew he had taken something and it was taking effect.

Todd guided me over to the hay bales and we sat down.

He took a small bag of white powder out of his pocket and demonstrated what to do by sticking his finger in the powder and rubbing it around his gums. He had a bottle of beer and took a long gulp of it. He handed me the packet of white powder, nodded encouragingly with that sloppy smile and I dipped the tip of my index finger in until it was coated with the white powder. I took one more glance at Todd for reassurance and then did as he had demonstrated. He handed me his beer to take away the bitter taste.

Todd smiled at me and nodded for me to take more, but I handed him the bag back.

'I'm fine,' I mouthed.

Todd put it back in his pocket and got up and walked over to the bar. I sat and looked at the bodies floating about the barn, I saw Reese and Kiefer, and Reese's friends, all dancing and laughing. Through the sea of people, I was sure Kiefer had not seen what Todd and I had taken. Todd came back with a beer for me. I took a sip and just as I put it to my lips, I felt the electric pulse of the drug. It was so unfamiliar, so new to me. I turned and smiled at Todd, and he pulled me into an embrace. I took another sip and I knew all I needed to do was dance. I stood up and pushed my way through the crowds to the centre of the dance floor, pulling Todd behind me. The music seemed to move in time with us and I felt like I wanted to break free and run through the fields. I tilted my head back and felt the warm summer night air filling the barn and the heat and sweat from the bodies next to me.

* * *

A few hours later I was coming down from the drug. My mouth was dry and making a small robotic movement. I sipped more beer and then bought a vodka and Coke. At the bar I could see Nancy was there in a full embrace and snog with Minty. I thought about how Todd and I had yet to cement anything, even talk about it. I didn't know how he felt about me, I was seven years younger than him. He probably only saw me as a child. Yet why had I always felt something more?

I felt a hand around my waist. I knew it was him.

'Come on,' he whispered, sounding more sober and together than I had heard him all night.

I turned and he put his arm around me so I was almost cocooned within him, so much so that we were able to walk straight past Kiefer completely unnoticed. I took a moment to steal a glance at him as we passed and saw how happy he was then with Reese and his friends, hands in the air, dancing to the music.

Once outside, Todd took my hand and pulled me to the side of the barn. I had imagined this scenario a hundred times and now his soft warm lips were on mine, exactly as I had hoped they would be. I melted into his embrace. When I felt him pull away I opened my eyes and he was looking down at me and smiling. He took my hand and we walked away, the sound of the heavy bass fading into the night.

25

NOW

I let the hot water from the shower envelop me and stood there for as long as possible. I had napped for maybe five minutes, but it was enough to get me through the night with Mason. Truth was, I shouldn't have drunk the Negroni and champagne. That had tipped me over the edge. I was still reeling from the fact that the room bore the number that haunted me from my past and I was struggling to comprehend how that could be a coincidence. Was it possible that Mason had known somehow, that bringing me here was a way to make me feel vulnerable?

I dressed in a simple black knee length dress with red heels. I walked out of the door and stood and looked at the number once more, shook my head in disbelief and headed down to the bar.

Mason was already there with a bottle of champagne chilling on ice next to him. I felt for a moment as though I wanted to turn and run, but where would I run to? I looked through the masses of windows in the bar and could just about make out the density of the woods.

Mason looked up as I arrived next to him.

'Tell me you are suitably refreshed because I am told this is the best champagne in Belgium and I cannot possibly drink it all alone.'

I smiled and took a seat on a stool. He was wearing a white shirt, open at the neck, with a crisp grey suit jacket and trousers. He smelt freshly showered, of mint and lemons.

'Good rest?' I watched Mason look me and up and down. 'You look very nice,' he said softly.

'Thanks. Yes. I feel much better. You?'

Mason popped an olive in his mouth. 'Yes, I sat in my boxers and watched the sport channel. It was lovely, actually.'

'Okay, thanks for that.'

'Oh, sorry, I forgot where I was for a second.' Mason let out a small laugh. Then he turned to me. 'Sorry, Frankie, I didn't mean to imprint that image on your mind.'

'It's okay. It's good that you're relaxed. You work hard.' I took a long sip of champagne.

Mason nodded. 'Yes, I do.'

I picked up an olive and examined its size and shape before popping it in my mouth.

'So, what do you do for down time? I take it you're not a sport channel kinda girl? This isn't work time now so feel free to talk about you. What are your favourite foods? Who inspires you? What do you want to achieve, what's your biggest regret?'

My heart pounded at the word regret. I sat open mouthed, wanting to speak. I wanted to tell him that my biggest regret happened twenty years ago and I would do anything to go back and change the past.

'Come on, Frankie, don't go all agog on me now. Details make my job a whole lot easier, besides, I like to know the intricacies of everyone. And...' he paused to tap the side of his head. 'I have a very good memory.' Mason smiled and his piercing blue eyes fixed right on me.

I sat and thought back to that day in his office when he offered me the prosecco and I had too much to drink before I headed down the pub. Had I said too much then?

'Don't look so horrified. I just want to know the little things, stuff that will make a difference when we're working together. I want to know if you have a phobia of spiders or you won't tip a waiter if the service was poor but it wasn't necessarily their fault?'

'So, fairly specific,' I laughed.

'Yeah, maybe.' Mason ate another olive. 'But you may have noticed, I'm not like normal bosses, this is how I keep my staff.'

'That's because you get them drunk on a Friday and they forget how awful you are all weekend until Monday.'

'Ha! Yes, you've got me, how many employers have you had that have done that for you? Staff are the most important aspect of the business and if I can't look after you guys to the best of my ability then who will look after my business, hey? I can't run this thing on my own. I was treated horrifically in jobs as a young lad, I just couldn't see that working for me as an employer. What *has* worked is that if I give all those little extras to my staff, like good coffee and breakfast, subsidised lunches and a few free drinks at the local pub after a long hard week, I have found that I have only lost two employees in three years. And one of those was because she had a baby and decided she loved him more than my croissants.'

'And the other one?'

'Oh, he was a total prick. There was no amount of freebies or flexible working that was going to save that one.' Mason stabbed at an olive with a toothpick. 'So, come on, Keegan. Spill.'

'So, I'm Keegan now?' I smiled and raised an eyebrow.

'Yeah, I heard Fish calling you it. I kinda like it.'

I smiled and looked past Mason across the room. 'Well, what is there to know about me? My favourite drink at the moment is a Negroni.'

I paused as I thought and I was pleasantly surprised at how Mason waited for me to continue without commentary. 'I have a penchant for Spanish music, if I hear the Gipsy Kings I go to pieces, it reminds me of my youth.' I took another moment to pause. 'I love to bake but haven't done it for so many years I fear I may have forgotten how. I like badminton but I haven't played in so many years. I have lower back problems from carrying two babies, and I should do yoga but I choose not to. Yet, I don't know why.' I was on a roll, and continued with barely any pauses. 'I hate people who talk really loudly in restaurants and I love honesty. Real grafters, salt of the earth folk, you know where you are with them. And I love my kids and I should spend more time with them but I don't because I have to work and as much as I love the flawless organisation of a working day compared to the wretched harrowing chaotic world of parenting seven days a week, I wish I had the choice. I wish... I wish there was a choice so I could decide, then maybe I would know, for sure. Am I working because I have to or because I can't bear to stay at home and watch another episode of *Paw Patrol* and wet wipe another stain off the carpet whilst juggling a million household chores and wondering if I would actually, indeed, be better off at work.'

I blew out a big breath and looked round the room to see if anything had changed while I had been monologuing. It felt a relief to have said it, but I began to panic that I had perhaps over-stepped the mark.

I looked at Mason's expression, which was taut with emotion, empathy? Sympathy?

'I... anyway, you asked.' I laughed loudly and took a long gulp of my champagne and watched Mason arrange himself in his seat, still not rushing to say anything but this time I was silently urging him to speak up.

'It seems there is a lot to know about you. I knew you were a complex character when I met you. That's why I employed you, I think. Other than the fact you have an outstanding CV, I like someone with depth to them. You have depth. I guess we are all

constantly facing dilemmas and problems though and I can understand how life must be very hard for you sometimes, the decisions
we need to make and the choices you are faced with.' Mason
cleared his throat and took a sip of champagne. 'So. Why don't you
start by talking me through this obsession with the Gipsy Kings?'

I sat back in my chair and laughed a laugh so loud it momentarily attracted the attention of half the bar.

Mason smiled a sultry smile and I relaxed into the chair and
began to tell him about the time I was seventeen and worked in a
Tex Mex restaurant and the Gipsy Kings were on repeat for the next
two years of my life and became the soundtrack to my youth. He
listened with intent and intrigue and we laughed and talked some
more and ordered more olives and then some very strong Belgian
beer arrived. We made it to a table to eat and there was more
drinking and soon the night began to become very hazy as I once
again lost all inhibitions. The shackles of parental responsibilities
were gone, the sadness of the last twenty years had lifted, and I was
once again Frankie, the girl about town, who knew everyone, who
could hold the banter and laugh at herself. It felt so good that I
didn't want the night to end.

* * *

January 1999

*I made it through Christmas without you. It was painful in every way.
Painful to swallow, painful to see Mum and Dad's taut expression as we
ploughed through a day on autopilot, wondering if we should do the stuff
we normally did: make the trifle you loved every year, get the board
games out after lunch. It seemed a bit silly playing with just three, but we
managed half an hour. I received an odd look when I suggested setting the
table for four and leaving your space there. They didn't object but it felt
weird and I regretted it the moment I sat down and had to stare at an*

empty set place, all the while expecting you to bound through the door as though you had just popped out. I made it through that lunch, my toes curling to stop myself crying. Mum and Dad had seen enough of that these last few months. I had to be the strong one now. I booked in for a few more therapy sessions without telling Mum and Dad. They have each other. I didn't see them talk but occasionally I would see Mum reach out and grab Dad as though she might fall and he needed to catch her. He always would and then he would fold her into his arms, I would watch them from the doorway sometimes then retreat with that aching emptiness into the shadows.

I opened my eyes and the room was still dark. I was used to waking early for work and, with or without alcohol in my system, I would mechanically rise at a reasonable hour. I thought I had been through enough in my time to handle the aftermath of a drinking session, I had got up and worked through hangovers from hell, I had gone straight into work on no sleep and worked through until the next night. But nothing could prepare me for a hangover from Belgian beer. The first thing that struck me was that I couldn't remember how I got back to the room last night. The second was that I could feel pain. When I looked down, I could see scratches on the inside of my legs.

* * *

I showered, wincing at the pain from the sore marks on my inner thighs, then I took a moment to look at the severity of them once I was dry. I found some Sudocrem left over from a family holiday in my toiletry bag and slathered some on the red marks. I dressed in an orange and yellow pattered wrap dress, tights and boots. I wrapped a chunky cardigan around me and found my way down to the restaurant where I was meeting Mason. I felt my stomach go tight as a young staff member met my eye. The flutter of her eyes and the serious expression made me wonder if she had been on duty last night and whether I had done or said anything to cause a scene or embarrass myself. I could barely look at her and instead I flashed her my room card and found a table in the corner. As I walked, I could see heads moving, were they turning towards me? Did people recognise me?

I could feel the expanse of the wood next to the windows, the weight of its wonder pushed itself against the glass, the endless depths within it calling to me. I felt the effects of last night's drinking, hard. My body felt almost weightless as though I might float away. I aligned the cutlery next to the napkin and forced a smile when a waiter poured me a glass of water. When he walked away I drank it in one and used the napkin to pat my lips. I felt the familiar post-drink sweats sweeping over me and the room felt as though it were closing in.

My breathing became rapid and then, just as I went to stand to race to the toilet to prevent the panic attack I could feel building, Mason appeared, striding confidently towards me.

'Keegan, no need to stand on my arrival,' he said with a wide smile.

He sat down.

'How's the head?' He leant to touch my forehead and I found myself jolting backwards. I had no idea, still, what we did. If we did? How was I supposed to ask that kind of question, here, now?

Mason gave a small laugh and picked up the menu.

'What's good? We have a bit of a busy day, so I'd stock up on the carbs. Unless you're one of *those* girls?'

'No. I need carbs,' I said, eyeing up the cheese, meats and breads a few feet away. I stood and went over to fill a plate. When I returned the waiter had brought coffee.

'How do you like your eggs in the morning?' Mason said with a wink.

I furrowed my brow. Mason assessed me for a second. 'It's a joke, Keegan. I ordered them poached with sourdough.'

'Great,' I said biting into some gouda cheese and bread.

'Frankie.'

I looked up.

'Do you wish to talk about last night?' Mason looked solemn.

The bread in my mouth felt incredibly dry and I struggled to swallow it. I felt the sting of the scratches on my thighs. I looked guiltily into my plate of food and swallowed painfully.

'It was the Belgian beer and the day's travelling, it knocked me for six. I knew the beer was strong... I just... did we...?'

'Did we what? We were eating dessert and you said you were going to the toilet and I didn't see you for the rest of the night.'

I laughed. Part relief, part nerves, still unsure where the second half of the night went. And not for the first time either. 'Well, I woke up in my room safe and sound,' I said breezily.

'If that's what you say, but that's not how my version of the night went. You see, I went to your room,' Mason said seriously. 'I waited an hour and persuaded the concierge to open your door to check you were okay. He kindly did so and when we looked in, you weren't there.'

* * *

For the second time on our trip so far I had abandoned Mason. I was now standing in the ladies' facilities, holding my wrists under the cold tap, trying to calm my nerves. How was it possible to have a complete blackout, to not remember massive sections of an evening? I didn't drink to excess all the time, but it seemed recently things were spiralling out of control. Things felt like they were unravelling because of the toy car, the texts, my doubts over

Damian and I. Then there was the person I was desperately avoiding. I wasn't sure how, but I knew I needed to pull it together.

I looked at myself in the mirror. 'Get. A. Grip,' I said to myself slowly.

* * *

I met Mason back at reception.

'Is everything okay, Frankie?' Mason's brow furrowed with concern, he almost looked in pain.

'Look, Mason, I don't know what you think you saw or what you think happened last night but I was drunk. It was that simple. I had obviously popped out of my room to get something when you came to try and find me, but I know I woke up there this morning, so all is well. I have a bit of a hangover but nothing some more Belgian bread and cheese and a vat of Orangina won't solve. I'm ready for the day and you needn't worry about me.' I leant into him and placed my hand on his arm. 'But thank you for your concern anyway, it was very sweet.'

I felt the look pass between us as my hand remained on Mason's arm for a few seconds. Maybe it was the hangover, our close proximity in the foyer or the softness of his suit jacket, but he held my gaze for a few seconds, and I felt fully in control of us right then as my stomach fizzed with a strange unfamiliar excitement.

* * *

The morning passed in a dreamlike haze as though I wasn't a participant but an observer of my own behaviour in an all-male meeting. I surprised myself at several times during the presentation they gave, piping up to make valid points and asking questions which gained me more than one nod of approval from Mason. By the end I was receiving firm handshakes from all three men and as I shook the final man's hand, I felt a touch from Mason in the small of my back. I turned and his eyes met mine and for just a second we were the only people in the room.

We walked out of the building and once outside in the cool autumn air I could smell a range of unfamiliar smells, all of which were tantalising my taste buds. I was suddenly ravenously hungry.

I was about to stride on up the road, back towards the station where we would catch the taxi to our next appointment, when Mason grabbed my arm and swung me round right there in the street.

'My God, Keegan, you were unbelievable in there! What happened? You charmed those men right out of their comfort zones, they were practically giving us the products for free. I think we have secured a very good relationship there. I am leaving you in charge of all their calls in future.'

I laughed, there in the street I felt a million weights lift from my shoulders. I saw his face suddenly look as youthful as it ever could. He was smiling a full smile I had never seen before.

'Come on, I smell bratwurst and fried onions, let's grab some before the next meeting.'

* * *

The second and third meetings of the day went as well as the first and Mason congratulated me as we climbed into a taxi to take us back to the hotel.

'I'm looking forward to dinner with you tonight. Maybe don't disappear this time?' He looked over at me with his head leaning against the back seat of the cab.

I looked down and saw the multi-coloured flash of his socks, showing his sunnier side. A part of him I felt I wanted to know more about.

I swallowed, and in my mind's eye I allowed a brief image of Damian at home, then I turned to Mason.

'Me too.'

Mason smiled and then he closed his eyes, the bob of the cab lulling him into a light doze. I squeezed my hands together and I felt the tingling sensation rush into my gut and I was thrust back to another time when I felt this way.

I woke to a hazy light sneaking through the half closed curtains in Todd's bedroom. I was in a double futon bed in an attic room in his parents' house. It was a minimalistic room, not because he was trying to be trendy but because that represented who Todd was. Around me were torn cigarettes and tobacco on top of a vinyl record; some house tune Todd had been playing me last night and one he was adding to his collection. He was still only a bedroom DJ but hoping to break out in the new year into some local pubs and clubs. In the corner was last month's Mixmag magazine, Fat Boy Slim grinning against a background of yellow smiley faces. There was a coffee table at the end of the bed with a small TV on it and next to that, the bottle of vodka we had been drinking when we got in.

I sat up, from under the dark grey duvet, and pushed a few pillows behind my back and neck. I could feel the after effects of the night before. I had felt Todd's presence next to me all night. It wasn't invasive, we were synced in our waking and sleeping and occasionally I would feel his firm arms around me, his soft breath on my cheek. He was kind, gentle. He didn't push me to do anything

I didn't want to do and I woke with a kind of happiness I hadn't felt in a long time.

He kissed me softly then padded downstairs, topless in jogging bottoms. I could hear the distant sound of his parents performing what I presumed were their usual weekend rituals and I felt my gut tighten at the thought of them questioning Todd about who was here and the prospect of having to meet them at some point.

He came back into the bedroom with a tray of tea and toast.

I picked up Todd's t-shirt from next to the bed, which smelt heavily of smoke and his aftershave, and pulled it on.

'Are your parents wondering who you have up here?' I asked coyly as Todd handed me a cup of tea.

'Nah, they are used to me bringing people back.'

I looked at him over my tea.

'Not like that,' he said quickly.

I nodded and took a sip of my tea. He smiled a wide grin and his eyes, which still seemed stoned from last night, were half closed.

'How's ya tea?' he asked through that grin.

'Good. How did you know how I have it?'

Todd laughed and sat down on the edge of the bed. I shifted my legs.

''Cos you told me last night,' he laughed again, 'it was the last thing you said to me before you fell asleep. Strong, milk and two sugars.'

'Oh yeah, I did,' I said dreamily as the hazy memory floated back.

Todd leant in to kiss me, no warning.

'God, you are cute.' I could smell the intoxicatingly sweet scent of last night's alcohol on his breath.

I kissed him back. 'Cute?'

'Yeah, there's nothing wrong with cute. Sorry, do I need to say, "You're such a sexy woman"?' Todd said in a deep husky tone and I looked back up and laughed at him.

'No, that's weird.'

'You're not like other girls, are you, Frankie,' Todd said seriously all of sudden, 'You have this aura. It's addictive.' He took my cup and placed it on the floor, then he straddled me over the duvet and kissed me long and hard.

* * *

After that day we were inseparable, much to Kiefer's dislike. But as I reminded him, I couldn't live my life by his choices.

'I wouldn't expect you to like Todd anyway,' I shouted at him the following weekend as I stood in a lime green baby doll dress and trainers. We were going to a night club in the next city: me, Nancy, Todd and a few of his mates.

'You won't get in with your hair like that,' he said, pointing at my long bunches, 'You look about five.'

I was trying to look like Baby Spice, but I didn't tell Kiefer that.

Reese winced, then gave me a sympathetic smile. 'I like your dress,' she said sincerely.

* * *

Just outside the club, Nancy's hand was draped through my arm and Todd and his mates were walking behind us. Minty was having a night off to recover from the massive bender last weekend.

I saw the bouncers stop a girl at the door and watched as she rummaged in her bag. I could tell she was being ID'd. I pulled my arm from Nancy and subtly pulled the bunches out of my hair, wrapping the hair bands around my wrist. I flicked my hair forward and shook it up from the roots then flicked it back so it was full of body. Then I pulled my baby doll dress down at the chest, exposing a patch of bare breast, just before we approached the step where the bouncers stood. The girl stood to the side looking forlorn.

They looked down at us from their step. I could hear the bass line from one of my favourite tracks. The speed I had just taken in the car was now bringing me up, I was itching to get inside.

'Evening, lads,' I said with an inordinate amount of confidence.

'Ladies,' one bouncer replied and stood aside to let us through. I turned to see Todd and his two mates walking in behind us as the bouncers eyed them for any sign of trouble. Todd caught my eye and smiled. I blew him a kiss and with Nancy on my arm once more we burst through the double doors into an electrifying expanse of multi-coloured lights and smoke billowing from a machine. The DJ stood high and proud on a stage, the crowd was screaming and whooping as the track built to its crescendo and we nudged our way through the sea of bodies, all sweating and moving in time to the music. The beat stopped, the DJ threw in a spin back and the track kicked in. The house lights went on full, then the strobe went into full throttle. The thick heavy bass pulsated through the crowds, into our bodies and our veins. I threw my arms in the air and saw Nancy and Todd do the same.

Then we just danced.

I sat down opposite Mason at dinner, having just returned from the ladies'.

'Good, you came back.' Mason looked visibly relieved.

'I'm not as drunk as I was last night,' I smiled and tucked my hair behind my ears and looked at the menu. 'But there's still time,' I said quietly and from behind my menu and heard Mason sniff a laugh out.

'Grilled mussels it is, then,' I said, 'and I'll just stick to the champagne tonight.' I laughed at the absurdity of the sentence. 'How will I cope when I go home and have to deal with bog standard chardonnay?'

'How the mighty will fall,' Mason smiled. He was sitting back casually in his chair. He always appeared fairly relaxed but he always had that look of concentration etched across his face, the face of a businessman with a hundred tasks flying through his brain. But now the slightly furrowed brow had gone.

'How is the fam?' Mason said with a hint of sarcasm, as though he didn't actually want to know.

'Yes, they are good.'

It was as good an answer as I could manage based on the fact I had only texted Damian twice since I had been away, once to remind him to pack Pixie's school t-shirt into her gym bag and the other to tell him there was bread in the freezer. Always carrying the emotional labour even though I wasn't in the house or even the same country.

'Good, good,' he said, looking anywhere except at me. I could feel this thing building between us, I was unsure what to do with it or how to move it forward.

'Do they miss you, when you're away?'

'Yes, I suppose they do. I choose not to speak to them, you know, FaceTime and all that nonsense. I feel guilty. I miss them. But I worry that if they see me or they hear me, especially Maddox as he is so young, they won't understand.'

'Yes, I see.' He took a drink of champagne. 'Absence makes the heart grow fonder.'

I took a swig of the drink and just smiled with my eyes. I wasn't sure that absence was doing anything other than driving Damian and I further apart.

Mason put his champagne glass down. 'Look, Frankie. I don't mean to pry and you can tell me to get lost if you like but I just wondered, if all isn't well, you know, at home, you could say and I won't judge you.'

'Well, that's very perceptive of you, Mason.' I put my glass down, now empty, and felt the swell of the alcohol do its work. 'I don't really know is the honest answer. I suppose we are just going through what every couple at this stage in their lives goes through, dealing with huge mortgages and bills and kids and activities and endless to-do lists and well, truth is, Damian,' I cleared my throat, 'that's my husband—'

'Ah, so he has a name. I have never heard you mention him before.'

'Which is why you are asking?'

Mason nodded.

'Damian and I, we are drifting in separate directions.' I didn't know why I was telling Mason this. Was it because I felt comfortable in his company, or was it because I needed to make him aware there was some possibly of my status becoming single sometime soon?

'He doesn't really know what he is doing with his career and he always seems a little lost when he's with the kids. It's like he woke up one day and this family had been planted in his life,' I laughed, 'a bit like that film with Nicholas Cage, *Family Guy*, where he wakes up, having lived a millionaire bachelor life, and is suddenly a car salesman living in the suburbs and married to his childhood sweetheart.'

'I know the very film. Great actor, too.'

'Yeah, well, for the first half of the film he resents what he has been given, doesn't he, so he is always walking around with that lost expression, asking his kid how to change a diaper.' My laughed fizzled out. 'It's a bit like that, I guess. Like we are all an illusion and he should be somewhere else, anywhere than where he is, with us, living this fairly uneventful life.'

'Does he... drink? You know, to compensate for his miserable life with you and the kids,' Mason said sarcastically.

'Oh God, no. Beer, yes, but Damian can't really drink. If you give him a spirit, he's completely unrecognisable. I've seen it once. It was not pretty.'

Mason nodded and filled my glass up with more champagne. 'And is that how you feel, Frankie? That your life is uneventful?'

'I hope not,' I said placing my glass down on the table a little too hard. Mason reached over and put his hand around mine on the glass. I looked at it and then up at him, my stomach rolled a somersault and I felt my body quiver.

He pulled his lips in a tight smile and let go of my hand.

'Everything is a phase, Frankie. Nothing is forever.'

'I know. I'm sorry I haven't talked much of my family before. I guess I like to remain professional.'

'It's okay, I get it. But you know, for this bit, tonight, I'm not your employer, you don't need to be anything other than what you are. If you want to go for a midnight run in the woods, I'm not going to stop you.'

I shot him a look. He had confirmed my fears. I had discovered my red shoes and dress under my bed covered in mud.

'The receptionist said she spotted you heading out that way last night and you looked like you were pretty interested in the woods and well, I couldn't help noticing your arm.' I lifted my arm. 'It has a scratch.' Mason pointed.

I looked and just below my elbow I noticed there was a long red scratch.

'I figured, since you were missing half the night, maybe that's where you went. Is there some affiliation with the woods? Something you missed on your CV, maybe?' He looked away and smiled absently at a passing waitress.

'I... I don't remember,' I lied as the images of that night twenty years ago came flooding back.

'Frankie, are you ok?' The room felt as though it was closing in. I looked up and Mason's voice sounded as though it were under water.

'Keegan, don't bail on me again. We can call it a night if you like?'

I took a deep breath, touched Mason's hand across the table and said, 'I'm fine. Let's eat.'

* * *

We filled up with mussels and frites and champagne, mixed in with plenty of water. I didn't want a repeat of last night.

Mason put his knife and fork together on his plate and wiped his mouth with his napkin.

'Is there no one at home for you, then?' I asked.

'Only my mum. She's seventy-six so I kind of have to care for her a little bit.' Mason's phone pinged and he pressed a few buttons. 'Oh, look, that's her now, always checking in.' He smiled.

'So no girlfriend, that's what I'm getting at,' I said.

'I know, and not so subtly either.'

I looked up at Mason with wide eyes and a cheeky grin.

'Oh, come on, Frankie, I think you have me worked out by now. Fifty-two, no kids, no ex-wife.'

'Oh heck, you're gay?' I put my hand over my mouth.

'I wish it were that simple.'

'Okay, care to elaborate?'

'Not really. Just that there never has been anyone.' Mason looked at me and narrowed his eyes. 'Okay, Keegan. Prepare yourself, I'm about to monologue. My father left when I was very young, my mother raised me but suffered terribly with depression her whole life, inflicted by her own poor upbringing. Times were hard, my mum grew up and took many of her frustrations out on me.

'I haven't ever been able to love anyone, Frankie. I just don't have the capability. Women have tried.' Mason paused to laugh at this and I offered a small smile in return. 'I don't know, I guess I am just as messed-up as the rest of them.' He laughed but it sounded hollow.

Then he leant forward and whispered, 'Anyway, enough of that. How about some pudding. I have heard the molten chocolate pudding here is to die for.'

* * *

January 1999

I live for the day when I see you again, for how can I not. Not when I have so much to tell you, to show you.

There can't be such a thing as never again, or nothing. You were once so physical, so present. I live for the day when you walk through a door or pick up the phone to call.

Sometimes I hear a word muttered, the tone of your voice so familiar I turn and expect to see you there but it's not you. It's someone else, different age, slighter build. I search their features for a sign of you. It could be you, how you would be now. I am trapped with the memory of the last day we spent together. That was the day to say goodbye. But I never knew. Why must these emotions catch me off guard? There is still so much to say.

I'll save it for another day.

29

NOW

'I think a night cap is in order after such a successful day, don't you?' Mason said as we reached the bar.

'Just a tea for me. Mint,' I said, not wanting to lose control. I felt perfectly inebriated.

'Mint tea it is. Sensible choice.'

Mason ordered a large brandy.

I tried to stifle a giggle when it arrived in a large oversized glass and he began to swirl the golden liquid around.

'What?'

'It's a bit of cliché, isn't it? Big boss man orders large brandy in a comedy sized glass and swigs it at the bar.'

'I am a walking cliché. What can I say? Here's your tea, Keegan, drink up.'

The barman placed a large glass with a handle before me and inside were bright green mint leaves infusing in steaming water.

'Looks good. Very healthy. You're a better woman than I am.'

I laughed. 'I try. Anyway, you fill your boots. I won't judge you. I am sure you're as fit as a fiddle under all that.'

Mason looked down at his buttoned up shirt and then back at me again. 'Are you flirting with me, Keegan?'

I smiled, the rush of the champagne still in my body. Every now and again I saw the flash of woods. But which ones? My mind was awash with images of trees. A place I had been, recently, yes, according to Mason and other witnesses. But back then, I had sought safety in them. I pushed the images away and focused on this thing that was building between me and Mason.

'I wouldn't know how to flirt,' I said nonchalantly, trying to bring myself back to the moment. Mason gave me a friendly push.

'I don't believe that for a second. I think you would know exactly what to do.'

'I'm thirty-six with two kids. I don't do flirting,' I said.

'Oh, I think you do,' Mason said. 'I just think you don't know you are doing it.'

'Shall I put it on my CV then? Professional flirter.'

'You don't tell people you're a professional flirter. That's the mystique of the professional flirter. People never know. Until they have been flirted with.' Mason wiggled his fingers.

'Okay, I'm taking this all on board. From a man who knows what he is talking about, I presume?'

'I couldn't possibly say, Keegan.'

'Should I call you Valentine?'

'Well, that depends, doesn't it, Keegan,' Mason laughed.

I pushed away my cup of tea, still full, and stood up. Suddenly I felt like a night cap. 'Do you know what, I don't believe I have seen your room. I will be a bit upset if you got the bigger suite.'

Mason looked at me for a second and then downed his brandy.

'Are you sure you wish to see my suite, Frankie. Because you know, once you have seen my... suite, there's no unseeing it.'

'Oh my God, that's hilarious, are we really doing this? 'Cos, you know, I just really want to see your suite.'

Mason stood up, took me firmly by the hand and began escorting me from the dining room.

'Come on, you, let's go.'

I felt the excitement rush through me like a jolt of electricity.

* * *

Inside the lift Mason and I stood close together and I felt the butterfly sensation of his fingertips on mine. There was another couple in the lift so neither of us spoke. We arrived on the second floor and all four of us walked out together. The couple gave us a polite goodnight nod and headed in the opposite direction. Mason and I walked in silence past my room and towards his. He pulled out his card from his right pocket, still clutching my hand, and then pressed the key to the door.

I gasped as I walked in.

'I knew it.' I let go of Mason's hand and walked round the lounge area which had slightly open sliding double doors leading to a neatly made up super king size bed. Two sofas and a reclining chair were in front of me, with a sixty inch LED screen on the wall. To my right was a desk with a chair and a mini bar.

'Right, what are we having?' I wandered over to the mini bar and fridge.

'There should be a nice champagne in the fridge,' Mason said, his voice soft and small.

I spun round and walked to the fridge.

'Oooh, expecting company, were we?'

'Well, one is always hopeful.' Mason stood with his hands in his pockets and shuffled his feet.

I opened the fridge and pulled out the bottle of champagne. I found two glasses and laid them on the bar.

'Let me do that.' Mason's voice was behind me and he took my elbow with one hand and relieved me of the bottle with the other.

'Well, it was a little heavy,' I laughed.

Mason skilfully opened the bottle and poured two glasses of the fizz. He handed one glass to me and held the other close to mine so they clinked.

'A little night cap, Keegan. To us. Thanks for today, you were a star – I couldn't have done it without you.'

'Oh, I'm sure you would have found a way,' I said.

'Frankie.' The sincerity of his voice made my heart beat so hard I could feel it in my throat. I gulped the champagne.

'You're beautiful.' Mason was looking into my eyes. 'I have nothing to lose here, you have everything to lose.'

I stood still as Mason moved an inch closer, then another inch, until his face was closer than I had ever seen it. I was thinking about what could happen and that now was the time to step backwards, put the glass down and walk away. And yet, I didn't.

Instead I took the glass out of his hands and placed it on the counter as my lips moved closer to his.

30

AUGUST 1998

I was lying in bed. It was half past twelve. I should have been at work five hours ago. I had woken with a head that felt like it was stuffed with cotton wool, I felt tingly to the touch, feverish. But it wasn't a fever. It was self-inflicted. I had rolled in at six in the morning with every intention of sleeping for an hour and then getting straight into the shower and heading to work but a shadow had enveloped me and I couldn't bring myself to get out of bed. So I pulled another sicky. I had rung in and heard the manager's weary reply, as I was obviously not the first young employee to call in sick on a Saturday morning.

The guilt was lying heavy on my chest. I hated letting people down. I liked my job. I just wanted to do it on my own terms, in my own time, not when I was told to. I knew that wasn't conducive with society but neither was going out all night and spending the little money I had on vodka mules and getting into nightclubs. The drugs were free. I didn't have to pay for those. Todd took care of it because he took care of everyone, because that was his job. He didn't need to worry about having to ring in sick, if he didn't fancy working he didn't have to. But that's because his job only involved walking or driving a few blocks to a punter's house to present them with a bag of green herbs.

* * *

After the club we had driven to the Breakfast Club, a sort of come down venue where people were engulfed by oversized bean bags and comfy sofas. There was a DJ playing the sort of house music that kept you moving if you wanted to keep on a high for a bit longer. I had just sat there and let the beat impact my body without moving. I had drunk an insipid coffee. There was no food because no one had an appetite.

* * *

The door opened an inch and Kiefer stuck his head round. I was just a face cocooned by a duvet.

'Not working today?' he asked.

'Rang in sick.'

'That's not good.'

'Oh, sorry, goody two shoes, I forgot you never do anything wrong.'

'Alright, come down, queen, I was just concerned. It's not like you to miss your job, I thought you loved it?'

'I can love a job and still be ill.'

'Summer's nearly over, Frank. You will be going to college soon, you can't carry on like this.'

I didn't reply.

'You're not ill.' Kiefer shut the door and the sound made me flinch. It was true, I loved my job, but the thought of standing in the hotel, talking to customers, serving breakfast and having to inhale eggs and bacon was already making my stomach turn. I vowed never to call in sick again. Besides, I needed the money. I needed to keep funding the nights out somehow.

I closed my eyes and fell into a fitful sleep.

31

NOW

I ran along the corridor, my dress slightly hitched up, the scent of the aftershave clinging to me and the whispered warning still ringing in my ear: 'Are you sure, Frankie, are you sure?'

I didn't stop running until I was at my door, a few moments from Mason's, but as soon as I hit the key to the lock, I ran into the room, shut the door and leant my weight against it. I stabilised my breathing, threw my purse on the bed and walked to the bathroom where I turned on the shower full blast. I stripped and got under the almost scorching water and remained there until I felt calmer.

Why did I feel so full of hatred? Was it because I knew I had initiated the move to Mason's room, then the kiss? He said he had wanted it too. Maybe more than me. But then something had clicked, a distant faraway voice of Pixie or Maddox, I wasn't sure, but they were there, my kids, my loves, the reason for everything. Whatever was happening with Damian and I, whatever he was doing or thinking, I couldn't throw everything away.

I sat on the bed in my towel and saw there was a text message. It was Mason.

Everything is cool, Keegan. See you 8 a.m. sharp for breakfast meeting

So, if he was able to just push all those feelings aside, then so must I.

A few seconds later another text pinged through.

Kids missing you

Damian was doing his usual, removing his own feelings and projecting them through the kids.

I knew I was a little drunk on champagne and I was incredibly tired. I needed to sleep. Damian was fine, the kids were fine.

I didn't do anything with Mason, that was the important thing, our lips met and then I panicked. I was swept away in a moment of lust, that was all.

* * *

I had set my alarm for 7.30 a.m. as a precaution, thinking I would definitely wake up before then, but I did indeed wake as the alarm pounded its intrusive bleeping into the room. I pressed it off and automatically went to the messages to check there were none from Damian.

I showered and dressed and was out of the door by 7.55 a.m.. As I closed my door Mason was walking towards me from his room, his brief case swinging next to him.

'Morning, Keegan.'

I closed my door. 'Back to Keegan, is it?' I said dryly.

We looked at one another for a few seconds, his face looked so youthful today. I realised I was staring.

Mason laughed and put his arm around me, a friendly hug this time. 'Come on, let's get you some breakfast.'

* * *

We sat down in the dining room and Mason ordered us coffees. He began eagerly tapping on his phone, the first business messages of the day. Then he dropped his phone into his briefcase and looked at me.

'Let me go and grab your daily intake of carbs this morning, you sit tight.' He stood up and headed off to the breakfast buffet cart.

The waiter came along and moved Mason's chair in to get past. As he did, he knocked over Mason's briefcase, sending a few items flying.

'Oh, I am sorry, miss.' The waiter stooped to begin picking things up.

I shooed him away. 'No, it's fine, I'll do it.' I pushed my chair back, fell to my knees and stood the briefcase back up. I saw that a small diary, two pens and Mason's mobile had fallen out. I gathered them up and went to drop the items back in, but as I did, I spotted another phone, a much smaller model. I looked up over the table and saw Mason still at the buffet bar so I lifted the second phone up and looked at it as I tried to piece together why Mason would have two phones. Surely one phone can carry all the information one man needed for work. I thought perhaps he used one for personal calls, but he had his one large phone at dinner and had received a text message from his mother. I was mulling over all this information when I looked up and saw that Mason was making his way back from the cart. I threw the stuff into the bag, stood up and brushed down my skirt.

'Everything okay?' Mason placed a plate of pastries, cheese and ham in the centre of the table.

'Yes, fine, thanks,' I said, forcing my face into a smile.

* * *

Mason and I flew home in virtual silence, no doubt each of us wondering what the other one was thinking. I couldn't think of any more things to say to him that I hadn't already said before.

We parted at the airport. Mason kissed me lightly on the cheek and brushed his hand against the side of my other cheek.

'Look after yourself.'

I smiled up at him and tried to disguise the tears that I knew were glistening in my eyes but it was too late, he had clocked them. I blinked and one fell. He wiped it with his thumb. I closed my eyes and he kissed me again on the other cheek. I thought to myself, this will be it, I will go back to Damian today and enjoy the rest of the weekend with my kids and come Monday I will have to forget that any of this happened between me and Mason. Because it was for the best. This was how it had to be. Anything else was too confusing.

* * *

The kids came running like a herd of animals and almost bowled me over at the door. I paused there with them wrapped in my arms and just inhaled them. Damian stood behind them in the hallway, leaning against the wall. I stood up and then my senses were taken over by something else. I wasn't sure but I thought I could smell cleaning products. I carried Maddox on my hip and Pixie skipped next to me wittering on about auditions for the Christmas school play.

I entered the kitchen and was taken aback at the sight. It was spotless.

'Kids have been fed,' Damian said as he took in my expression. 'I've booked Aimee to babysit, I thought we could go out and you could tell me all about your trip?' I instantly felt deflated. I had thought about the trip all the way home, pushing out the bit where I discovered two phones in Mason's briefcase. I realised it was entirely plausible that a man of Mason's status would have two, maybe more, phones. And Damian telling me we were going out for dinner was the equivalent of him getting a pin and popping the balloon I had cocooned myself inside where only thoughts of Mason and the hotel and food and the streets of Liège were allowed. Now my feelings were as stark as the spotless kitchen I stood in, as I tried to deal with the reality of going out for dinner with my husband.

'I'm tired, Damian. I've been travelling—'

Damian butted in, 'I know, I thought just a quick early dinner. We'll be back by nine. I've booked Aimee already and she's looking forward to it.'

'It's alarming, isn't?'

'Eh, what do you mean?'

'That a girl of her age wants to spend so much time here with our kids, when she should be, I don't know?'

'Getting wrecked like you were, you mean?'

I raised my eyebrows at Damian. 'I was always fairly sensible compared to most, and you can hardly talk.'

Damian moved around the kitchen island and straightened a few pamphlets as if to highlight again how well he had done while I was away.

'Well, for whatever reason, Aimee enjoys spending time here. She likes us.'

I thought about the zoomed in image of me and Damian on her laptop screen, and I wondered if she liked us a little too much. It hadn't occurred to me before that she might have a little crush on Damian, or even me.

'Okay, well, I'll put the kids in the bath so they are ready for bed when Aimee gets here and then we can go. Why don't you go and unpack and get ready?' And then Damian gave me a half smile. He scooped the children up who immediately protested, then suddenly, I was alone in my very quiet and tidy kitchen.

32

NOW

I stood in our bedroom with my case from the trip and I thought how time was such a strange concept, neither real nor hypothetical and how it felt like only a second ago I was just here, packing to leave. I looked at the sheets. I could tell they had been replaced with clean ones while I was away, a job I had intended to do before I left. The scent of the floral washing powder was filling the room. I looked round and realised that it also looked tidier and cleaner than usual, which was such a rarity because it was the one room I just didn't have enough time to focus on and was usually a dumping ground for all our washing and anything that needed sorting out.

I laid the case on the floor, opened it up and began to pull out the bits of washing that needed to go in the laundry basket when out of the corner of my eye I saw something glistening. I moved over on my knees and picked up a small pink studded earring with the back missing. I examined it for a moment or two, trying to ascertain when I could have dropped it, and then it occurred to me it wasn't mine at all. I didn't own any pink studded earrings.

So if this earring didn't belong to me, and Pixie didn't have her ears pierced, it had to belong to another female. As I sat on the bedroom floor, which Damian hadn't ever cleaned since we had got together, I didn't need to spend too long trying to work out exactly what was going on here. I already had the image of Harriet from a few doors down in my head. Of course, he was shagging her, why wouldn't he? And this dinner, this taking me out was obviously his way to cover up the guilt that he was shrouded in. I thought about the almost kiss I had with Mason and knew that whatever was happening with Damian and I right now and whomever this earring belonged to, she had been in my bedroom and that trumped my near miss with Mason.

* * *

I sat opposite Damian in the restaurant as he fiddled with his beer and rattled on about all the activities he and the kids had got up to while I was away.

We nibbled some olives and dipping bread and Damian asked about the trip. I made sure to make eye contact as I described the meetings, how well I did, how Mason was super impressed and in fact how I had surprised myself. I asked about the kids, if they had any play dates so I could establish when exactly Damian was able to shag another woman in our bed, but he assured me the kids had stayed with him the whole time. Apart from when they were at school, of course.

'And your room was nice?' Damian asked. How could he ask that when he knew exactly what he had been up to when I was away? But we continued to dance this routine of politeness, asking the right amount of questions to dig deep enough without alerting each other to the fact that neither of us trusted one another right now.

'Yes, the room was lovely. Spacious. Comfy.'

'Bet you didn't want to come home?' Damian gave a wry smile.

'Well, I'm here,' I said dipping a piece of bread into the pool of oil and vinegar.

'Everything okay, the kids okay?' Damian motioned to my phone on the table.

'No word.'

'Great.' He looked around. 'Mains should be here soon, I'm famished. Are you hungry?'

I was not at all hungry.

As Damian wittered on about a work project that was in the pipeline I barely listened. The waiter brought our food and we ate in near silence.

When he had finished, he put his knife and fork together. 'You've not eaten much,' he commented.

I looked down at my risotto, which had a small dent in it.

'I'm just not hungry as I thought. Must be all that Belgian beer.'

Damian eyed me over his glass of wine. 'Oh really, you drank a lot of it then?'

'A few.' I looked towards the window.

'Listen, Frank.' I felt my stomach sink. Was this it, was he about to tell me what had happened? Did I need to prepare myself for breaking up, or was he about to beg for forgiveness and I needed to prepare myself for counselling and months more of awkward meals like this while we found ourselves again as a couple?

'I've been thinking about stuff while you have been away. I guess your absence gave me the space to gain some perspective.'

I swallowed hard. 'Right.'

'Well, yeah, I realised how things have started to evolve and realised how much the kids need you, they really missed you when you were gone and well, I just think I'm ready to go back into the workplace, you know, do a proper job. I can still keep tinkering away on these little projects but I know it's been unfair of me to expect you to work all this time, even though I know you prefer it and it's saved us a hell of a lot on childcare. Maddox starts school next year and I think it's really important for one of us to be at home for them. I feel after I have done it all these years, I figured, maybe you'd like to be there for them. Maybe cut your hours, or look for something part time?'

I played with a leftover piece of bread. 'You want me to leave my job because you are suddenly geared up to go back to work all these years later when I have been holding the fort.'

I looked at Damian and he looked back long and hard. His eyes seemed darker than ever. 'Be careful up there, Frankie, it's a long way to fall.' He continued staring as though he was looking straight through me.

'You can't freak me out with your staring eyes, Damian. Why exactly should I be the one to quit, after everything I have done to climb the ladder to success while you sat around and contemplated your life for the last God knows how many years?'

'You're right.' Damian put his glass of beer down firmly on the table. 'You couldn't hack being at home full time, which is why you were back at work as soon as you stopped breastfeeding. Your demons won't allow you to sit at home with the kids. Especially in the winter, once the darkness sets in, you aren't well enough. I see it in your eyes, Frankie, the pain and the suffering are still there and I am really sorry about what happened to your brother and the other person but at some point you need to accept that you should have done way more therapy than whatever measly amount you did after it happened. It's traumatic and all this time later you haven't dealt with it and it haunts you every day and therefore haunts me and soon it will haunt the kids. It's become part of the fabric of our life, this thing that you carry around with you every day. I want it gone. I need it gone to be able to thrive in this relationship. Right now I am suffocated by you!' Damian's voice was loud enough to attract a few stares from fellow diners.

'Oh, do you know what, Damian, you are so self-righteous, go fuck yourself.'

Damian stood up and threw down his napkin.

'Well, you sure as hell won't!' He hastily put some notes on the table. 'Enjoy dessert.' He grabbed his coat off the back of the chair, downed his beer and as he wiped his mouth he gave me one final glare and then walked out of the restaurant.

* * *

I felt the rage almost consuming me. Damian had only ever walked out on me in a restaurant once before, many years ago, and we vowed to never do it to one another again. I looked around and caught a couple of diners swiftly looking in the other direction. I felt myself getting hotter and felt the strain from my clenched jaw. I was furious that Damian could think I would possibly want to give up my job that I worked so damn hard at. Mason was happy for me to be flexible with my hours but to reduce them right down was never going to work for that role. I loved my kids more than anything. But Damian was right, I did find the monotony of being at home all day with both kids tiresome. It was too many hours in the day to think about the past. Kiefer was my brother, of course I was never going to get over this, and no amount of therapy was going to bring him back.

I gulped back the tears and felt the burning sensation in my nose and throat.

A waiter appeared and filled up my wine glass. I could feel the weight of his thoughts, and I gave a meek smile as he slipped away back to the waiter station. I could see him muttering something to his colleague. The humiliation did not subside. I was going to skip dessert, there was no way I was going to stay sitting alone, but there was no way I was going to go home and face Damian. I wondered what Aimee would think, seeing him come home alone? Damian would have made up an excuse for us but still she would have questioned my absence.

The notes on the table were more than enough to cover the meal so I stood up and began gathering up my belongings. But something caught my attention from the window. At first I presumed it was Damian, that maybe he had had second thoughts and was standing all forlorn at the window, waiting for me so we could get a cab together. I felt a mild moment of relief. I couldn't stand arguing and I was too tired to go and spend the rest of the evening propping up some bar.

I turned and looked at the figure staring through into the restaurant. They had their hands pressed against the window. They were wearing a black hooded coat, pulled right up over their head and almost covering their face, and if I hadn't known those eyes from all those years ago I would have looked the other way and carried on collecting my things, but they were staring straight at me, the way they had so many times before. Although it had been twenty years, there they were again, locked on mine as though a day hadn't passed.

* * *

I stumbled back towards my chair and clipped my ankle on the leg, and I gasped out in pain. I could see the waiters looking over at me, too immature in their ways to run to me and check if I was okay but intrigued by the car crash of a dinner date they were voyeurs to. I fell back into the seat, my legs felt like jelly. I took a final swig of the wine and looked anxiously around to see if anyone else could see the figure at the window. Finally, the maître d' passed by and touched my arm.

'Madam, can I get you anything?'

'Yes, it's a silly request but can you, could someone possibly go and check the...' I pointed towards the window but there was no one there. All I could see was a gentle lash of rain and a few bright car lights.

'Madam?' the maître d' continued.

'I... I'm sorry, I just saw someone, pressed against the window, it alarmed me.'

'Well, there is no one there now, madam.' He looked towards the window.

'Oh, okay.' I looked down at my wine and went to take a final gulp but there was none left and the bottle was empty.

'Can I get you a drink?'

'A brandy?'

'Of course.' The maître d' strode off towards the bar, said something authoritative and gesticulated towards the staff and they scarpered to opposite areas of the restaurant.

I sat wringing my hands and looking anxiously around.

The maître d' returned with my brandy and I thanked him.

'Madam, if there is anything else I can get you, do not hesitate to ask.'

'I don't suppose you could call me a taxi?'

'Of course, madam.'

I slowly sipped the brandy while looking uneasily at the window.

A few minutes later I felt a hand on my shoulder.

'Madam, your taxi, it is here now. Can I escort you to the car?'

'Yes, please,' I said eagerly. I was usually so street savvy but today I had no intention of walking an inch in the street alone.

He walked me to the cab and opened the door for me. 'Goodnight, madam,' he said and closed the door.

'Where to, love?' the cab driver asked. I sat for a moment and considered the last words Damian spoke to me, the way in which the meal ended and what would be waiting for me at home, the dreary aftermath of an argument, neither of us wanting to break the silence or apologise for what was said, instead each retreating to our own corners of the house, far away from disappointed looks and angry sighs.

Then I thought about the streets of the town tonight; people lurking in dark corners and alleyways. I leant forward and gave my home address to the driver.

I stole one last look behind me at the restaurant and the window where I was just sitting. As the car jerked and the diesel engine chugged into gear, I saw for a moment, there in the shadows of a shop doorway next door to the restaurant, the black hood, and as we turned the corner the person stepped forward out of the shadow, pulled down their hood and confirmed my fear.

* * *

Damian was slouched on the sofa when I got home, watching some war series on Netflix. He turned to look at me and for a moment I thought he would turn back to the TV, ignoring my presence.

'Did I leave enough cash to cover the meal?'

'Yes,' I said.

I knew Damian had done a job recently for a friend who was setting up a business from scratch – he had helped him to design his website and install some safety aspects and so I knew that was his way of showing off what he had earned as well. I was having trouble working out what Damian wanted or where exactly he was at, right now, I couldn't understand why he would want to spend his hard earned money on me while he was clearly sneaking around behind my back, but after our cross words I had no intention of furthering our discussion. If he had done something behind my back and in our room I wanted to have more proof than an earring and a secretive exchange in the neighbour's garden. I had intuition and I could sense the changes we had gone through as a couple and the distance that was opening up between us, but I needed to know for certain.

'Was Aimee okay?' I thought about my last interaction with her and my face zoomed in on her laptop.

'She seemed fine. I paid her the full amount.'

'I'm sure she was very happy with that. I'm going to bed.'

Damian turned back to his TV show.

* * *

In our bedroom, I walked over to my dressing table, where I had put the pink crystal earring in a tiny pot I used for spares, and pulled it out again, I tried to imagine if Harriet seemed like the kind of woman to wear such a thing, whether her forties style would accommodate such bling.

It vexed me how Damian talked about my therapy and how I hadn't done enough. The proof for me was sitting in that safe in my wardrobe, I poured out my feelings back then and then locked them away. Although the way the past seemed to suddenly be careering into my present, and with who I had just seen at the restaurant, along with the text messages, I knew it was time for me to seek closure.

33

SEPTEMBER 1998

I had just started college so I calmed down on the midweek nights out. Todd was understanding of this, and when his parents had gone away on a minibreak to France, he invited a few friends round for a dinner party. Todd was cooking a mushroom tagliatelle. It felt like we were a proper couple. I wanted to prove more than anything to Kiefer that this was what Todd and I were about, making steps together, not just out raving every weekend. This felt like progress, the stuff real couples did.

Nancy and Minty were coming, which I was really happy about, and a couple of Todd's other mates would be coming over too, which didn't feel as nice because the two didn't fit. Todd referred to them by their surnames, Soames and Lofty. Minty referred to them as Zig and Zag from our favourite breakfast TV show because they looked like a couple of pie-eyed gurners. I didn't even know what their first names were. I only associated them with Todd out in the clubs or at a party getting wrecked. I wanted to have a relaxing dinner party where there would be chat over the food, someone would bring a pudding, Todd would pour wine and maybe we'd end with a spliff and a game of charades. None of my gang had our own flats or houses yet, so when someone's parents went away it wasn't just anyone who was invited over. It was only people you really trusted, who weren't going to trash your house or do anything totally stupid. Which was why I was a little wary when I heard that Lofty and Soames were coming over. They weren't close friends of Todd's. They were dealers. Except they didn't stop at pot. I could see it in their eyes, that vacant glaze. They looked as though they were well on the way to losing the plot.

* * *

I opened the fridge to put the white wine in to chill. Todd's parents had one of those huge Smeg fridges with the Union Flag on it. Todd's dad had said when he bought it a year ago, 'Son, we are in the midst of a very important political and cultural epidemic and this fridge is my contribution to that.'

I asked Todd what his dad meant. Todd took my hand and said, 'This is Cool Britannia we are living through. We are part of something. Can't you feel it, Frank?' he said as he held my hand, 'In your heart, in your mind, when we're in the club, it's all around us.'

'I just thought that was the drugs,' I said, seriously enough that Todd laughed really loudly and then drew me in for a hug.

'Oh, Frankie, you are so sweet.'

Todd still hadn't actually said that we were an item, nor had he referred to me as his girlfriend. But we were spending every weekend together and now days like this during the week when his folks were away, so it felt as though we were, in fact, going out.

* * *

I went all out that night. I laid the table properly with a glass for wine and one for water like I did at the hotel. I folded the napkins and put a dessert spoon next to the knife and fork. Nancy and Minty were bringing a pavlova.

Todd came in just as I was finishing, his Timberland boots scuffing against the wooden floor of the dining room. He was smoking a spliff and handed it to me.

'Wowsers, babe, cool. You're a pro. Proper little wifey.' He bent down and put his arms around my waist, he was a few inches taller than me. A giant of a man really, and stocky too. I smiled, and kissed him, inhaling the scent of him mixed with the alcohol and tobacco on his breath.

* * *

Nancy and Minty arrived bang on 6.30 p.m. carrying a bottle of red wine and their pudding offering, then we all stood in the kitchen sipping the wine and pretending to act like connoisseurs and saying things like 'it has a good nose' and 'notes of raspberry and chocolate'.

Todd started to cook the tagliatelle while Nancy and I sat on the sofa in the lounge. I gave her all the gossip on Todd and I, and she about herself and Minty. We barely saw one another these days without the boys there too, so we began making plans for a girls' day shopping, plotting our trip starting at the Body Shop for lip balms and then Our Price for some music and Dolcis for some knee high boots for the winter.

Time was ticking on. I felt certain Soames and Lofty wouldn't show, and felt a surge of relief when Todd called us in for dinner and we all settled around the table. We got stuck into the pasta. I stole intermittent glances at Todd which he caught and then smiled at me.

'Oh my God, this is so good, Todd,' Minty said. 'Fair play, man, I can't cook for shit.'

'Yeah, that's why we eat so many burgers. I am going to turn into a burger,' Nancy scoffed.

'We don't eat that many burgers, babes?' Minty said.

Nancy laughed. 'Oh no, just the three times last week, four if you include McDonald's.'

'The best burgers,' Todd and Minty said in unison and clinked their wine glasses. I shot a look at Nancy and we both smiled. I looked at Todd. He appeared so relaxed, this seemed like the real him. I had completely forgotten about the other invited guests until the doorbell rang. I felt my body physically shrink down and dread hit the pit of my stomach. I looked at Nancy who gave me a look of sympathy.

Todd jumped straight up and went out to the hallway. I could hear the muffled deep voices of Soames and Lofty.

They came through and sat down at the table, Minty stood up and shook their hands in his usual infectiously jovial manner, apparently unperturbed by the invasion of our party of four.

Soames was small and fidgety. He had a rough little beard that was neither stubble nor fully grown. He always wore a black beanie cap. Lofty was tall and blond, with pointy features; he wore a sports sweatshirt with light denim jeans, white sports socks and Nike trainers. They were an odd looking couple, yet rarely seen apart. They both nodded their greetings at me and Nancy as they got comfortable, and Lofty instantly began skinning up at the table. I shifted in my seat and tried to suppress a sigh, but it came out anyway. Lofty looked up at me slowly, acknowledging my despair. I wanted to scream at them to get out, to tell them they were ruining what was a civilised dinner party. Todd offered them a plate of tagliatelle, but they declined. Minty offered them a glass of red, but they both asked Todd if he had any beer. With Todd headed into the kitchen I took a moment to steal a glance at Nancy, who breathed in really hard and widened her eyes at me.

'So, why do they call you Minty then?' Soames asked out of the blue and with a hint of laughter in his voice.

Minty went on to explain how he was actually called Paul Hodgkinson, but he was always eating polo mints, at least he was when we all first met him, and that's how he got his nickname which stuck and now it's just who he is.

Todd returned with three beers and I found myself narrowing my eyes at him for switching to beer after we were all having a nice time on the wine. If Todd noticed he didn't make an issue of it. Soames sniggered at nothing in particular and I found the atmosphere, which had been warm and pleasant, was now prickly and uncomfortable. He licked his rizla and looked at me as he did, the tip of his little pink tongue just visible. I turned away in disgust.

'Come on, Nance, let's clear these away,' I said and we left the dining room and returned with the pavlova. Todd, who had said he was looking forward to it, was now wiping his nose and shaking his head as Nancy cut it up and offered him a slice. I looked at Minty for confirmation. He squeezed his lips tightly and began eating his pudding. I didn't need to ask him to know he had seen cocaine disappear up the noses of Soames, Lofty and Todd in the time we had been in the kitchen.

We retired to the lounge, Nancy and I got out the Scrabble, toked on a spliff between us and fell about laughing at the darkness of the words that Nancy was putting on the board.

I tried to catch Todd's eyes a few times but he was chatting animatedly with Soames and waving a spliff around. Lofty went to the hifi and put on a mix tape from his pocket, then Todd and him were off, dancing like nutters.

Eventually Nancy and I gave up trying to play a chilled board game and slouched into one of the oversized couches with a beer each.

'No hot rocks on my folks' rugs,' Todd slurred, pointing with a spliff which instantly dropped a huge rock onto an old and expensive looking red and black oriental rug.

'What the...?' Todd said, falling to his knees and blowing at the rock which had already burned out, leaving a small charred hole behind.

Lofty's loud high-pitched laugh punctured the air.

Soames called Todd over to a chair in the corner of the lounge. We ignored them for a while, carried on talking, but then Minty pointed and I could see Lofty was holding some aluminium foil with a lighter underneath and Todd was bending down and inhaling vapour through a small tube.

'I reckon it's time to say goodnight. That shit is too heavy even for me.' Minty stood up and Nancy followed.

'Sorry, Frank, do you want us to stay, or come with us?'

'No, it's fine,' I said quickly. 'I'll stay, make sure he's okay.'

I walked them to the door. Minty went first and Nancy stood on the step. 'It's not okay, Frank, what he's doing. He could end up an addict.'

'I know,' I hissed, 'I'll keep an eye on it.'

'It's not your responsibility,' she said, and turned and went down the step.

I closed the door and went back into the lounge where Todd was completely comatose on the chair. Lofty and Soames were standing up.

'We're off,' Lofty said and patted my arm. 'Take care, sweetheart.'

Soames just looked at me with those dark glassy eyes.

I spent the night asleep at Todd's feet. When he finally woke at 6 a.m. he was disorientated and panicky. I got him some water and took him up to bed.

'You're a great girlfriend,' Todd said groggily as he fell into a slumber. I lay awake next to him all morning, watching him sleep, and despite the let-down of the evening, I felt high on love.

34

NOW

On Monday morning I had been sitting at my desk for twenty-five minutes when Lil and Fish arrived and walked over.

'Tell us, how was it? Did you have a great time? I've always wanted to go to Belgium. Babes, shall we go to Ghent next year? It looks amazing,' Lil said to Fish who nodded in approval.

'I was mostly in meetings, chatting to clients, that sort of thing,' I said.

Mine and Lil's eyes met; she smiled awkwardly and then slipped her hand through Fish's arm.

'Oh, come on, you can't ignore that Belgian beer – my God, I would have been downing that by the bucket load,' Fish laughed, rescuing me from Lil's look.

'Well, that's because you have no decorum,' I said flatly.

'Yeah right, fair play,' Fish joined in when he finally understood the flavour of my response.

'Well,' Lil said, raising her eyebrows. 'So glad you had a nice time. Come on, Fish.' She pulled at his arm. As they walked away, Lil shot me a quick look over her shoulder. I shook my head in bewilderment.

Penelope arrived at her desk opposite mine. She looked tired and gaunt.

'Morning, Penelope,' I said loudly to her back.

'Morning,' Penelope said quietly, turning my way slightly as she carried on unpacking items from her bag. 'How was Belgium?'

'Yeah, it was great, and we nailed a couple of deals too,' I said cheerily.

'Oh, well done,' Penelope said, without much enthusiasm.

She then turned around, faced my desk and looked directly at me.

'And your kids? Were they happy to have their mummy back?'

I was taken aback. Penelope was never usually so forthcoming. I could see now I was looking at her that her eyes looked a little red and bloodshot. I couldn't find the confidence to ask her if she was okay.

'Daddy kept them busy and I was only gone a couple of days,' I said and tried not to narrow my eyes, but after Lil's funny look and detecting malice in Penelope's tone, I was beginning to wonder if the women in this office were jealous of my relationships with my male colleagues.

'Well, that's just lovely. You should bring them into the office one day. I'd love to meet them.'

I smiled. 'Did you ever think about having kids?' I had been reluctant to ask, but with Penelope taking an interest in mine, I was suddenly intrigued.

Penelope paused before answering.

'Do you know what, Frankie. I would have loved kids. But someone took that choice away from me.' Penelope looked at me for a second and then she tilted her head towards the ceiling. I looked up, wondering if she had spotted a leak, then I realised she must be talking about God.

'Right.' I sat rooted to the spot and just nodded earnestly.

'Anyway. Mason behaved himself, did he?' she asked when I thought the conversation was over.

I felt my heart thud and my face redden. 'What do you mean?' I felt as though I were unable to conceal any of the shame.

'I mean, the man likes a drink. He didn't get you up dancing on any tables or walking the streets until dawn?'

I laughed a feeble laugh, out of sheer relief. 'No, not at all. He was...' and I paused for a second, but long enough for Penelope to tilt her head slightly to one side as she awaited my reply, 'a gentleman,' I said quickly.

'Well, there we go. He can behave himself.' And yet Penelope stayed looking at me for one or two more seconds. I broke the stare by looking across the office where I caught Stella's eye. I tried to give her a look to encourage her over to rescue me, ask me out for a fag, but she turned her head towards her computer and began typing.

I let out a sigh. My thoughts turned to the end of the day when I could have a glass of wine. The weekend had taken it out of me. I felt off-kilter. I could do better than this.

Half an hour later my desk phone rang, I could see it was Mason's internal line.

'Hi, morning,' I said as cheerfully as I could.

'Morning, how's things, back into the swing of it?'

'Yep, all good.'

'I wondered if you would pop along and see me in my office. Whenever you can is good. No rush.'

'Ok, I'll just finish this report and then I'll come.'

'Great. See you shortly.'

* * *

I stood outside Mason's office and knocked as I always did.

'Come in,' Mason called, I could see he was sitting at the far end of the conference table.

'Hey, grab a drink.' He pointed to the fridge.

I picked out a sparkling water and sat down in the chair next to him.

'How are you?' he asked.

'I'm good.'

'Did you sleep well, recovered from the all the travelling and monumental sales pitches?'

'Ha, yes, it was great practice.'

'If that was practice, I'd like to see you in full throttle. It was great, Frankie, you should be so proud.' Mason looked at me for a second, his eyes trying to say something his mouth wasn't.

'Thanks.' I looked down at my hands, knowing that this was all small talk, an aperitif to the main course which was building up. Mason had told me all this already, I knew he was happy and proud.

'It's my birthday, tomorrow,' he said softly.

'What? Why didn't I know this?' I was surprised he hadn't mentioned it when we were in Belgium.

'I'm sure Penelope will be sending a card around later. I'm having a dinner party at my house this weekend. You should come. Bring your husband.'

'What? Really?'

'Yes, I don't want him getting grouchy because you are off spending all this time with me working. Let him meet me.'

'You're weird.'

'No, it's perfectly normal thing to do, I often invite colleagues and their husbands.'

'Even the colleagues you almost kissed,' I said quietly.

'In Belgium.'

'So what happened in Belgium really does stay in Belgium.'

'If that's what you want?'

'I don't know what I want, Mason.'

'Well, that's okay too. You have a lifetime to decide.'

I sniffed out a laugh. 'That's a fairly profound statement.'

'I like words. I read a lot. You don't see me when I'm tucked up in my bed at night with my teddy and books.'

'Conjuring up that image now.' I looked to my left and squinted my eyes. 'PJs or no PJs?' I quipped.

'Now you're asking.' Mason tried to smile but it looked forced. We could both feel the strain underneath the banter. What we both wanted but couldn't have. 'So, I'll see you at eight on Saturday then?'

'You're hopeful?'

'Maybe.'

'Okay. 8 p.m. Saturday. I'll drop the reports from the Belgium trip on your desk later.'

'Wow, speedy work.'

I stood to leave.

'You're a brilliant asset to the company. I don't think I could do without you now.' Mason stood up as well and was suddenly very close to me.

I looked at him for a moment, gave him a small smile and then turned to walk away. As I did, I felt the air suddenly become a little icier and a small shudder crept its way across my back. I pulled my cardigan around me a little tighter and walked away without looking back.

* * *

I left the office at lunchtime, stopped at the delicatessen on the high street and picked up some cheese for supper. Only when I had left the shop did I realise I had unconsciously picked up Damian's favourite. The weather was unseasonably warm, one of the rare yet most enjoyable times of autumn, when there was a short window to appreciate the warmth muddled with the array of oranges and yellows falling all around you. Distracted, I realised I had taken a different route back to the office, one I didn't usually take, and I found myself on a part of the street I hadn't walked down for years. I had purposely kept away from it for so long because I was terrified of what I might find. Or who I might find.

I was now in the shade. All the sunlight had gone and had been replaced with dark grey shadows from the buildings on this side of the street. On the other side of the road I could see I was approaching the big superstore. The back entrance was next to a long wide alley. It was densely populated day and night. Druggies, drunks. The homeless. My heart began to beat faster and my mouth became dry when I realised where I had inadvertently found myself. I was already halfway down the road, I could have turned and run the other way, got back to the roads I knew best, which I trusted to keep me safe these days. But something drove me on, an urge to see what I had been hiding from for too long. The text messages, the birthday card, the feelings that were brought back. I knew what was out there, usually lurking in the shadows. I could see plainly the whole side of the street was lit up by the midday sun but I hung to the right, feeling some protection from the buildings next to me. I felt the flight or fight instinct kick in way before I saw the figure crouched in the opening to the alleyway. And when I did, I stopped so suddenly that the person walking behind me collided with me.

'Sorry, sorry,' I muttered as they tutted and skirted round me. I pushed my back against the wall, felt the protection of the concrete. As I stood with my hands pressed against the craggy wall, as though my presence had been felt, the figure lifted their head.

And for the second time that week I looked into the eyes of the person I hadn't seen or spoken to in almost twenty years.

35

NOW

I decided to risk another session after work with the office crew in the Chambers. I didn't wish to get close to them, but I needed to get them on my side. Specifically Stella, who seemed to be a bit distant, and Lil, who couldn't stop herself giving me long looks across the office. Penelope was a complete enigma. I decided I wasn't ever going to understand her. I was feeling shaken after my lunchtime encounter and a quick drink before I went home would calm my nerves. I kept my time in the pub short, limited myself to two drinks. There were a few raucous protests from Fish, and Lil eyed me suspiciously. But I stuck to my guns and proudly finished my second drink and headed home to begin my weekend with my family.

* * *

'Thanks for getting this cheese,' Damian said as he sliced the Cambozola onto his crackers in great chunks.

I almost said to Damian, who I was still cross with for storming out of the restaurant and leaving me with the figure glaring through the window, that I had not intended to pick up his cheese, it was merely a habit. Perhaps something that encompassed our relationship more than we would care to realise.

'We've been invited to Mason's birthday dinner at his apartment on Saturday night,' I said casually.

'Birthday dinner?'

'Yes. Birthday dinner.' I could hear the tension in my voice mirroring Damian's.

'Why are we invited? You've been working for him for like five minutes and he doesn't know me.'

'Well, that's the point of a dinner party, to get to know people. I guess once you start to mix business and leisure you've made it.'

'What do you mean?'

'I mean, Mason thinks I'm a valuable member of the team. I've made great progress in a short period of time and he sees loads of potential in me. By going to this dinner on Saturday night it shows I am committed to this job as a lifestyle choice as much as just a job.'

'Why can't it be just a job? Why must it be your life?' Damian pulled an expression I considered to be a little immature.

'Because jobs are part of our lives. We can't just separate the two. I come home and still think of to-do lists and I sit at my desk at work and plan meals for home. It's all encompassing. This is the best way, Damian. If you just embrace it, life becomes a little easier.'

I watched Damian's face contort as he chewed over my words.

I pushed the thoughts of the past few weeks aside, the bits I didn't want to think about, the text messages, the card, the earring on the floor. The face of the person I had seen on the way home. Twenty years is such a long time to miss someone and not speak to them. But equally I was terrified what they thought of me and how I could possibly atone for what had happened all those years ago.

* * *

'And you're sure he definitely said for me to come?'

Damian stood in our bedroom on Saturday evening.

'Damian, I've said it a hundred times and now Aimee is booked, if you don't want to come, don't bother, but I have to go.'

'I don't get it. It's his birthday and you're his employee and yet he wants you there?'

'It's a free meal, he is bringing in a chef and we get a night out and you get to finally meet my boss. It's all good!'

'Fine,' Damian huffed, struggling with his tie.

'Are you sure you want to wear that thing, why don't you wear an open collar and that blue suit jacket, it's just a casual dinner.'

The doorbell rang and I looked at Damian, as I was poised half in a pair of tights.

'Right, I'll get it then,' he huffed, throwing the discarded tie on the bed as he left.

'Thanks,' I called feebly after him.

I finished getting ready and put on a blue vee-neck dress with some silver sparkles, scooped in the middle to create the 'thinning look'.

Damian came back upstairs. 'You're wearing that, that's dressy and you're telling me not to wear a tie?'

'I just don't think anyone will be wearing a tie, that's all. Besides, we match, you're wearing the blue suit jacket and this is blue. It's fine, Damian, stop stressing.'

* * *

We arrived downstairs to Aimee looking as keen as she always did.

'Wow, Frankie, you look very nice,' she said and I tried to gauge anything other than innocence in her voice. Perhaps I'd raise my concerns with Damian tonight after a glass of wine or two. Maybe he could find a device to install in the house so we could watch her. Or was that crossing a boundary?

I grabbed a few last minute items and threw them into my handbag. All the while I couldn't help but notice Aimee's gaze was on me. I stopped racing around and stood in front of her. I put my hands on my hips for extra effect; I had heard it showed assertiveness and power.

'How are you, Aimee?' I asked super confidently boarding on sarcastic. I saw Damian turn his head out of the corner of my eye. Aimee didn't seem to notice any tone to my voice.

'I'm good, thanks, Frankie. Very busy start to the school year. I got picked for the hockey team!'

'The hockey team, wow, is that... good?' I saw Damian turn his head to look at me full on this time. 'I mean, I don't know, I hated hockey at school, all those big grey pants, freezing my arse off running around on pitch and then the fear of being hit in the shin with a hockey stick.' I wrinkled my nose.

'We wear thermal underwear, jogging bottoms and hoodies and shin pads. I really like it. I didn't get picked last year because...' Aimee looked down at her feet, 'because, well it doesn't matter.' I looked at Damian and we exchanged a concerned look; it was the most genuine interaction we'd had in weeks. We both recognised that stunted response of a young girl trying to say something. I suddenly felt an enormous amount of sadness for Aimee and guilt at my poor attempt at a power trip.

I made a mental note to check in with Aimee later after the party, to make sure she was okay. Maybe there was something else going on that I needed to know about. I was leaving her in charge of the two most precious things in my life, after all.

* * *

I pressed the apartment button.

Damian had laughed and laughed in a sort of semi-malicious tone when I said it was the penthouse.

'Of course it is,' he snarled.

The front door made a small buzzing sound and we walked into a grand foyer with lifts to the right and stairs to the left.

We stood in silence as the lift climbed the twelve floors to the top. Damian looked at his shoes, flicked some specks of white from his shoulder and ran his hands through his hair, all acts of a self-consciousness male about to meet his wife's high-powered boss for the first time. But something prevented me from reaching down and grasping his hand with mine and giving it a small squeeze of reassurance.

As soon as the lift doors opened, we heard a loud raucous laughter.

Damian looked at me with disdain and let out a sigh. I felt the bubble of irritation rise inside me.

I led the way out of the lift and double checked that Damian was with me, just in case he decided to pull another stunt like the one at the restaurant. There were only two apartments on the top floor. Mason's was the one to our left. The raucous laughter continued to come at us loud and strong. I rang the doorbell, which this time rang out long and shrill. A few seconds passed and a woman swung open the door. Her hair was blonde and shoulder length; she flicked it from one side to the other as she spoke.

'More guests! Hooray!' I put her at about fifty because of a few wrinkles around her eyes. She was tanned and wore a black dress with a gold-trimmed plunging neckline revealing half of her breasts, which were small and flat. She continued to fling her hair from side to side and I noticed she wasn't wearing any shoes. I wondered if that was the policy. She stepped aside to let us through.

'I'm Kate.' She held her hand out. Damian thrust his hand into hers too quickly for my liking, and when she laughed Damian and I clocked one another as we realised who the raucous laugh belonged to.

'Oh no, silly, I was taking your bottle, I'll pop it in the fridge to chill!'

'Oh, right.' Damian handed over the bottle of champagne I had agonised over for ages in the supermarket, trying to decide which one would taste delicious at a reasonable price.

'Come through,' Kate said, looking at neither of us and instead inspecting the bottle of champagne. I watched her closely.

'Oooh, lovely' she said at last. Mason had specifically said not to bring presents, but a bottle was general dinner party etiquette. Never turn up to someone's house empty handed was my motto.

Kate walked us down a long hallway with rooms leading off on either side. All the doors were closed, then we were through to a large open plan lounge, kitchen and diner. The kitchen was to the right with a large dining table on the other side. To the left was a huge lounge area with low flat sofas, a huge white coffee table in the centre and a massive LED TV screen mounted on the wall. I noticed the very same painting that I had seen in the restaurant when Damian and I had celebrated my new job. I figured this was the original. I became mesmerised in the different swirls of Mediterranean colours of orange, blues and yellow.

'Our three year old kid could do better than that,' Damian whispered into my ear.

'It's a surrealist piece, I picked it up in Italy about twenty-five years ago, guess I always knew I'd be a bachelor as I have never been able to get any woman to love it as much as I do.' Mason's confident voice came from behind us and we both swung round. I could see the look of horror etching its way across Damian's face.

'You must be Damian?' Mason held out his hand which Damian shook firmly, asserting himself and hoping to rectify his insolent comment.

We both took in Mason who was head to toe in black tuxedo dress complete with a black bow tie and maroon cummerbund. As I looked about the room I could see another five or six men all wearing tuxedos and one curly haired man in orange trousers, purple shirt and pink tie. We all turned to look as he made his way nosily past us.

'Back in a second, darling, total disaster with the music system.' He skimmed past us and Mason smiled. 'That's Mo, he lives in the suite opposite.'

Mason patted Damian on the back. 'Great to meet you, bud. Thanks for being here tonight. It means a great deal to have Frankie here. Has she told you how wonderful she is at her job? A complete natural, don't know where she has been hiding all this time.' Mason looked over at me, 'Good to see you, girl.'

I glanced at Damian who looked as though he was chewing on something that wasn't there. Then he started to do that thing he does when he wants to assert his authority over another male; he started rubbing his nose and pushing his shoulders into his back. I looked on as this horror show began to unfold before me and I quickly turned to Mason.

'So, where's the punch?' I said, 'This is a party, right? Got to be a bowl of punch somewhere?'

Mason laughed. 'Can't say there's been a bowl of punch at one of my parties since 1987.' Then he gave Damian a light slap on the back. 'Right, let me show you where the beers are, unless you're a champagne man? Obviously, the whisky comes later. What can I get you? You name it.' He began escorting Damian away. I was left standing in the doorway wondering what the hell to do, still undecided about removing my shoes, then I heard a voice behind me.

'Madam, can I get you a drink?' There was a young waitress in a white shirt, black skirt and a long black apron down to her shins balancing a round black tray on her palm. There were three glasses of champagne on it.

'Oh yes, champagne, definitely.' I took a glass and drank half. A second waitress appeared with a tray carrying something nibbly. I felt my stomach rumble at the sight of it.

'Crispy beef in lettuce parcel, madam?'

'Oh yes, please.' I grabbed one and when they went by a minute later, I grabbed another. Kate's raucous laugh found its way over from the other side of the room. I occasionally eyed Damian who was being shown the bar and its entire stock by all accounts.

'Great suite, isn't it?' I heard behind me. It was Mo, back and holding a stack of CDs. 'Yet can you believe he doesn't own one piece of decent technology? Not even a docking station. A hifi, that's what he has! I mean, I just had to go back and scour though my early nineties CDs to find something worthy of listening to. You need ambience at a party, don't you think? Even if it will end up being the Corrs!'

Mo held up a CD with the faces of the three beautiful Irish women on the front.

'Ridiculously attractive women,' I said, deadpan.

'Annoyingly so. Never quite trusted them. Steely eyes, all of them,' Mo replied.

I laughed.

'Where's your drink?' he asked.

I looked at the empty champagne glass in my hand, unaware that I had finished it.

'Erm, looks as though I drank it,' I said, perplexed.

'Finally, a woman who isn't on a fucking detox! Come on you, bar!' He threw his arm through mine. 'But first, some Steps I reckon?' and we walked over to Mason's old hifi system, where Mo put in the CD.

About twenty minutes later Damian found me on the sofa with Mo, reminiscing over music from our youth. I was three glasses of champagne in by this point.

'Ahh, my husband. Mo, this is Damian.' My voice was already a little slurred.

'Hello, mate.' Mo held his hand out.

Damian took it, nodded and smiled. 'Good to meet you, Mo.'

A large lady in a red dress came and sat next to Mo and the two huddled together and began bitching about another woman on the other side of the room.

'What's the deal here? It's bloody pretentious as hell. Could your boss be trying any harder to impress me with his extensive collection of vintage wines and spirits? Honestly, Frankie, and why the hell did you tell me not to wear a tie, every bloke here is in a tux!' Damian hissed.

'I'm sorry, I didn't think it would be that kind of soiree. And what's with you getting your hackles up when Mason came over? I actually thought you were going to start beating your chest and pissing in the corner to mark your territory!'

'What's wrong, Frankie? Some women may say that's a good thing?'

'No, Damian,' I leant forward and hissed. 'It is not a good thing. Not a good thing at all. I am here to prove myself a worthy part of Mason's organisation. He didn't have to invite me. No one else from my office is here. It's an exclusive invitation. If you can't stop acting like a total Neanderthal and just support me then you may as well just piss off now.' The emphasis on the 'piss off' made Mo turn his head from his heated conversation and look at me. I caught his eye and flashed my best smile.

'Drink up, my kindred spirit!' he called over, raising his glass.

I raised my glass.

'Oh, Christ,' Damian said spitefully.

'Damian, hear what I said, buck up or fuck off.' I whispered it this time so as not to attract any more attention. Damian stood up and walked back to the bar. I watched him slap Mason on the shoulder this time. Mason was chatting to another man but he immediately stopped and began requesting the barman to mix more drinks. I noticed this time it was some sort of spirit and I thought back to our time in Belgium and how I had told Mason that Damian was not a heavy drinker. He had told me he had a supreme memory, yet I watched my husband being handed another drink and then Mason turned and smiled his most sparkling smile.

We were seated at the table with little name plaques in front of us. I was between a man named Duncan who had been Mason's finance director at his last firm and a woman named Louise who was his badminton partner at his local gym. She was pleasant enough and we got through the starters with some light chatter about her three grandchildren and her holiday home in France. The conversation wavered on me for a little while until I gave Mo, who was sitting just two places away, 'the eye' and so he swept in, told Louise that his dinner neighbour, Clive, owned a chateau in Burgundy and she was off like a shot.

'Thank you. I was about to gouge my eyes out with my dessert fork,' I said.

'Oh, don't do that, darling. Those forks are far too pretty.'

I laughed long and hard while Mo smiled modestly.

Then a noise brought me to a complete standstill. I looked over. Damian was laughing so loudly he was now rivalling Kate. I narrowed my eyes at him and then Mason caught my eye and raised his glass at me. I excused myself from Mo who was tucking into his in between course sorbet palette refresher and left the table. I began opening various doors along the corridor we had come down when we arrived. I found the utility room, a small spare bedroom, a huge luxurious bathroom with a roll top bath and was just about to go in and touch up my face when Mason arrived at the door. He motioned for me to go in and when I did, he followed, closed it and locked it behind him.

'What are you doing?' I hissed.

'I'm just checking in.' He began to edge closer to me.

I took a step back so my back was against the sink.

'I saw you ply Damian with alcohol. I told you he wasn't a very good drinker on the hard stuff.'

'Did you?' Mason moved another step towards me.

'Yes, and you told me how you are so good at remembering stuff, the incidentals about people.' I took a side step just as Mason reached me, then turned towards the mirror and checked my makeup.

Mason was behind me leaning against the sink. A loud knock came at the door.

'Just ignore them,' Mason whispered, close to my ear.

I swung around so our faces were inches apart and I was thrust back to the moment in Belgium in his suite when I almost kissed him.

'What are we doing here, Mason? You can't be in the bathroom with me, what if that's Damian waiting outside? How are we going to pull off leaving together?'

'Staff meeting?' Mason said in a cheeky hushed tone.

'No, seriously.' I began pacing. 'This is not cool.'

'Hey!' Mason said and raised his hands up, 'Okay, I'm sorry. I'm just checking everything is okay. Things seem a little tense between you and Damian. I thought bringing you both here would distract me from just you. But I'm afraid it has had the opposite effect.'

I closed my eyes and took in a deep breath.

'Keegan.'

I opened my eyes.

'While you're here. Check this out.'

He walked over to the other side of the bathroom, pressed a tile on the wall and a door handle popped out. Mason depressed the handle and a door opened into another room. I peered inside and saw it led into a huge master suite with a super king size bed. All greys and whites and blacks.

'So, this is where you snuggle up and read at night, is it? With your teddy bear?' I said as I made my way towards the bed and felt the fabric; the softest Egyptian cotton, no doubt.

'PJs off,' Mason whispered next to me. 'Always.'

I breathed in and wondered what would happen if it was just Mason and I here. I thought about how I had stopped myself going through with anything with him in Belgium. It was the ideal opportunity; all that time alone together and yet... I didn't.

'I need to check on Damian,' I said, and edged my way back into the bathroom. Mason stood up straight and smoothed his shirt down.

'Yes. Of course. I'm just going to close this door and leave through my bedroom.'

We stood face to face for a second, Mason on the bedroom side of the door, me in the bathroom, looking at one another. He blinked slowly and sighed.

'It will be as though it never happened.' he shut the bedroom door. As he did, I watched as the handle to the door once again disappeared as though it was never there. I was alone in the bathroom, pondering over Mason's words as though whatever this thing had been between us, had ended. A mixture of sadness and relief swept over me.

* * *

I made it back to the table and now Damian, who seemed to be the life and soul of the party, was standing up telling some anecdote, swishing his glass around, and spilling his drink onto the table. The waiters kept trying to clear up round him until Mason shook his head, indicating that they were to let him be. I had to admit it had been a long time, if ever, that I had seen Damian this drunk. He wasn't even this drunk on our first holiday or our wedding. Kate was laughing so uncontrollably it had turned to snorting, which only seemed to egg Damian on even more.

The waiter arrived with our mains, a lamb dish with a delicate ratatouille sauce and a neat square of dauphinoise. I ate mine with intent, trying to ignore Damian's outrageous display of drunkenness which had attracted the attention of most of the table. I could hear lots of intermittent swearing as his glass was raised over and over again.

'Your husband is quite the entertainer.' Mo sidled into me. 'Everything... okay there?' he asked with the most seriousness he had used all night since he had informed me that Steps were still his favourite band. 'I'm going to take him over a glass of water.'

'I...' I was about to tell him not to bother but Mo was up and out of his chair and next to Damian. I watched as Mo said something quietly and Damian stopped talking and looked up at him.

'Hey guys, it's Buddy Holly. Hey, don't go getting on any planes, son... what's... water? I don't need... did my wife send this over? Frankie... where's the vodka... can anyone mix a Negroni here? It's all my wife wants to drink... it's fucking pretentious as hell but that's what being a corporate wanker does to you... get off me, man... I said...'

Damian put his hands on Mo's chest and pushed him forcefully. Mo stumbled backwards and hit the floor. I put down my knife and fork and raced round to the other side of the table just as Mo was standing up and dusting himself down. Damian was swaying about telling everyone he was okay, completely oblivious to the fact that Mo was just getting himself back on his feet. I tended to Mo first.

'Are you ok?'

'God, yes, I'm fine babes, it's your obliterated husband you need to check. Sorry to ruin your night but maybe he needs taking home?'

'Listen, you were the most interesting person here,' I said, helping him up.

'I'll get your number off Mason. We'll go for brunch, darling. Just get that husband of yours home.'

We kissed each other on the cheek and I took Damian's arm and told him we were going.

'Going? You come all the way here to play dinner parties and as soon as I get a drink inside me you decide it's time to go.' Damian pointed his finger at me. 'You, you, you, it's all about you.' Damian swayed from side to side; he looked as though he could barely hold his head up. What the hell did Mason put in his drink?

'I spend all day at home with our kids so you can fulfil your... dreams.' Damian threw his arms out wide to emphasise the word. 'Everything we do is because of you. My whole life. Runs. Around. You.' Damian poked his finger hard into my chest.

Everyone had stopped eating and talking and they were all watching us. Steps played on, the lyrics for 'Tragedy' coming through loud and proud.

'I think that's enough, mate.' Mason approached Damian.

'You! Mr Valentine with your suave penthouse and bottles of champagne, taking my wife to Belgium a few weeks after you met her, what do you think I am? A blithering idiot? I know your game, sunshine.' Damian stumbled back and a burly man I had seen hovering about all night stepped in and grabbed his elbow. He looked like he could be a bouncer, and when Mason gave him a nod, I realised that was exactly what he was – some sort of personal bodyguard.

Before I knew what was happening, Damian was being escorted on his way past the dining room into the hallway.

'Shall I call you a cab?' Mason spoke softly.

'I think you've done enough,' I hissed at him. 'I'll take it from here.'

I took Damian's arm from the burly man, grabbed our coats from the coat rack and headed out into the foyer where I called the lift. We stood for a few seconds. When I turned round Mason was in the doorway. Was he gloating or genuinely distressed by the turn of events? I truly didn't know any more.

Outside it had started to rain. I put my coat on and tried to place Damian's coat round his shoulders.

'Oh, piss off, Frankie.' He shrugged me away and his coat fell to the floor.

'What the hell have I done? I got a job, I like my job, I took us to Mason's house to celebrate that and you act like a complete idiot and embarrass me in front of everyone!'

'There you go again, it's still all about you. What about me?' Damian prodded his chest.

'What about you, Damian, where the hell are you these days, hey? 'Cos I sure as hell can't get through to you.'

'That's 'cos you don't bloody try, Frankie, you're either at work, thinking about work or in your bloody dark place mulling over what happened twenty years ago. It's time to move the hell on!'

I stood and looked at Damian, my hands clenching and unclenching, my palms getting damp from the drizzle.

'Get over it? That's all you've wanted, isn't it, for me to just be this happy-go-lucky wife with zero baggage and no grief to compete with your endless issues. We're just a mess, Damian, look at us, there is no room for either of our problems in each other's lives. You haven't got time to think about the sadness that engulfs me daily and I haven't got the time nor the inclination to worry about what the hell it is you're playing at these days.'

'Trying to find a way, just trying to find a way.' Damian threw his hands in the air.

'We have drifted so far apart. I don't know you any more.' I got closer to his face so I could smell the alcohol. 'And do you know what, I don't trust you either.'

'Then what is the point?'

'There isn't one.'

'So I'll just go, shall I?'

'Yes. I think that's best.'

'Fine, Frankie. I'm beyond done anyway.'

I saw a taxi with its light on in the distance and hailed it.

Damian watched me.

'I'll walk,' he said as the taxi approached and I got into the cab, feeling a pang in my stomach from everything that had been said. The years of the build-up, the hidden resentment and the hiding of our emotions. It was all leading to this anyway.

'Where to, love?' the taxi driver asked and I gave him my address then turned to watch as Damian strode away unsteadily in the rain, his jacket over his head.

* * *

I stepped out of the taxi and instantly felt the heel of my shoe crack and break.

'What the hell?' I pulled the broken shoe off and then the other one and stood on the cold pavement as the rain soaked through the soles of my tights.

'You alright, love?'

'Yes,' I sighed. I handed the driver some notes, shut the door and fumbled for my keys as he drove away.

I opened the front door and stood in the hallway, expecting to hear a child cry out in their sleep. The weight of the silence closed in around me. I pushed the door to as quietly as I could until it clicked. I didn't double lock it as I wasn't sure if Damian would be making his way home later. I shivered under my rain soaked jacket so I removed it and hung it on the bannister. Goosebumps were on my skin and I rubbed my arms, then I pulled off the sodden tights. I couldn't get a sense of where Aimee might be, there was no light streaming through from the kitchen; sometimes if we were back very late she would doze on the sofa in the snug with the door ajar to hear the children. But the door to the snug was closed. My first instinct was to check on the kids as I always did when I got home and they were asleep.

The stairs were dark and only a thin strip of light from the main bathroom lay across the top landing. I placed my foot on the first step and then my heart leapt as I saw a figure appear from my bedroom door and steal across the landing. I initially thought it was Pixie but my brain quickly worked out that the figure was not as slight as Pixie and that it was Aimee who had made a dash from our bedroom. I stood frozen on the stairs, feeling like an intruder in my own home, unsure whether to make my way upstairs or retreat to the kitchen. Or perhaps I should do what should have been the obvious first choice, confront Aimee and demand to know why she was in my room. I continued up the stairs; the desire to check on the children was still strong. As I reached Pixie's room I came face to face with Aimee.

'Oh, my God,' Aimee said in a stage whisper and threw her hand to her mouth, 'I didn't hear you come in.'

'Are the kids okay?' I whispered, pushing past Aimee into Pixie's room. I moved over to the bed. I could hear heavy breathing coming from the high rise bed as I approached the ladder. I stood on one step and leant in to look at Pixie curled in the foetal position, sleeping peacefully.

I headed out of the room, passing Aimee who hadn't moved from the landing.

'I didn't hear you come in,' Aimee whispered again as I went towards Maddox's room. I tiptoed over to his bed. His bed clothes were a tangled mess, and he lay in the middle on them, snoring softly. I touched his head, it was slightly damp around his hair line as it usually was when he slept so heavily.

I came back out into the hallway.

'Has everyone been okay tonight?'

'Yes, yes, fine.' Aimee looked flustered.

'Okay, I'll see you downstairs. I need to change.'

I walked to my room, switched the main light on and quickly scanned around, looking for anything that seemed out of place. Everything looked as it was before I left. I could only imagine Aimee had been using my en suite. Or perhaps she had been dozing on my bed, although the bed sheets were still pulled taut.

I changed into pyjamas and comfy socks and went downstairs to find Aimee stood in the kitchen with her coat on and laptop bag in her hand.

'So, was it a good night?' Aimee looked at her watch. I looked up at the clock. It was only just after ten.

'Yes... I had a headache. I left Damian there. He was having a good time.' I imagined Aimee was getting used to one of us arriving home without the other.

'Right...'

I paused for a second as I considered asking her outright what she was doing in my bedroom. Aimee was near the doorway, occasionally pushing her glasses back up the ridge of her nose. She wasn't like other girls her age who would be glued to their phones. I thought about her comment earlier in the evening and how I was going to check in with her but I could feel my head starting to hurt and the stress of what had happened at Mason's was constricting my thought process. I needed to get into bed.

I pulled out some notes and handed them to her.

I saw Aimee out of the front door and then collapsed into bed, dreading the start of tomorrow, knowing that Damian and I were no more.

* * *

February 1999

You always talked about what a major event the millennium would be. Well, people have started talking about it already. Parties are being planned. They say it could be the end of everything as we know it, that computer systems will crash and create a total economic crisis. I know you would have loved to have been here for that. The party. The end of the world. We could have seen it through together, the way we did with everything, head on. Even when we weren't together, when you were with your friends, and I with mine, we were still one, the same. I wish so often that we could have just had one more day together so I could have said all the things I needed to say. I didn't know I needed to say them then, but since you're no longer here, I have so many things to say to you. They say to tell your loved ones regularly that you love them because you never know if that will be the last time you see them. I was with you until the end, but I will never know if you heard me, the things I whispered to you in those final moments. I hope you heard them, I hope they brought you some comfort. I hope you are safe now, happy. Who knows what awaits us after this life, a conscious existence or an existential floating through different dimensions until one day our souls meet again. It's too big, all of it. Too big for me to imagine. When I try to think where you are, I feel giddy and I have to stop thinking immediately.

I have stopped the therapy now. Nothing that anyone can say will make me feel any other way. Nor do they know the very thing I hold onto the most, maybe it is what is causing the blockage, maybe once I say the words out loud then maybe things will start to get better. Maybe I will be able to grieve for you instead of holding onto so much frustration.

Maybe if I start by writing the words down first. Maybe that will

help me say them out loud one day. But for now, they can stay hidden
here in this journal where no one will ever see them.

It was me. It was my fault. I caused the accident.

I caused your death.

You're dead because of me.

37

Nancy called round the next day. I had left Todd at home in his bed still recovering. His parents weren't back for a few more days but I needed to get away from the house after everything I had seen. I needed to speak to Nancy.

We sat at the table drinking tea. 'How are you? Last night was mental. Is Todd okay? Does he do that stuff all the time?'

I wanted to tell Nancy that it was the first time and the last time. I wanted to say he wasn't going to do it again. I wanted to say it was just a phase. I wanted to remind her that so many of us used marijuana and the odd amphetamine and didn't move on to anything harder. But there was no point. Some people were predisposed to this kind of stuff. Todd was probably one of those people and maybe he was always destined to go down this route. But I would try to do whatever I could to help him.

'So, what will you do?' Nancy sipped her tea.

'What do you mean? Do?'

'You can't date a druggy, Frankie?' She put her mug down and looked at me with her best grown up, serious expression.

'He's not a druggy,' I said, not even believing my own words.

Nancy raised her eyes at me.

'He's not, he's just going through a phase!'

'He's what, twenty-two? He needs to be going through a sorting his life out phase, not a throwing it all away phase.'

'I don't think you should give him such a hard time, Nancy. Minty isn't so bloody perfect.'

'Minty *is* perfect, thanks. I love him.'

'You what? You love him?' I pulled my head back in surprise.

Nancy laughed. 'Yes, I love him, he's sweet and kind and *so* funny. I mean, he just makes me laugh, like all the time. What more do I need in a boyfriend?'

I smiled. Minty was all those things. 'Yes, he's sweet. It's still weird you two hit it off. I mean, it's Minty.'

'I know, but he's different to how he is when he's with you lot. He's softer. I mean, it must be the same with you and Todd?'

'Yes. No one sees the real him except me,' I said.

'It's nice, isn't it?' Nancy looked dreamily into the distance and I couldn't help but snigger. She slapped my arm. 'Don't be a doofus!'

'I know, I know. It's sweet, I get it. We both have "actual" boyfriends.' I used air quotes and Nancy fell about laughing.

'I can't believe you actually just did that!'

Nancy looked up as Kiefer came into the room. He pulled his lips together and did a half smile with his eyes.

'Hey, Kiefer,' Nancy said, still laughing.

'My sister amusing you, is she.'

I frowned at Kiefer with his curt words. Had he been listening at the door?

'What's your beef?' I said.

'Who do you think?' Kiefer said, opening the fridge and taking out wafer thin ham and eating it straight from the packet.

Nancy looked down at the table and fiddled with a huge daisy ring on her finger.

'Todd is a good person and if you just got off your damn high horse there Kiefer and—'

Suddenly he was at my side leaning right into my ear.

'I don't need to give that piece of scum anything, do you hear me?' Kiefer said through a clenched jaw.

I sat back, feeling the force of his words.

'Why are you being so mean, why can't you be happy for us? What has Todd ever done to you?'

Kiefer pulled the chair out opposite us and sat down. Nancy shifted uncomfortably. Kiefer spoke much more calmly this time.

'It's not what he has done to me, Frankie. It's what he could do. To you. The guy is a junkie, he hangs around with the wrong types. He has no direction, his focus is all about getting hammered. He is leading you astray and I don't like it one bit. You need to back off.' Kiefer pointed his finger on the table to emphasise each point.

'You're wrong, Kiefer. He has plenty of direction. He loves to cook and, well, the drugs thing, you've got to admit, it's pretty entrepreneurial.' I looked at Nancy for backup. She nodded and shrugged her shoulders.

'He picks up some gear, take it round his mate's house, exchanges it for money and splits the money with his man. A monkey could do it.'

I looked down at the table. I was starting to feel defeated. Kiefer had it in for Todd and nothing I could say or do would make him change his mind.

'Well, I guess we'll just have to wait and see then,' I said quietly.

'See what?' Kiefer leant forward in an exaggerated way, 'You planning to elope or summin'?'

I shook my head. 'Just get off our case, Kiefer. Go and see Reese.'

Kiefer pushed the chair back so it scraped against the floor and walked back towards the door.

'Just try not to get into any trouble, won't you, Frank, yeah? Use your intuition.' He tapped the side of his head. 'Don't get suckered into anything you think is dodgy. You're a clever girl. Don't let that bozo drag you down.' And he walked out of the kitchen.

Nancy blew out her breath. 'Phew! He's got his knickers in a twist about your Todd.'

I smiled. 'My Todd.'

'Yeah.' Nancy smiled and pushed me playfully on the arm. 'Your Todd.'

I smiled some more as I liked the way it sounded. He was mine. I was his.

'Ahh, don't worry about what your bro there says. Just be happy for now. Todd's a decent human being. When he's not with those scumbags Zig and Zag. He'll come through this. And then Kiefer will be gutted he made out Todd was such a nonce. I think you two are gonna make it.'

'Really?'

'Yeah, why not? Because Kiefer says you won't? I know he's your brother and you two are close, but he doesn't know the future. All I can see is good things.' Nancy made a circle with both her hands as though she were looking into a crystal ball.

I smiled and tried to see what Nancy was envisioning but all I could hear was my big brother's parting words.

38

NOW

I had asked Mason for the morning off, to take Maddox to preschool and Pixie to school while Damian removed some of his belongings from the house. He had arranged to go over to a friend's whose house had an annexe in the garden. It was the right amount of time and distance we needed to get things into perspective and decide where we needed to go next.

'You need to ask Aimee if she can help out after school a few days. I can't bring both the kids back to the annexe every day. It's too small. I'll have Maddox on his days off from nursery. This is going to cost us, Frankie,' Damian said sternly, and I didn't ask if he meant financially or emotionally. I felt it was all too late now anyway.

* * *

I arrived at my desk just after midday with a sandwich and a bottle of sparkling water. Fish was in full sales mode on his phone while walking around the office but still managed to give that look which said, 'Why are you late?' I sat down and looked at my desk. Immediately my eyes were drawn to an envelope with my name on the front. It just said 'Frankie'. Presuming it was from Mason, I ripped it open. Inside was a white piece of paper with grubby marks over it and the words

Don't keep hiding from the past. You know where to find me.

I blew out a long breath. I did know where to find them.

I saw a shadow fall across my desk. I slipped the note inside a folder.

'Everything alright?' Fish said.

'Yeah.'

'Can I get you a coffee?'

I smiled and then felt a wave of tears well up. 'Yes, that would be great.' I tried really hard to push the tears away.

'Okay, Keegan, back in a tick.'

Damian's leaving should have felt like a breath of fresh air so why did I feel like a weight was suddenly lying heavy on my chest?

I glanced over and saw that Penelope was at her desk. She looked subtly over her shoulder and I was aware she could see I was upset. She would have known I wasn't here this morning and Mason would have informed her it was for personal reasons. I didn't want her to know anything about my life. I didn't want any of these people to know anything about my life. I couldn't cope with sitting at this desk with all these strangers sussing me out, trying to assess who I was based on a morning off and a look of exasperation etched across my face. They didn't know me. I half longed for my phone to ring, for it to be Mason asking me to come to his office, but it didn't. Fish dropped the coffee off with a simple smile.

I got down to work, occasionally peeping at the note inside the folder. I mulled over the scruffy handwriting, the dirty fingerprints all over it.

I managed to complete a good bit of work and after an hour I called the preschool to check Maddox was okay as he had left the house with a slight sniffle. Then I put the basic ideas together for the hot sauce and sent an email to the designer to create a mock-up label.

* * *

Somehow I managed to make it to 4 p.m. and got out of the main door only to bump into Mason as he was leaving his office.

'Frankie. How is everything?'

'Great, I have to go, sorry, I need to get the kids from our babysitter.'

'I know, I know, it's fine. I just wanted to check that you are okay? After the party?'

I looked at Mason and I thought back to the night. The image came back to me of Mason taking Damian off and pouring him a drink.

'Damian was wasted but I'm not entirely sure whose fault that was.' I raised my eyes.

Mason smiled, 'Yes, sorry about that, I guess I was just in the party spirit, and I didn't want Damian to feel uncomfortable.'

'When you weren't sneaking off to the bathroom to find me, you mean?' I said, just as a colleague from finance came down the corridor.

Mason nodded an acknowledgement to the man.

'My door is open, any time, just come and see me,' he said quietly.

'What are we doing?' I hissed.

'We're not doing anything. That's the frustrating part,' Mason whispered.

I shook my head. 'Look, I like you, I respect you, I bloody fancy you, yes...'

'But?'

'I can't do this, Mason. This thing, whatever it is we're doing. It has to end.'

I pushed past Mason and headed out of the front door into the cool late afternoon air; the sun was already disappearing. I turned and I could see through the glass windows that Mason was still standing there watching me. His hands in his pockets. Then he turned and headed back into his office. A metre or so behind where Mason had been standing was Penelope. Panic set in as I thought about how long she could have been standing there and what she may have heard. I turned away from the window, pushed my head into my coat and began walking.

As I walked home, I made sure I took the route that wouldn't take me past the supermarket and the alleyway. I made it home by 4.30 p. m., safe in the knowledge that I was only going to need to pay Aimee for an hour of her time after school.

As I rounded the corner to our house I did a double take at a car that looked like Nancy's silver Lexus heading away in the other direction. As I stood there and watched it work its way around the corner, I was certain I could make out her profile in the driver's seat.

Nancy lived on the other side of town on the leafy outskirts, why would she be driving down this way and then not even pop in?

I opened the door and heard the raucous chorus of two over-tired and hungry children. Maddox came running at me. 'Mammy, Pixie hit me wiv her pencil case.'

'No, I didn't!' Pixie shouted.

Aimee appeared in the doorway. I scooped Maddox up and stroked his forehead and kissed his wet cheek.

'Hi,' I said to Aimee with a big sigh.

'Hi,' she mirrored back. With a grin. 'I think they are getting hungry; they had a snack.'

'It's fine, thanks, Aimee, I'll sort their dinner now. Thanks for doing this, should only be for a few weeks until we get some childcare in place. Damian has to be away for a little while after school hours, so...'

I trailed off. Aimee looked at her feet then back at me. I wondered if she had already been upstairs and seen that most of Damian's clothes had gone from his wardrobe.

'I can help out, it's not a problem, I mean, if you want me to. I would only be at the library after school, so it's not a bother.'

'Okay, thank you, Aimee, that would be a real help.'

Aimee came down the hall past me and put on her trainers.

'And thanks, Aimee.'

As she opened the door I remembered Nancy driving off down the road.

'Hey, did my Nancy pop by at all just now?'

'No, I haven't seen her today.'

'Okay, not to worry.'

'But we have literally just got back from the park. Stayed right up until the last bit of light. I'm sorry, they are really tired now.'

'Oh right, so Nancy could have rung the doorbell while you were out?'

'Yes, I suppose,' Aimee said, grabbing her coat and giving Maddox a high five.

I waved at the door with Maddox in my arms then went to the fridge and found some pesto and cheese. I put some pasta fusilli in a pan of water and began chopping tomatoes, red onions and olives for a salad. Pixie's favourite.

Once everything was prepared and on, I texted Nancy.

Hey, did I see you drive down my road earlier?

Maddox came careering into the lounge and was running around my feet. Once I was on my phone I decided to check social media and emails, I was distracted by some posts on a friend's page, a family holiday she had just come back from.

'Hey, Mummy, look at me!'

'Yesssss,' I said in the absent way I couldn't help; it became an unconscious act and I hated myself for it.

'Mummy, look, look, look what I have!'

'Yes, Maddox, lovely,' I said, ignoring him. I continued to scroll.

'Mummy. Mummy. Mummy. Mummy.' Maddox bashed his ladybug ride along into my legs.

'Ow, Maddox, that hurt Mummy's... what have you got there, Maddox?' I put down my phone and bent down to his level and took out of his flailing hand what was obviously to me a freshly rolled marijuana joint, but to a three year old was a small toy gun or sword. The joint end was twizzled around and sealed, as though it had been rolled ready to smoke and forgotten about. Damian and I hadn't smoked joints for years, not since before the children.

'Thank you, darling, Mummy take that.'

'Oooooohhhhhh,' protested Maddox. 'My sword!' I took a plastic spatula from the kitchen side and handed it to him.

'Go and find some flies to slay, my fly slayer.'

'Okay, Mum.' He scuttled off on his bug.

I put the spliff to my nose and inhaled. A million memories engulfed me and I was suddenly drowning in nostalgia. I put the spliff on the shelf where the wine glasses were kept, too high even for Pixie to reach, and tried to work out who had dropped it.

My phone pinged a text and I looked at it, it was from Nancy.

Hey babe. On my way back from town so just swung by but you weren't in. Obvs. x

I bashed out my reply.

You must have just missed me. Everything ok?
I'm fine. How are you?
Not so good. Damian moved out

I waited a good three minutes before the reply came.

How do you feel about it?

Pretty shit. It's not what I wanted or expected. He got totalled at Mason's birthday dinner party and completely embarrassed me

Shit. I didn't know that

Course you wouldn't. Why would you?

I meant Mason's birthday. Didn't know you were going to his house

Yeah well, we did and it was awful. I had to practically carry Damian out after he completely insulted me in front of everyone

Let me know if you want me to come over for a drink

Sure, thanks. Can come to you?

There was a break of about two minutes before Nancy's reply came.

Harry is away for a few weeks and the builders are here at the moment. It would be good to get out of the house. Can I come to you?

Great. Tomorrow night

Sure. Take it easy, don't stress too much. It will all work itself out

Thanks

I put my phone down on the side. Many people say that text messaging is bad for relationships as it's hard to decipher precisely what the other person is saying without being able to hear their tone of voice or, even better, to be able to read their facial expressions. I felt an ache of unease after the text rally with Nancy, and I couldn't quite put my finger on why.

I served the children's dinner, much to Pixie's delight, bathed them, read to them for a while and said goodnight, leaving Pixie with her lamp on to read the latest Matt Haig book. All the while I was doing these tasks, ones I had done a thousand times before, I was carrying with me a feeling; a regret, a doubt, I wasn't sure, it was as though I had forgotten to do something. Once the children were tucked up in bed, I had a shower and tried to pinpoint my doubt. I thought about how I felt about Damian and him leaving. It was too soon to feel anything significant. I would see him often enough and right now it was like an ordinary work evening when we wouldn't spend time together.

After my shower I headed downstairs in a t-shirt and jogging trousers and stood next to the cooker. I sniffed the air for gas and checked all the appliances. I checked that the back door was locked and then I stood still in the same spot where I had been texting Nancy just a few hours ago. I began to replay the conversation in my head and then picked up my phone from the side. There was a text from Damian.

Kiss the kids goodnight from me x

I went straight back to the texts between me and Nancy from earlier. I scrolled through the messages and reread the part where Nancy said:

I meant Mason's birthday. Didn't know you were going to his house

I hadn't spoken to Nancy for a few days. I hadn't told her about Mason's birthday party invite and what was blatantly obvious to me now was that even in our hurried text rally, I had not once mentioned that the party was at his house.

I woke with a start. I heard a fierce wind outside. But what had woken me sounded like a loud bang.

I was used to sleeping peacefully these days because both children slept so well. For a second I presumed Damian had come home, that we would be having some sort of discussion about 'us' in the middle of the night and I would be going into work exhausted again. I looked at my phone; it was 1.30 a.m..

I knew Damian kept a baseball bat under his side of the bed. We'd never played a game of baseball in our lives, he bought it purely for protection. I presumed all men had some sort of weapon they kept under the bed for 'that day' when they might need to release their inner Joe Pesci.

Even when Damian wasn't there, I still slept only on my side, leaving a significant gap in the bed. I rolled over to the other side, grabbed the bat and tiptoed down the stairs. When I reached the hallway, I thought I saw a shadow through the glass pane in the front door. I froze, cursing myself for not bringing my phone. Perhaps I should go back upstairs to call the police? The shadow disappeared and I took a few more steps forwards.

I looked through the peep hole. I couldn't see anyone, but I was sure the noise came from outside. I raced upstairs two at a time and grabbed my phone from the bedside table. I was going out. I reached the front door and opened it slowly, peering round the edge into the night. The front step was illuminated by the porch light and I could see clearly what the commotion had been. Again, to my right, the plant pot I had only just replaced was on its side and smashed. As I came out from behind the door, I could see the second bay tree also on the floor and the pot smashed. I stole a look along each side of the road but I couldn't see anyone. With my heart pounding and my feet freezing, I quickly stepped back into the house, double locked and chained the door and went to the kitchen. I instinctively pulled a bottle of wine from the fridge, poured myself half a glass and drank it down hurriedly.

I poured a second glass and began to relax a little. I sat on the sofa in the kitchen and began to mull everything over.

Just as the letter on my desk at work had said, I needed to confront my past. It also said, 'You know where to find me.'

And I did.

I knew that by lunchtime tomorrow I would have all of this cleared up. The person who had been trying to mess with my life these last few weeks was about to be stopped right in their tracks.

40

SEPTEMBER 1998

I was in a basement flat filled with smoke so heavy it was like being on a country road when foggy. I couldn't see anyone in the room. I was stoned. I had skipped college to be here.

I didn't know whose flat it was. I couldn't remember now. But I was sure I knew what was going to happen next. And I had to make sure he was okay. Because I loved him. He hadn't told me, but I knew. When you love someone, you protect them. I knew he didn't really know what he was doing and that this was just a phase and I knew he would come out the other end and we would be happy and healthy and get married and have children and everyone would say, look at those two, they've been together since they were kids, now that's true love. I knew our kids would be cute and funny with messy crazy hair like his but I wouldn't try to control it and I'd let them run wild in their bare feet and we'd take them to festivals and keep partying and our kids would fall asleep in our arms next to the fire. He'd be holding one and I would be holding the other one and we'd look at one another over the flames and the fire would reflect in his eyes and then he would smile the smile that engulfed his whole face.

'Frankie.' A voice came through my thoughts.

'What?'

Someone handed me tea. But it wasn't him. We had been sitting together, so close, and now he was gone. I needed to find him.

Then I saw him through the smoke. Todd stood up and walked across the room and then someone followed him. I was too stoned to move, but I knew what was happening, and I knew I had to go and make it stop somehow. My homing beacon kicked in and I needed to be where I could relax in my own room and sleep. I summoned some strength and lifted myself out of the chair. I stepped over a sea of bodies on floors and legs poking out from sofas and made my way out of the front door.

41

NOW

I woke up with hazy vision. The shower had done nothing to ease the dull ache in my head. I had promised myself one drink to help me get back to sleep but that turned into finishing the bottle at 2 a.m.. I headed downstairs. It was still dark outside but I had to check I hadn't dreamt it, that there were two smashed pots. And as I opened the door I could see that they were still there on the floor as I had left them last night. But then there was something else, something I hadn't seen last night; maybe it was too dark to notice, but even as I thought the words, I knew I was kidding myself. I had stood for a good thirty seconds on the doorstep assessing the damage last night and I knew I wouldn't have missed it. A small green car. Another toy Mini Cooper, identical to the one I had in the house, was on the top doorstep just by my feet. So this couldn't be the same one. And I realised that when I looked out of the door last night the intruder had still been close by and had left it after I had closed the door. I shuddered as I bent down to pick it up.

From the kitchen I could hear one of the children stirring and moving around upstairs. I took the first Mini Cooper toy car from the nook in the kitchen and put it on the counter next to the one I had just found outside.

Then suddenly I could see it all coming back to me in flashbacks and I had to grab the counter and focus on my breathing for a few minutes. I focused on the colour of the white surface, the clock ticking on the wall, anything other than the feeling of my body flooding with terror. If this was what they wanted, to punish me by terrorising me, then they were succeeding.

I knew it was time to get this over with. Once I got my breathing back to normal, I looked at the wall whilst I still clung onto the counter and thought about everything that had happened to me. I wondered if it had something to do with the twenty year anniversary and suddenly felt middle-aged, and I wondered if the person who was trying to scare me had maybe had some sort of an awakening.

I had allowed myself to let go of any repetitive thoughts over the hotel room number in Belgium. I decided it was just synchronicity. In this great big universe we exist in, some things are just that.

I clung to the counter; my fingertips had started to turn white.

'Mummy, are you having mental cramps?'

Pixie's voice was behind me. I spun round.

'No.' I smiled at her mix up of words. 'I was just stretching out my legs. Are you ready? Have you brushed your teeth?'

'Yes, but Maddox has spilt toothpaste all over his top.'

I let out a huge sigh then tried to cover it up with a smile to Pixie. I headed upstairs, dealt with the toothpaste situation and helped Maddox get dressed. By seven thirty I had them assembled by the door for Damian to collect and take to breakfast club.

When Damian arrived I could see he looked tired, as though he had been up all night. He had dark streaks under his eyes. At least I had the magic of makeup to cover up my bags after only four hours' sleep. I stepped back away from him, conscious that I might smell of booze.

* * *

I made myself walk the route to work I wouldn't normally take. I stayed on the other side of the road from the supermarket and stole a look down the alley and saw three figures standing there; I didn't recognise any of them. The sun was low in the sky, obscuring my vision to my right. I squinted to see more but I couldn't. I felt a pain in my head and wished I had taken some paracetamol before I left for the office. The business of the street unnerved me and I longed for the sanctuary of my desk. Then, out of the corner of my left eye, I saw a figure approaching the alley carrying a plastic bag. I was pretty sure I knew the contents. For some reason, I decided to smooth down my skirt under my coat before checking the traffic and making my way across the road.

One of the figures was crouched next to a small Staffordshire bull terrier who was curled up in a pile of blankets. I bent down to pet him.

'He's sweet, what's his name?'

'Blue. 'Cos of his colour.' The man had several front teeth missing and spoke with a lisp. 'Don't suppose you got change for a night in the hostel?' He got to his feet and paced about with his hands in his pockets.

'Oh, erm, yes.' I reached into my bag, took out my purse and handed him a note.

'Ahh, thanks, cheers, means a million.' He bent down and showed the dog the money. 'Look, Blue, we can sleep in the warm tonight.' Blue sniffed the note and I smiled at them both. As I observed this act of love I felt as though I too were being watched. I looked up to see a man leaning on the wall of the alleyway, his eyes on me.

I nervously stepped past Blue and his master and found myself face to face with a rough beard and bloodshot eyes.

'Francesca. Long time, no see,' Todd smiled and spoke in the same tone of voice I had always known him to have; soft yet slightly gravelly. There was a slightly pungent smell coming from him that was a mixture of alcohol and body odour. Even though he looked more gaunt than when I knew him, I could see a flicker of the man I remembered behind those smiling eyes. I felt a fluttering inside my stomach, a muscle memory, maybe, of the way he had made me feel every day for those few months twenty years ago.

I looked down at my feet.

'And still as shy as you always were.'

'I wasn't shy,' I said. 'Just unsure of myself. I know myself better now, thank you, Todd,' I said assertively.

'Well, you look good for it.' Todd stopped looking at me and took out nothing more than a stump of a rolled cigarette, or possibly a spliff, from behind his ear. 'I don't suppose you still...'

'No, nothing,' I said with no tone to my voice. I glanced along the street hoping I didn't see anyone I knew.

He lit the rolled cigarette and immediately I smelt the scent of marijuana.

'I would invite you in, but I've not cleared up.' Todd pointed to the alleyway.

I smiled because I felt uncomfortable standing at the edge of the alley that Todd was referring to as his home.

'So, shall we walk instead?' I suggested.

Todd nodded and pointed in the direction of the top of town where there was a large green park and plenty of benches. I typed out a quick message to Mason explaining I would be half an hour late. His response came back promptly.

Sure, no problem. Hope everything ok x

We walked in silence as we navigated our way through the morning crowds and over the pelican crossing to the green. I gestured to a bench nestled between two large oak trees that was dappled in hazy autumnal light. It seemed like such a romantic spot to sit, somewhere a young couple might meet on their lunchbreak, away from the hustle and bustle.

Todd sat down with a sigh that bordered on a groan, and I was aware that there was a possibility he could be in pain. I sat about twelve inches away from him.

'I got your note.'

Todd nodded. 'Uh huh.'

'It was you then?'

'Who wrote the note? Yeah, course.'

'So what's the deal. Why are you trying to freak me out?'

Todd zipped his coat tighter up to his neck and hunched his shoulders. 'I see you all the time, Frankie. I know you know where I hang out... live, whatever you want to call it. And I know you saw me at the restaurant that night. Your husband stormed out and left you alone.'

'And why were you there?'

'Taking a stroll.'

'Right.' I snorted. 'Why wait all this time to start trying to freak me out? You know where I live?'

'Of course I know, I am the eyes and ears of this town. People ignore me, they think I am scum, I get overlooked, trodden on, stepped on, stepped over, spat on, beaten up.'

I sucked in my breath. Todd's words were hitting a nerve.

'But I still know people. And it doesn't take many conversations to work out where you're living. This town isn't so big,' Todd said.

'I'm sorry things are so bad for you, Todd,' I said.

'I didn't tell you this to make you feel sorry for me, but where people don't see me, I see them. I hear everything too. Stuff you wouldn't believe, conversations, people having affairs. I saw a girl raped once.'

I recoiled at this information.

'So what do you do? Just walk around the town looking for

things to discover. What made you suddenly start on me after twenty years?'

Todd was quiet for a long time. He let a loud sigh.

'You were the nicest person to me. You were always there. Until, well, you know. And it's tough. I've been on the streets nearly three years. It's getting tougher. My parents disowned me after everything and things got worse over time. I couldn't seem to keep a job. I never really got my own place.

'But I see people, they know who I am, but no one stops to say hi, check in on me. I can get in a hostel some nights, but I save it up for winter mostly. I have pains, all over. Some nights I feel like I can't breathe. I itch. The winter is so cold. Cold like you have never known. Everything hurts. I'm falling apart. I don't know how much longer I can go on.'

'So you thought you'd get my attention by trying to terrorise me?'

'I'd hardly call it that?'

'Then what do you call it, Todd?'

'It was a letter, I thought if I added a bit of something to it, to get your attention. You know I was never one for soppy love letters.'

'But what about everything else, the birthday card, the text messages, the car through my letter box.'

Todd looked at me and frowned. 'What? Not sure what you're talking about there. I wrote you one note because I have reached the point where I am not sure I can carry on any more.'

I edged closer to him on the bench. Todd glanced sideways at me. How could I think he was the one behind all of this. This was my Todd. And we were sat here together as though a day hadn't passed. Except that I had allowed many days to turn into years.

'Okay, Todd.' I started speaking slowly and carefully. 'You're telling me you haven't done anything except send me a note at work. Yet you admit you know where I live and you saw me out eating dinner with Damian and you know he's my husband, yet you're claiming innocence over everything else?'

'I was outside the restaurant by pure fluke, I don't stalk people. I am far too tired for that. I had been beaten up. Kicked on by some trashy youths. I took a stroll until they left and my mates got back.'

'And how do you know where I live then?'

'I spoke to Reese, she told me where you worked as well. But I've seen you walk into that building enough times already. You forget this town is small, people know people. I don't know the exact house where you live. Just the road. Very nice. Very up and coming.'

'It does us,' I said with a sniff.

'And you have kids?'

'Two. But don't think I'll be telling you what school they go to,' I said too coldly. I regretted my tone.

'I'm no paedophile,' Todd said with clear offence.

I looked at him, tried to assess his thoughts, his feelings, his motivations. What had gone on between us all those years ago? It was surreal to be sitting next to him after so much time had passed. As though those years never happened.

'So you didn't post a Mini car through my letter box?' I needed to be clear on everything.

'How the hell would I post a Mini through your letter box. I told you, Francesca.'

And the way he spoke my name gave me the same fluttering in my stomach as it had when I was sixteen, and then it was as though we hadn't had twenty years without contact.

'I don't know your house. I just know you live on the posh road.' Todd squinted at the hazy sun.

'It's not posh.' I kicked my heels on the grass. I wanted to edge even closer to Todd, to take his hand in mine.

'Well, it's posher than my digs.'

I let out a small laugh. I thought about who Todd was all those years ago. A druggy, a skag head, a dealer. But also a lover, a friend, a trusted companion. I chose my friends well. Regardless of what we did, where we ended up, we told the truth. We didn't hide things from one another. Even when Todd started using, he didn't try to hide it from me, that's what I loved about my gang the most. Me, Kiefer, Nancy, Minty, Dave and anyone else who hung about the Chambers pub or wherever else we were, we all knew who we were and we loved each other anyway. Regardless of what happened to drive us apart, I knew that there was a bond that we once shared and a bed we had lain in together.

'Okay,' I said quietly. 'I believe you.'

I noted the jitter of fear which pelted through my body, reminding me that if Todd was telling the truth, there was still someone out there who wanted to hurt me.

The sun had moved as we sat and now there was only one ray that came through the trees and hit the spot between us. I saw Todd lift his head to the light and I did too. Bonds from our youth are stronger than anything I have ever known. And even though the burning flames from a first love will fade, the remaining embers can live on and the warmth can suddenly catch you unaware. Especially when the love was stopped short before its time. And so there we were, two old friends, two old lovers, sitting on a park bench drinking in the warmth of the gentle morning sun.

42

NOW

I arrived at the office with a muddle of emotions. I had embraced Todd for a whole minute or so. I ignored the musty smell from his clothes and tried to remember he was still the same guy underneath. My first love. The guy I had loved so furiously that I would have done anything for him. Except in the end, I didn't. I couldn't.

I said I needed a little time to try to figure out how I could help him. I gave him enough money to get him into the hostel for the next seven nights but there was always the risk he would use it for drugs. The money was nothing to me: a cab fare home on a Saturday night, or a takeaway.

Mason was at his desk on the phone, he gave me a subtle thumbs up without even changing his facial expression as he spoke. I thought about the difference between the two men. The ex-lover I had just been with in the park, homeless, stinking of booze and sweat, who lay on the urine soaked concrete of an alleyway, his shoulders hunched with the cold. Then there was Mason, who always smelt so fresh, who always knew what to say. People knew of him and everyone seemed to respect him. He ran a successful business and could stay in a five star hotel every night of the week if he wanted to.

Back at my desk images of Todd and I together as our younger selves kept coming back to me, the short time we spent together as a couple; just a few months had felt like a lifetime.

I sighed and looked at the mass of emails waiting for replies. But I was still reeling from the interaction with Todd. I had been here in the same town as him for all this time, the town I grew up in, and there he was, living rough.

His departing words to me that morning were: 'Look after yourself, Francesca.'

Here was a man alone and vulnerable, who could be murdered as he slept, and he was telling me to take care of myself. I knew I had to do something to help him.

But I didn't know what. I couldn't bring him into our home, put him in the spare room.

Now I knew it wasn't Todd behind the terrorising I also needed to focus on what to do next. The car was a defiant act; someone wanted me to know that they were thinking about that night twenty years ago. But were a couple of texts and a toy car through the door enough to bring in the police? What else was there to do? Sit and wait for something more serious to happen? I needed to remember back to that Friday night, when I was so drunk in the pub and Penelope said I was talking to someone, a man. I had thought she meant Todd, that was why I froze when she gave the description. But now I knew it couldn't have been him. Not after I saw how fragile and ill he looked now and how he had given me his word.

My phone pinged. It was a text from Damian.

Mislaid my keys. Need to grab a few bits from the house. Can I come to reception and get them at 3?

I bashed out my reply.

I'll be home at 4.30, can't it wait until then?

I don't really want to be in the house at the same time as you. I'll be in and out before you get home.

Fine. I'll leave them at reception. Can you leave in the usual place when you've finished?

Yes

I sellotaped the key to a Bliss compliments slip so it didn't slide about and attract attention, then I opened my drawer under the desk, retrieved a white envelope and put the key in it and sealed it. I went to reception and handed it to Carys and asked her to give it to my husband Damian when he arrived.

I flopped back down at my desk and a few seconds later Penelope sat down at hers.

'Hey,' I said.

'Is everything ok? I saw you at reception just now?' Penelope inquired.

Venturing out from behind my desk was a rare occurrence. I was usually so busy between the hours of eight and four that I would only have time to nip to the loo and often missed my lunch break.

'I had to leave my key at reception for Damian. He has lost his, can you believe it?'

'He's a man, isn't he?' Penelope said with a smirk and I made an effort to laugh longer and louder at her joke than was absolutely necessary because it was the most she had ever interacted with me. I felt sorry for her, especially knowing about those cuts on her arm. I wondered if there ever was a man in her life. Perhaps those cuts were the result of the breakup. Was there ever a right time to ask these things?

Fish swung by with a coffee and I looked up to thank him. Behind him I could see Lil looking at me. Her hard stare suddenly broke into a beaming smile when she saw I was looking right at her. It was clear to me now there was some envy there because Fish gave me attention; brought me coffees and water.

'He's a diamond, your man,' I said loudly and raised my coffee cup.

She grinned and giggled, and I hoped I had done what I needed to do to assure her I wasn't about to steal her boyfriend from under her nose.

For the rest of the morning I managed to throw myself into my work and ignored all passing thoughts of worry. Just before midday, Penelope told me she was leaving site for a meeting, which I found rather refreshing as usually she barely kept me in the loop as to her whereabouts. I wondered if she was finally beginning to accept me and no longer saw me as a threat.

The next thing I knew it was 3.30 p.m. and my phone pinged. It was Damian.

Thanks for keys. In usual place. I'll have a good hunt for mine later. Might need to get some more cut

Whatever he needed to do he had done it pretty quickly. I knew it was a good thing that we were keeping out of each other's way, at least until we could reach a point where we could try to understand whatever it was we were afraid of truly saying. If it was the end then we both needed to be able to communicate that and then make the relevant decisions that would be the right ones for all of us. If there were such a thing as a right decision.

I sat back in my seat, stretched my arms up and glanced round the office, as I did, I saw Lil was looking at me again; her serious expression once again morphed into a gleaming smile.

Penelope came back into the office and slid into her desk.

'Good meeting?' I asked.

Penelope gave me a thumbs up whilst immersing herself with something on her phone. Was I imaging the change in her behaviour again?

My phone pinged again. This time it was Nancy.

We still on for tonight girl?

I typed out my reply.

Still on. I'll do snacks, bring wine

Of course! Laters x

* * *

I arrived home and straight away began looking around the house to see what Damian had taken or done. The children were being looked after by Harriet and she said she would give them their tea. I wasn't sure how I felt about Harriet having my kids. Was she the one Damian was playing away with? I made a mental note to cop a look at her earlobes later to see what kind of earrings she wore.

I headed upstairs to see if Damian had taken any more clothes, but the contents of the wardrobe looked the same. Back downstairs, in the study by the front door, I noticed a few drawers had been left open, and even though I was annoyed with Damian for sweeping through the house like a whirlwind without a care for anyone but himself, I still did the dutiful thing and went around closing them all.

In the kitchen I poured myself a glass of wine and contemplated texting him exactly what I thought of him.

The doorbell trilled through the house, dragging me from my thoughts and rescuing Damian from the onslaught of my feelings.

I pulled off my suit jacket and walked to the door clutching my wine.

I had barely pulled it open when Pixie and Maddox both ran at my legs, nearly knocking me over backwards.

In front of me stood Harriet. I had still never formally met her. Images of her and Damian together kept flashing into my head, yet here she was delivering my children back to me.

'Hi, I don't think we have met properly. I'm Harriet.' She flung her hand out towards me. She was still rocking that forties vibe with a tight pink long sleeved woollen top tucked into a beige pencil skirt. She wore long feathery earrings today, a complete contrast to the small pink studded earring I had discovered in my room.

'Oh.' I transferred the wine from my right hand to my left and took her hand in mine.

'Really nice to meet you,' I said through the biggest smile I could fit on my face. 'Hope they behaved!'

'They are adorable. Both scoffed their dinner. I made a soya mince cottage pie, they didn't seem to notice it wasn't meat, I'm vegetarian you see.'

'Oh well, that's good then, isn't it, kids. What do you say to Harriet?'

The kids started sing-songing their thank yous, then disappeared into the snug.

'Sorry I'm a tad earlier than five, I'm going out tonight.'

'Right,' I said dully.

'I see you're on it already?' She motioned to the wine.

I raised my eyebrows and did a tight-lipped smile. 'Yep, caught me out there I'm afraid.'

'Oh, I don't blame you, it's hard being on your own, isn't it?'

I was floored for a second. Damian had moved out less than forty-eight hours ago and here was Harriet trying to show empathy for my situation.

'Kids can be challenging. Especially having two of them,' I said, feeling like I had hit the back of the net when I watched her face crumple. My two kids trump your one, I thought, as I flashed her my best smile.

'Well, anyway,' she looked round and did a shiver. 'Better get back and get ready. I'll see you next week.' She turned slightly towards the path.

'Great. And thanks for having them, bye then,' I said.

'Oh, it's—'

I didn't hear the last of the sentence because I kicked the door to with my foot and the weightiness of the metal hitting the frame reverberated around the stark hallway.

'I made a soya mince cottage pie, I'm a vegetarian,' I mocked in a squeaky voice to myself.

'Mummy, who are you talking to?' came Pixie's voice from behind me.

I peered through the glass to see if I could see Harriet still on the doorstep, but it was all clear.

'No one, darling.' I turned and stroked her hair. 'How was school?'

We began walking back towards the kitchen together.

'Well, Mummy, you are not going to believe what happened today.'

'Go on, sweetie, tell me.'

* * *

After I had put the kids to bed, there was a light knock on the door.

I quickly pulled on a pair of jogging bottoms and a light grey flannel top and opened the door.

'Well, girl, you're a sight for sore eyes,' I said as Nancy opened her arms, a carrier bag of wine over one arm. 'Let's get this cracked open.'

And the sight of alcohol and my best friend were the only things I needed right now. I knew as that as soon as I could get another drink down me, all my worries would evaporate.

43

I threw myself back into college. I needed to get the grades, I wasn't going to be one of those people who skived off to get pissed and high all week and came away with nothing to show for two years of studies. I wanted to do something with my life. I hadn't heard anything from Todd for a few days, not since I walked out of that flat. His absence was an ache that came and went only when I could distract myself.

I came home from a late seminar on Wednesday to find him sitting on the doorstep. Mum and Dad were in as usual, watching *Neighbours*.

I stood there with my Benetton bag on one shoulder looking down at him. He looked okay, tired but okay.

'I don't want to do that stuff again, Frank.'

'So don't do it,' I said, kneeling down to his level, pleading with him. My intention of playing the role of hardened girlfriend from our three day break fell by the wayside. My insides were exploding with joy, the fact he had come for me, he wanted to stop, meaning he wanted me more than that stuff.

'I want to. I do. But you must understand it's like no other experience on earth. I think to myself I won't do it and then it's there and my God, it's so good. But this, this feeling afterwards, I'm terrified I will become an addict. I don't want that. Because, well, the thing is... I want you more.'

I closed my eyes for a second so I could absorb his words.

I sat down on the step next to him. 'So, what shall we do?'

Todd looked at me, put his arm around me and pulled me into him. He smelt like fresh linen and soap. 'See, this is why I love you. You're so pragmatic and—'

'Hold on, did you just say what I thought you said?' I interrupted Todd and turned my body to look him.

Todd smirked. 'Yes, I did. I called you pragmatic.'

'Yeah, and the bit before that? Are we going to just skip over that bit as though it never happened?'

Todd feigned confusion then said, 'Oh right, that bit, yeah,' then he leant over and said it again, only this time it was a whisper in my ear. I fell into his arms and felt sheer joy and happiness. The only thing I wanted was Todd. I knew he needed me. And I would be there for him. No matter what got in the way.

'I've missed you, girl.' Nancy poured wine, wearing her standard outfit of three quarter length jeans and kitten heels, even though it was freezing out. Her curly hair was bunched up in a high ponytail and I thought how she still looked like a teenager.

'What have you been up to?' She handed me a glass.

'Just been feeling a bit numb about it all really,' I said, thinking about Damian.

'Yeah. So, tell me about Mason, how was the trip?'

I paused for a second, because Nancy had clearly just side-stepped around me talking about Damian which, between two friends, was clearly more important than news on Mason. I was aching to ask her how she had known that mine and Damian's argument happened at Mason's house.

'You knew I was at his house with Damian, how would you know that?' I asked as I looked at Nancy sipping her wine. She swallowed and let out a small cough.

'I have a great imagination. Of course hotshot Mason would host a dinner party at home. I presume he resides in the penthouse suite? Very Richard Gere in *Pretty Woman*.'

I shrugged. 'Not quite like that, Nancy, but yes, he has the penthouse.'

'Eeeek! Was it amazing, I mean, what kind of furniture does he have?'

Relief swept through me. Why was I doubting Nancy? She was my best friend. We understood each other perfectly.

'Why are you so fascinated by Mason Valentine? How's things with you and Harry?' I sipped my wine.

Nancy waved her hand. 'Oh, he's away at the moment, but that's for business. Not back for another week. It's nice, actually.'

'Not missing him?' I asked.

'We've been together ten years. What is there to miss? The snoring, the mess.' Nancy started looking around the kitchen, avoiding eye contact. I assessed her for a second, trying to work out what was going on.

'Did something happen with you and Harry?' I said quietly.

Nancy shook her head and pulled her lips down. 'Nope. Everything dandy. I fancy a fag, do you fancy a fag? Cheeky midweek ciggy?'

I smiled and shrugged, 'Why not.' I wasn't averse to the odd ciggy these days, since Stella at work had dragged me back to the dark side.

'I'm just going to go for a waz, the fags are in my coat pocket. Crack them open.' Nancy jumped down from the stool and clicked off to the hallway and the toilet. I pushed myself away from the island and walked round to the chair her coat was slung over. I rooted around in the right-hand pocket and felt only a packet of chewing gum. I put my hand in the left pocket and sucked my breath in as my finger came into contact with something small and sharp. I pulled my finger out and there was a tiny dot of blood on the tip. My hand had already brushed against the cigarette packet so I lifted them out, placed them on the side and then went back in to find the offending object that had pricked me. I went in with my thumb and forefinger and felt the familiar shape of an earring. As I lifted it out and looked at it I clamped my left hand over my mouth as I stared at the piece of jewellery that was already so familiar to me. I had the other one to the matching pair in the box on my dressing table.

I threw the earring back into the pocket, ripped open the packet of fags and found a lighter in a drawer. My head was awash with thoughts; if Nancy had one earring in her pocket then she was missing the other one. A million reasons were catapulting through my head. Could it have fallen by the edge of the bed weeks ago when Nancy and I were in my bedroom going through some of my old clothes for the charity shop, and maybe Damian had moved the bed and...

'Oooh, you're keen!' Nancy came clicking back into the kitchen as I stood poised with a cigarette in one hand and a lighter in the other. She went to the back door and opened it and I walked round to shut the kitchen door so none of the smoke would go upstairs into the kids' rooms.

Nancy sat back in her chair and took a cigarette from the packet. I took a ramekin from the cupboard to use as an ashtray.

All the while my inner monologue was screaming at her. 'Why were you in my bedroom when I was away in Belgium, is this why you knew Mason had the dinner party at his house, is that why you don't want me to talk about my separation. Are you fucking my husband?'

'Gosh, it's gone cold now, hasn't it?' Nancy put her arms around herself.

'Yes. Makes you glad we're not homeless,' I said with a slight shake to my voice. I felt I couldn't even look at Nancy. My mind jolted to thoughts of Todd, hoping he was safe and warm in the hostel.

'Well, it was touch and go but we did alright, kid.' Nancy took a long drag on the cigarette and blew a smoke ring. 'The likes of Todd and co didn't do so well, I know.'

'I saw him today,' I said bluntly.

'I haven't seen him for a while, last time I saw him he was parked up on a bench at the top of town with a load of winos,' she giggled, and I narrowed my eyes at her.

'No, I mean I really saw him, I met him at the park. I gave him some money for a hostel this week.'

'God, Frankie, why? That guy was a total crackhead and nearly took you down with him. He doesn't deserve any of your time.'

'We were in love once, Nancy. And he came to me to reach out for help. Said he's had enough of being on the streets.'

'Well, I don't know why you are so nice, but you are.'

'You think I'm a pushover?' I thought of the earring in her coat pocket.

Nancy frowned and sucked on her cigarette.

'No,' she said as she blew the smoke out. 'I just think, well some people are never going to come good. I mean, he was fit at the time, and you guys were cute, but he was doing all that heroin!' Nancy wrinkled her nose and I eyed her suspiciously.

Nancy was a girl I had known since I was eleven years old. We were drawn together because we were both growing our fringes out and sporting the biggest Alice bands our foreheads could accommodate. But there was no denying, as we sat downing red wine and smoking cigarettes as though we were still those pre-pubescent schoolgirls waiting for the boys to grow up and notice us, that something had shifted. I suddenly had doubts about my best friend, and I didn't know how to deal with that.

Nancy finished her cigarette, stubbed it out and started telling me about the pay increase she had been offered and the fact she was getting her nails done at a different salon this month because her usual girl was on holiday. As much as I usually relished these low level conversations where I let Nancy rant about the mundane aspects of her life, and I would nod along, just happy to be in her company, I couldn't help but think that today suddenly all that was gone, that Nancy had been here in this house when I wasn't and that I couldn't and shouldn't trust her.

I almost catapulted out of my bed as I heard the crash. There was a low moan from one of the children's rooms, but I couldn't make out which one. I ran to Maddox's room first, but he was sound asleep. I then scuttled down the hallway to Pixie's room. The hallway light was on and I could see immediately into her room. Her bed was a midi high rise with a built-in bookshelf and desk underneath. I remember the day we built it for her. I was pregnant with Maddox, yet I was so relaxed while Damian was the total opposite. His face was red and angry as he struggled with the instructions and keeping the Allen key in sight.

I looked into Pixie's room and what was left of her bed. I could see my daughter trying to sit upright, although the main frame of the bed had collapsed and had half slid off the side where the book-shelf was. I ran over to the bed and put my arms around Pixie who was sitting silently, still in shock and still half asleep. She automatically put her arms around my neck like she did when she was little, and wrapped her legs around my waist. I carried her away from the wreckage; my heart was thumping hard in my chest and my breathing was fast.

'It's ok, darling,' I whispered into her neck.

'Mummy,' Pixie murmured. I took her to my room, laid her down and tucked her in on Damian's side. With some light cascading in through a gap in the curtains and the hallway light I could see her expression, a look of confusion.

'It's okay, darling, you sleep in with Mummy tonight.' I stroked her head until she closed her eyes again and drifted off. I walked back over to her bedroom and hit the main light switch and assessed the carnage from the doorway, rubbing the back of my neck in bewilderment. I walked over to the bed, with the memory of Damian's angry face while trying to attach the pieces together and the sound of my laughter reverberating around the stark room that didn't have enough furniture in it yet to absorb sound.

I walked over to the bed that had slid down over the shelves. Pixie's beautiful books had been pushed off and a couple of their spines had been crushed. I bent to pick one up and saw a large silver screw lying next to it. Getting down on my hands and knees I found three more screws. As I stood up I ran my hand across the frames, finding the points where Damian had drilled them in until they were so tight the only way they were coming out was by reversing the mechanism on the drill. As I felt my way up and along the frame, I discovered more screws missing and some that were half out of the wood, ready to fall at any moment. I took a step backwards with my arms wrapped around myself, trying to work it all out. My mind rushed through a handful of plausible explanations, but in the end all I could see was Damian's angry face putting the screws in and then the same face as he removed them.

* * *

The first thing I did in the morning was call a locksmith and book them to come out after work to fit new locks on all the doors. It looked as though it might rain so I took the car and arrived at my desk weary and worried. I was terrified something might happen to the children while they were at school today or that Damian might suddenly decide he was picking them up. I kept clock watching all day and found every task I did arduous.

A few people were off with their annual head colds and I noticed Penelope's desk lay empty all day. I didn't ask after her, I relished the atmosphere without her. I went to lunch early to try to clear my head and my body automatically began walking to the supermarket and the alleyway next to it. I looked in and saw a body hunched into a sleeping bag. A scruffily dressed man was standing next to him. He looked at me, his body swaying side to side.

'Is that Todd?' I asked, pointing at the body on the floor. He didn't answer.

'Is that Todd?' I said louder, took his arms in my hands and almost shook him, but his eyes remained glazed over. I moved past him and into the alley. I bent down to the level of the hunched figure. The stench was so strong and pungent I had to cover my mouth and nose, finding some relief from the smell of the hand cream I had put on before I left the office.

'Todd,' I said through my hand.

'Urrrgggh,' came the voice. I pulled his head to one side and I could see he was barely conscious.

'Fink 'e took too much,' came a voice from behind me. It was the man with the dog called Blue, 'I told 'im it was too much but 'e wouldn't 'ave it.'

'What did he take?' I asked hurriedly.

'Usual, some crack too. Injected, I fink.'

'Oh God. Todd, stay here,' I said. I realised Todd hadn't used the money I gave him for the hostel. He had used it for drugs instead. I ran to the back of the Bliss offices where I had parked the car and drove it round to the road. I pulled up on the kerb.

'Er, you can't park there, young lady,' came the voice of the supermarket security guard employed to keep out the drunks, ruffians and homeless.

'Either help me or bugger off,' I said as I went back into the alley and tried to lift Todd up. The security guard peered at us. I squatted on my heels, already panting. For a man who was probably severely malnourished, Todd weighed a tonne.

'Are you helping or what?' I said to the floating head of the security guard.

He walked round and stood there with his hands in his pockets. 'Well, if it means he isn't going to be here any more.' He bent down and lifted Todd over his shoulder.

'You want him in here?' he said when he reached the car. I raced in front of him and opened the back door. Maddox's booster seat was there so I chucked it in the footwell and gestured to the back seat. 'Just lay him there if you can.'

The security guard threw him down with little care and I winced, but I knew Todd was out of it. I had seen him like that so many times before; it was strange to still be witnessing it all these years later.

I raced round to the driver's seat and accelerated down the road, out of the main town towards the hospital.

* * *

I left my details with the doctor and asked them to call me as soon as he stable, and made it back to work just as my hour was up.

I slid into my desk and tried to remain calm, focus on my work, but by now it was an almost impossible task.

I felt a presence next to my desk and looked up to see Stella, holding a pile of paperwork.

She looked at me, taken back. 'Good lunch break, was it?'

'Yes, rushed,' I said.

'Thought so – you've got mud on your shirt.' Stella pointed to my white blouse with the ruffle trim, which was now covered in a brown streak.

'What were you doing? Mud wrestling?' Stella snorted. I grabbed my scarf from the back of my chair and wrapped it round myself until it covered all of the ruffle.

'Yeah, something like that.'

'You coming to the pub at the end of the week? Freebie Friday!' Stella looked wide-eyed at me like an excited child. I unexpectedly rolled my eyes which Stella clocked.

'Take that as a no then?' She placed the pile of paperwork down on my desk and I could feel the vibration as it landed with force.

* * *

Two hours passed before I received a call from the hospital to say Todd was stable and would stay in tonight. I knew I couldn't visit him and it would be at least tomorrow before he was discharged so I put those thoughts to one side for now and concentrated on getting the children picked up from school.

I passed Mason's office just before 4 p.m.. He was standing near the open doorway flicking through a folder.

'I'm going now. Going to collect the kids.'

He let out a sigh and edged a step closer to me; his left hand was turned over as though he was reaching out to me.

I looked down at my feet. I knew how I felt about him, but it didn't seem right. Not when I had so many other emotions running high. For a moment I considered telling Mason everything. Maybe if I did he could simply rescue me from it all.

My instincts were telling me to throw myself into Mason's arms, to bury myself into his neck and to allow him to do what I knew he had been imagining us doing together all this time. Every look and twinkle in his eye, his thoughts were etched all over his face. He couldn't hide the passion he felt, and I had struggled as well. But now I was retreating from his outstretched hand that was offering me a lifeline. As soon as I placed my hand in his I knew all my problems would be gone. I would no longer need to worry about money, or who was trying to scare me, or what I was going to do with Todd, how I would help him. I knew Mason, with his years of life experience, his pragmatic approach to the world, his ever-growing love which was palpable and had become this force between us, would make my life so easy.

This tension between us had been building since the day I sat in front of him all those weeks ago but my mind was needed elsewhere. Even though the temptation was there to just fall into his arms, I had to walk away.

As I drove home I realised I hadn't heard from Damian all day. He was due to see the kids tomorrow after school, but I would make sure that wasn't happening now.

I collected the kids from after school club, but I was wary of Damian showing up. I simply didn't trust him any more.

I piled the kids into the car just as it began to rain and we arrived home to find the locksmith already there, waiting outside in his van. I scooped the kids out of the car and went round to the driver's side. He opened the door and stepped out.

'Hi, thanks for coming at short notice.'

'No problem.' The locksmith was a short man in his late fifties with greying hair. He followed us into the house with his box of tools and placed them down at the front door.

'What's he doing?' Maddox said loudly.

The locksmith raised his eyes to me as if to say. 'You'd better answer this one.'

'Silly Mummy broke the door so this nice man is going to fix it.' I used my mother-ease voice to assure Maddox that everything was fine.

'Oh, okay. I'm going to watch.' Maddox sat down cross-legged next to the toolbox.

I mouthed an exaggerated 'sorry' and offered to make him a coffee. I went through into the kitchen where Pixie was getting settled with her homework.

'What is that man doing, Mummy?'

'He is fixing the door,' I said absently as I started to search through cupboards for something to make for dinner.

'Did you break it?'

'Yes, I did, honey.'

'Like you broke my bed?'

'That was an accident too. I will be sending it all back and getting a new one. I think it was probably faulty.'

'I could have died, Mummy!' Pixie said with terror in her voice.

I breathed out unsteadily as the horrors of last night returned in a frightening vision in front of me.

'Well, maybe not died, but I will certainly be speaking very sternly to whoever was responsible.'

'Do you mean the man-yewell-facterers?' Pixie said slowly and carefully as she took out various pens and pencils from her bag. I let out a sigh and went over to her and put my lips on her head.

'Yes, the manufacturers.' I stood there for a few moments, just breathing in her loveliness.

'Shit, coffee!' I broke away from Pixie.

'Mummy, don't swear!'

'Sorry, darling,' I said, opening the cupboard, then I screamed and stumbled backwards.

'What, Mummy, what?' Pixie was up and by my side. I put my hand over my mouth. There at the front, next to a box of teabags, was a dead mouse.

'Mummy, errghh!' Pixie had both hands over her mouth.

I could hear drilling coming from the front door so I knew Maddox wouldn't hear the commotion.

'I know, it's disgusting.' I moved forward and prodded it. I was surprised to find it wasn't hard but still quite soft. I assessed the cupboard for holes, knowing that mice can squeeze through a hole the width of a biro but there was nothing, these units were still fairly new, installed when Maddox was a babe in arms.

Shaking my head in bewilderment, I scooped the mouse up with a carrier bag and threw it in the bin outside. I made the coffee and took it through to the hallway. I placed it on the floor next to the locksmith's box of tools.

'Not long now, love, I'll have this one finished in a mo and the other doors done in a jiffy.'

I smiled weakly as Maddox stood and reached up to be held. I picked him up and tightened my grip around him.

* * *

When the locksmith left me with a new set of keys I let out a small sigh of relief. But nothing made any sense yet. I knew Damian was frustrated and he was also angry at me for taking the job and throwing myself into it and therefore not paying any attention to us. But I couldn't understand why he would want to try to hurt the kids. I also wondered if the dead mouse was also another prank to add to the devastation he had caused in Pixie's room.

* * *

I had taken the broken bed away and Pixie was sleeping on just a mattress, which she said was fun because it felt like camping, even though we had never been camping.

That night, I checked on the children three times then I went around the house checking all windows. I stood at the kitchen window and shuddered at the thought of someone watching me.

I headed upstairs, double-checking windows on the way up. I sat on my bed and wondered about the last time I had felt this way – the grief, the frustration. The guilt. But it occurred to me that it had been twenty years since I had felt this scared. I had written in my diaries and filled up so many of them, only to lock them away. Yet again, the thought of them sitting in the safe was becoming overwhelming, as though they were calling to me. I perched on the end of my bed and stared at the safe in the wardrobe.

It was telling me it was time to face the past. I knew Damian thought I hadn't dealt with my demons, but I knew how I felt when I was pouring all my emotions out in those books, it was cathartic. So why did I feel as though it wasn't finished, as though after all those years of trying to make my grief go away it was still there?

I slid off the bed onto the floor and crawled to the wardrobe where the safe had sat untouched for years. Damian always complained, what a waste of space, we could use it for storing valuables. I ignored his rants. I twisted the lock backwards and forwards between the four numbers: 2461. Don't be scared this time, Frankie, I told myself. Just open the door and pull out the damn diaries. Nothing bad is going to happen. But I knew that by doing this I was bringing the past back. Yet with Todd suddenly in my life again, the anonymous fortieth birthday card for Kiefer, all the texts I had been receiving, I knew the past had already caught up with me.

The numbers clicked and the safe opened. I tentatively opened the door and saw the flash of coloured books, pinks, greens and blues. The memory of when I was handed them was so vivid it was as though it were yesterday when I had been told to take all the pain out of my heart and put it in the books. I let out a long sigh and slowly put my hand into the safe and took out the top book. The outside cover remained intact and they still almost looked brand new. The top book was green. I brought it to my lap and looked at it for a moment before opening it. My eyes tried to take in what was sprawled across the first page. I started turning the pages, seeing more and more of the same thing, yet unable to believe my own eyes. I took out a handful of notebooks and turned the pages again, trying to remember the angry and frustrated mind of a sixteen year old girl.

How could it be? How could I have not remembered what I had written? My entire recollection of my sixteen year old self was a total contrast to what I was seeing here.

I eventually found my way halfway through the final book where it all just stopped and there were blank pages all the way to the end. I looked at the first blank page, then stood up with the book in hand, went to my dressing table, took out a pen from the drawer, then sat down and began writing.

* * *

November 2018

I have tried so hard to make it all disappear, the thoughts, the anger, the frustration. I thought it had gone away, but with everything that has happened recently, I realised that it's still so raw. I can't believe you are gone, not now and not then. Twenty years have gone by and still I wake up every day and the first thing I think about is you. Sometimes I imagine what you would be doing now, what kind of job you would have, would you like hot or cold holidays, would you prefer books to films. You were so young when you went, that you hadn't even had time to become who you were going to be for the rest of your life or find out just what wonders were awaiting you. I bet it would have been something amazing.

I think about our memories. The stuff we did as kids, the laughs we had. The way we held hands in bed at Christmas when we were tiny, too excited to sleep but too scared to be alone in case one of us woke and found Father Christmas in the room with us.

Other times I think about the day you died, the way you were lying across the driver's seat, your head tilted to one side as though you had just lain down for a nap.

I think about the way my life is now without you in it, how I suffer every day without you. How I must think how to breathe some days. But most of all, beyond all of that I remember that day you died as though it were yesterday. I play it over and over in my mind, toying with alternative endings, trying to bring you back to life in my mind with all the 'if onlys' I can possibly imagine. But it's no good, no matter what ending I conjure up it will never ever prevent what happens to you in the end. The decisions we made did not come from you, you who were always so clever, so careful and diligent with your driving, they came from me. Forced upon you by me. I made those decisions; I made the things happen that led up to the crash. It was my fault you are dead and I cannot forgive myself, so I punish myself every day with the choices I make, the way I treat my body instead of taking care of it. But the thing is, twenty years later I have realised I can no longer keep on going like this, punishing myself. Because of course, I wasn't the only one to blame. There was someone else. All I can do now as I write this in my diary is say: this is my confession.

I am sorry for what I am about to do but I can no longer hold it in.

46

Todd had been off the gear for nearly two weeks. He said there were times when he thought about it but being with me made it all better.

There was a party coming up. I was nervous about it, and how Todd would be, if he would need to take anything stronger. When I asked Nancy if she was coming, she said she and Minty were taking a break from it all for a while, they wanted to try other things and had booked a weekend away in Skegness. I asked her what she intended to do in Skeg-bloody-ness in the middle of autumn and she said, 'Walk, talk, throw pebbles in the sea.'

I knew Nancy was always older than her years, so was Minty. I was happy for them. I would miss them at the party but I had Todd and he was trying really hard. It would be just us, me and Todd, and we would do all the things we did before he even looked at heroin. We would dance and laugh and then smoke and giggle. I couldn't wait. I had booked the day off work on the Sunday and the clocks went back so we had an extra hour in the morning to ourselves.

There was only one thing that was throwing a dampener on the night and that was Kiefer. He kept asking me if I was going and when I said I was, he would start rubbing his jaw and acting all stressed.

'Why, Frank, why? Why do you keep hanging around with that loser? You know there's talk of a raid?'

'There's always talk of a bloody raid, isn't that what you said made the nights more exciting? Just living in the moment, knowing they could be shut down at any second?'

'Yeah, well, I got a feeling this one might actually happen.'

'Todd isn't doing anything bad, Kiefer. He's clean.'

Kiefer looked aggrieved. 'Yeah well, you aren't going to be dancing all night on a spliff, now are you?'

'Oh, for God's sake, Kiefer, can you just give it a rest!' I shouted.

'I can't, Frankie. Don't you get it? You're my sister. You're all I've got!'

I frowned at him. 'You have Reese,' I said quietly.

'I mean you're my only family. Mum and Dad aren't exactly compos mentis most of the time. It's always been just us, hasn't it. You look out for me and I look out for you?'

I hung my head, feeling the effects of Kiefer's words. I knew he was a good brother, always had one eye on me, but since I had taken an interest in Todd he had become an irritation to me. I had begun to overlook his caring side and instead see it as an inconvenience.

I shifted uncomfortably from one foot to another. Mine and Kiefer's love for one another had always been a given, something undisclosed between the two of us. We never mentioned it, but we felt it deeply.

'I just want you to know, I am being careful. I will never do any of that stuff that Todd did, even when his mates are around trying to shove it down his neck. I stood by him and now he's off it,' I said.

'Whatever you say, Frankie. I trust you, I don't trust him. I never have and I never will.'

I just stood there. I couldn't think of anything else to say. I was never going to be able to change Kiefer's mind about Todd.

'Are you coming tonight?'

He shook his head. 'It sounds dodgy. Me and Reese and a few lads are gonna head out to Lola's.' Lola's was a club out on the bypass towards the next city. People went there after the pubs shut.

'It's gonna be a good night, sure I can't tempt you to go there instead of this party?'

'Nah,' I said straight away. I had my heart set on that night. I was sixteen. I made decisions and wasn't swayed easily. If I wanted to do something, I made damn sure it happened. If people cancelled or a night didn't happen it was essentially the end of the world in my eyes. I was blinkered. As much as I knew Kiefer loved me and cared for me, I had to do what I wanted to do and if that meant screwing his feelings once more, then that's just what I needed to do right now.

They discharged Todd the next day and I was to pick him up at 5 p.m.. I rushed through my day, barely able to concentrate.

I had been building up to what this day would entail, but I knew what I needed to do. I got home from work and made the futon up with fresh linen. I had slept the occasional night on that bed and it was a killer on the back, but I imagined it would feel like luxury to Todd. I looked at the bed and my mind was cast back to the days we slept on a futon at his house and I wondered if Todd would remember too.

I wondered what it would be like to have him sleeping here in this house with me, having spent many nights together as a couple. I knew I needed to forget about that for now, and just think that I was helping out a friend in need. To finish the job I started twenty years ago.

I raced home from work and Aimee handed over the kids and went home.

I had texted Damian to say we were all down with a stomach bug to keep him away from the house. He had a phobia of sick, always ran for the hills whenever one of the kids was ill, so I knew that this was the best way of not seeing or speaking to him for a few days.

I had no desire to get into any arguments with him just yet about all that had gone on. I had decided to deal with one thing at a time and had surprised myself with just how disciplined I was being. Since I had gone to help Todd a few days ago all the weird stuff just seemed to stop. It was as though now I had something to really focus on, helping Todd feel he had something to live for, it felt as though I had imagined it all. Except I knew I hadn't.

* * *

I had told the kids that Daddy was living at a friend's house because he had an important job to do and it was easier for him to sleep there. I decided I didn't need to overwhelm them with the intricacies of what was happening with us emotionally or my fears over Damian's current state of mind and what he was capable of doing. They were, as I had expected, fairly nonchalant about it and so far there had been very few questions except one from Maddox: 'What colour is Daddy's new bed?'

* * *

I had asked the nurse to tell Todd to wait for me in the car park and I had prepped the kids for his appearance.

'He won't look as neat and as well presented as me or Daddy.' As I used Damian as an example of what a real man should look like I shuddered at the memory of what had happened in Pixie's room.

'He's an old friend of Mummy's and he has fallen on hard times. We do not judge people when they are down. We help them rise up again.'

Pixie nodded firmly at me while Maddox looked on with a perplexed expression.

Pixie was all over it and had been doing some research online about the homeless. I had to remind her not to bombard him with her newly acquired statistics.

Todd got into the front passenger seat.

'Hi,' I said, unsure how else to greet him; a kiss on the cheek was out of the question with the kids in the back.

'Hey,' Todd said. He was pale and had dark rings around his eyes.

I introduced him to Pixie and Maddox, and he turned around in the front seat, smiled and said it was nice to meet them.

'Cool names,' he turned back to me, 'I always knew you'd have cool kids.' His voice was small and croaky. I noticed his beard had patches where some hair was missing. He was wearing the clothes he had gone to the hospital in.

I stole a glance at Pixie in the rear view mirror and she gave me one of her nervous grins.

As I drove us home I couldn't quite believe what I was doing. I had dreamt of doing these random acts of kindness before, just scooping a poor homeless person of the street and bringing them into my home, feeding them up and then getting them back on their feet, finding them a job and a home, but the reality of bringing a total stranger with dependencies and mental health issues was too much of a risk for the kids. Plus it was never the sort of thing that Damian would have ever agreed to. The only thing driving me on was that I knew it was Todd. I had to just keep seeing him as that cute lovable guy we knew all those years ago. He was in trouble from the day you met him and no one helped him out, I reminded myself. I should have been there for him. But in the end, I couldn't be. He's the same guy, I told myself. He didn't know any better. You're doing the right thing. I stole a look at him out of the corner of my eye as I drove, in that momentary glance he almost looked like the same Todd, and I felt my heart fill with sadness.

* * *

Once we were back home, I told the kids to go and watch some TV but they both insisted on following me round as I helped Todd settle in. Pixie was especially keen on being the tour guide and giving Todd all the mundane information about each room, such as: the cold tap in the downstairs loo was dodgy and the toilet upstairs only worked on the long flush, not the short. Todd smiled and nodded along until both kids got bored and went to pick out a film to watch.

Todd and I suddenly found we were alone in the spare room, both looking down at the bed I had made up yesterday.

'It's a futon,' I said with a laugh, 'like—'

'I know, Frank. I remember.' Todd looked at me and held my gaze and under all the beard and raw skin and the stench that was coming off him I could still see the old Todd.

'I remember it all,' he said. 'That night, what happened.'

'Don't,' I said quietly. 'I don't think about it any more,' I lied. I just wasn't ready to talk about it yet.

'Sure. What's the plan, then?' Todd asked.

'Well, I thought you could have a shower, have a bath, I bet you'd love a bath? I have some Epsom salts. Then I have cooked some supper. It's just spaghetti bolognaise—'

'I meant the plan, the big plan,' Todd gestured with his arms around the room, 'you saving me and all.'

'You asked,' I said with some offence in my voice.

'I know,' Todd said. 'That's the shittiest bit. I had to come to you, it should have been the other way around. I should have been looking after you. How can you do this, why would you help me?'

'Because you asked me to,' I said.

'And that's it? Did it ever occur to you that I am not a good guy?'

'Todd, shut up. You are a good guy. You have had a rough few years, but life can change, it doesn't have to be like that any more. I can't change what happened that night and why I couldn't see you again, but I can make a difference now.'

'And that will make it all better. Will it give you peace?'

I shook my head. 'There's no such thing with two kids in the house.' I tried to laugh off Todd's comment. He looked at me dead-pan. 'No, of course not. But it's not making things any worse is it? So why not? You need the help; I can help you!'

'And what about your husband?'

'He and I are separated at the moment. I don't know what's going to happen, but he is not going to come here any time soon, and that reminds me, please don't answer the door when I'm not here.'

'Hey.' Todd put his hands up. 'You don't have to worry about me, Francesca. I'll be the perfect house guest.'

'Okay. Great.' I smiled. The smell of him was now filling up the room around us. 'I'll go and run that bath.'

* * *

Half an hour later Todd came down, dressed in some old trackie bottoms and a t-shirt of Damian's that I had left out on the bed. I also left out razors and deodorant. He hadn't bothered to shave but the room instantly took on the scent of a freshly bathed person and so I was relieved.

We ate around the table; Maddox flashing looks across at Todd. I realised it must be very confusing for him and so I made a mental note to talk to him at bedtime, tell him that Todd wasn't someone who had come in to replace his daddy.

I had imagined that Todd would wolf his food down like a man who had been trekking the Andes for weeks, but he nibbled politely at the bread and ate less than a Maddox portion of spaghetti.

He looked sad and I realised it wasn't going to be the easy transformation I had anticipated, and I was suddenly panicked about what it was I was hoping to achieve here.

'If you need to rest, you're more than welcome to go on up,' I said looking at the clock. It was only 6 p.m. but he looked weary.

'Yeah, I should.' Todd looked at the kids. 'Dinner was lush, isn't your mummy clever?'

Pixie looked at me with one of her embarrassed smiles again.

Todd took himself upstairs and I cleaned and washed up and then got the kids in the bath. Once they were in bed, I walked past the spare room which was for now, Todd's room, and saw the light was still on. I knocked gently and opened the door; he had been lying facing the wall and as I entered he rolled onto his back and looked at me. He wasn't under the covers.

'Are you okay?' I whispered.

'Yep. I'm good,' he whispered back.

I moved a little further into the room.

'I know this will be hard, but honestly, just ask me if you need anything. I want to be here for you, Todd. Don't feel embarrassed or scared, okay?' I said in a slightly louder whisper.

'Okay, Frankie. Thanks. You're a good girl. You always were.'

I smiled and retreated from the room, pulling the door back to where it was.

* * *

I wandered around downstairs, checking and rechecking the windows and back door and front door. Then I realised I hadn't checked or looked at my phone for hours. There were seven voice messages. The first was from the hospital to say that there was a bag of personal belongings of Todd's that had been taken from his jacket when he was brought in which they had forgotten to give me and could I come and collect it. The other six were all from Damian. The first one began calmly and by the sixth one he was screaming down the phone. He had been reliably informed that I had been seen coming into the house with a man with the kids today and could I please call him to tell him exactly what the fucking hell was going on. Of course, it was Harriet who would have told him.

I quickly sent a text to Damian explaining that he must have been mistaken and someone must have crossed paths with us as we came home from the pharmacy today. I explained I had gone out to buy Dioralyte for me and the kids for our dodgy tummies.

His response was:

I'll be over tomorrow to check on my kids

'Fuck,' I said. I put the phone down, put my hands over my face and rubbed my eyes. When I removed my hands I let out yelp.

Todd was standing in the doorway looking at me.

'Shit, Todd, you scared me,' I walked a little closer. He was shaking. 'Are you okay?'

'Yeah, my body has gone into hypo I reckon. Don't suppose you have any ganj, do you?'

I laughed and then I suddenly remembered the spliff that Maddox had found and played with. I still hadn't worked out where it could have come from. But I had a sneaky suspicion it belonged to Damian.

We settled in the snug with the window open an inch. I let Todd have a toke first and then I took a few tokes. It hit me almost immediately, but it was nice and reminded me of the old days. We could have been back there together, just us two. We chatted quietly and I asked him, probably too many times, if he was okay. I watched him as he began to doze softly on the sofa and was taken back to the times we spent together; although greyer round the edges and looking the worse for wear, he still had that same face, those same eyes, that same mouth I had kissed a thousand times. I was almost tempted to climb on to his lap and remind myself of the tenderness. But instead I let the marijuana envelop me and as I started to fall asleep, I dreamt of another Todd and me together in another time.

Kiefer insisted we ate in the pub for his twentieth birthday, which had been a few days previously. We only ever ate together when it was someone's birthday and it was usually a takeaway at home. But Mum and Dad wouldn't come out on a weekday so we saved the celebrations for Saturday night. There was a pub just down the road from our house that sold Dad's favourite bitter and did chips in baskets, which Mum saw as a treat, so we met them there.

I was fidgety and kept thinking about the evening and what I was going to wear.

Mum had bought Kiefer a toolkit and wanted to give it to him. I remember how he declined the birthday pint of beer Dad wanted to buy him because he was driving, and a pint was too much. He had only passed his test a few months before and it was all still such a novelty. I watched Kiefer as he sat and ate his chicken, wiping the grease from his chin with napkin after napkin, and smirking at how he was making such a mess of it, but not caring because it was just us four and it was so rare we ate together. When we got up to leave and go off and do our separate things on that Saturday evening,

Kiefer off to Lola's with Reese and me off to meet Todd to go to the party in the warehouse, we both kissed our mum and dad.

I noticed then that as Kiefer leant in for a kiss, Dad's arm, always slightly shaky from the nerves that had taken over his life at such a young age, grabbed hold of Kiefer's as they embraced; as though he wanted to cling on to his son for a few precious seconds. And so he did, his hand a bony grip already slightly rigid with arthritis.

In this crazy wild journey called life, those are the things that stick in my head, the things I look back on and remember with such poignancy, despite all the big things we go on to do in life: get married, have kids, buy houses, travel the world. When I recall memories it's those moments that play out so perfectly in my mind: a meal, a chat, an awkward embrace.

A kiss.

The last kiss.

I had slept the entire night on the sofa and I felt like hell for it. Todd was still asleep on the opposite sofa. It was early, barely 6 a.m.. I knew Maddox would be up within the hour but I didn't wish to wake Todd who looked like he was having the best sleep he'd had in years.

For the first time in a long while I didn't feel like going into work. I decided to call in sick. Half the office was off anyway, and Penelope hadn't been in for days.

I went to the kitchen to make coffee. Even though it was early I texted Aimee to ask her if she could take the children to school today.

I was sure Todd would feel better if I collected his things from the hospital and that he would feel more comfortable having a couple of personal items close by.

I was surprised yet again when Aimee replied just ten minutes later. It was only just gone 6 a.m..

I looked up and saw Todd standing in the doorway. He looked like a small child, there in joggers and sweatshirt, his thick straw-like hair standing to one side. I didn't want to be imagining it but somehow, he looked better, like those eight or nine hours of sleep on a warm cosy sofa had made a huge difference to him.

'Hi,' I said softly.

'Hi,' he said and came to the island and took a seat.

'Coffee?'

'Can't remember the last time I heard that in the morning,' Todd said, ruffling his hair to try to straighten it out but making no difference. I had always liked it that way anyway, it was like a separate entity and not part of his body. I thought of how many times I had run my hands through that hair.

'You left some bits at the hospital so I'll go and collect them for you today,' I said as I busied myself with making coffee.

'Oh, right, thanks. It won't be much. Basic stuff. Did you, er... so do you need me to look after the kids?' Todd said with panic in his voice.

'No, it's fine. We have a babysitter. You just need to stay here and rest. I'll get Aimee to take them to school.'

'Oh, okay.' Relief permeated his voice.

* * *

Aimee arrived a few hours later. The kids were dressed but slightly perturbed that they were being taken to school by Aimee and not me.

I walked them outside. 'It's just for today,' I said, zipping up Pixie's coat and kissing her nose and ruffling Maddox's hair. I went and stood next to my car as I waved them off down the street. I turned instinctively to look at the huge bay window. I saw Todd standing there. He was staring after the kids. Then he turned, noticed me looking and slipped back into the shadows.

* * *

I drove to the hospital, parked up and paid for a ticket even though I was only popping in for five minutes. I headed to the area where Todd had been taken in. I walked through the double doors to the small reception desk where a woman sat.

'Hi, I have come to collect Todd Wilson's belongings, he was discharged yesterday?'

She reached down under the counter and pulled out a clear plastic bag and handed it to me.

'Thanks,' I said, looking down at the bag, shocked by the weight of it. I had expected a few insignificant items, a lighter, cigarettes, a beaded bracelet like the ones Todd used to wear when we were younger. When I looked down, I saw through the plastic a dark rectangular shape. When I turned the bag over and looked closer I could see it was a mobile phone.

* * *

I sat in the car, unable to move, just staring at the phone through the plastic. Todd had been unmoved by the idea of me going to the hospital to collect his belongings, he had made no claim to a mobile phone, but here it was in a bag amongst three lighters, a tiny dirty notebook, some screwed up receipts, and a supermarket gift card.

I took out the phone, and began to inspect it. It was turned off. It was a simple small Nokia phone. New looking. The screen was unscratched. I thought that was strange considering Todd had been living rough although it wasn't unusual to see the homeless with mobile phones; this type probably cost next to nothing to buy brand new. There were no fancy bells or whistles. It was for ringing and sending texts only.

It was a seamless action as I pressed the on button and it fired to life. No code. Without any hesitation or thought for what I was really doing or indeed might discover I took my own phone out and scrolled down to the messages I had received recently from the unrecognised number. I went into the info of the message which took me to the number. I pressed the phone icon and sat still for few seconds with both phones in my hand, mine in my right, Todd's in my left. I watched in sheer horror as the phone in my left hand sprang to life; vibrating and lighting up as my name appeared on the screen.

* * *

I would look back on the drive home and not be able to recall it at all. When I pulled up outside my house I immediately called the police who instructed me to stay in the car. Two police officers, one man and one woman, arrived ten minutes later and got out of the estate car rather too casually for my liking. They wandered over to my window with precision and no speed. My heart was hammering in my chest. I was paralysed with fear. Fear for having put the kids in danger by allowing Todd into the house, but also fear for what would now happen to Todd. None of this was his fault. If I had been able to help him earlier on in life, he wouldn't feel such injustice.

I sat shaking in the car. Terrified to go and face Todd.

The police took both phones and tallied up the messages. I explained our past, who Todd was to me, the anonymous birthday card, the replicas of Kiefer's car that came through my letter box late at night and on my doorstep. The male officer talked to me through the car door. I tried to focus on his words.

'There isn't anything of any threat on these messages so there's nothing we can do with regards to those. All we can do is escort Mr Wilson from your premises and drop him off somewhere of his choosing. Of course, if he shows up threatening you, call us immediately.'

I felt sick at all that I had done, how we had all slept under the same roof. I wondered what he might have stolen, then at the same time I felt sick at what I had put Todd through, I had promised to help him, he had reached out to me, but of course, it all had to have been a ploy to get into my house, where he had wanted to be all along. He said he knew where I lived, lying that he didn't know the exact house but only the street. Of course he knew my house. He had put that toy replica car through the letter box and the fortieth birthday card. Only he knew me well enough to do all these things.

I thought I was going to throw up.

'Just called for a couple of extra officers to help us remove Mr Wilson from the property. We don't know how strong he is,' said the female officer.

'He's big, but not that strong.' I thought how the streets had stripped the fat and muscle from him and how he was a skinny body on that tall frame. But the body was capable of amazing strength in times of stress and I didn't know how Todd would react.

Two minutes later another car appeared, and two male police officers got out. I felt terrible for all the fuss I had caused. Four police here just because of what I had done.

'Can you get out of the car, Mrs Keegan, and open the front door for us,' one of the male officers from the second car said.

'Oh yes, yes, of course.' I got out of the car and fumbled in my handbag for my house keys. I walked uncertainly to the front door, not knowing what would happen. The male and female officer went around through the side gate and I stepped back to let the two male police officers in.

'Where might Mr Wilson be?' one said to me.

'Erm, upstairs or in the kitchen?'

One police officer bounded up the stairs two at a time and the other walked through towards the kitchen. I saw Todd come out of the snug on the left; the door had been closed. He stood looking tired as though he had just woken, and cocked his head.

'Frankie?' he said as the male officer arrived back down the hallway from the kitchen. I saw the other officer make it down the stairs, then both of them were next to Todd.

'Frankie?' he questioned again.

'Mr Wilson, we're here to escort you from the premises. Can you come with us now, please?' and they each took an arm.

'What? Frank? Frankie, what's going on?'

I looked at the front door which was still open and the female police officer standing at the door. I presumed the other officer was still at the back door in case Todd made a run for it. But he was compliant, not making any sudden movements. Part of me wanted to hand him a wad of cash before he went or some food or water. I didn't know if he would end up back on the streets again tonight. He didn't have anywhere else to go. My mind was a muddle of emotions. What had I done? I wanted to reverse time to a few days ago when I went to talk to him in the park. I should have stayed clear of him and just called the police instead. But the biggest part of me wished I could go back twenty years and not have gone to that party with him.

There were smoke machines, huge speakers and girls skating round on eighties-style chunky roller boots with rainbow stripes down the side. There were large inflatables being thrown around the room, as though I was at a freestyle swim session at the local pool. There was a girl in the DJ booth I recognised from some other parties; she had pink hair in bunches, a white vest top, and was chewing gum, one headphone on her ear clamped underneath her shoulder. The top half of her body was bouncing up and down to the music, she leaned over mixing one record into another.

The dance floor was alight with everyone dancing, pure euphoria seeping from every crevice. I knew then I had made the right decision to come to this party and not follow Kiefer's advice.

Todd took my hand. A stack of upturned beer crates to waist height topped with a long piece of wood across the top served as a makeshift bar. There were bottles of water, cans of Pepsi, vodka mules, Hooch, Bacardi Breezers and even little bottles of champagne with straws. To the side were beers floating on top of an ice packed bin.

I pointed at a beer and Todd took two, dropping a five pound note on the bar. I was wearing an all-in-one jumpsuit, purple with white stripes down the side and my white knee high boots. Todd said I looked like someone from the seventies and that I looked cool. I took out two cigarettes from my white patent rucksack and lit them both, handing one to Todd. We saw some people we knew and went over to where they were dancing and talking. We tried to shout at one another over the music and then the speed I had taken in the car ride over here began to bring me up. Todd was going to wait, there was new dealer there with some ecstasy. Rumoured to be pure MDMA. A few minutes later Todd spied the guy he was meeting.

I found myself being drawn closer and closer to the dance floor, I was edging away from Todd. I could see him at the other end of the warehouse and I watched the deal take place. I saw Todd take something out of his hand and place it on his tongue then wash it down with a beer. I felt happy that he was going to be on the same wavelength as me. The DJ dropped 'Where Love Lives' by Alison Lymerick. Everyone's hands shot up in the air as the dance floor lit up with electrifying greens, yellows and pinks. I danced and looked around for Todd. He was still standing where he was, alone, sipping his beer. I gestured for him to come over, he didn't seem to see me. But then he looked at someone approaching on his left. I tried again to beckon to him, but whoever Todd was talking to had his full attention. I could see Todd was leaning into the person, talking in their ear. Then he pulled back and I could see Lofty and in the corner, in the shadows a few steps behind him, Soames.

Lofty was handing Todd a bag. Instinct kicked in, I lunged forward and pushed my way past the crowds of arms in the air towards Todd. Soames looked at me in surprise. Todd went to shove the packet in his pocket, but I knew what it was so I grabbed his hand.

'No,' I said firmly.

Behind me someone grabbed my other arm. I looked around, it was Soames, looking dodgy as hell.

'Hey, leave him alone,' he said.

I shook his arm off mine.

'No, you leave him alone,' I spat.

'You need to learn some manners, love. Let the man decide what he wants,' Lofty said slowly, his eyes half closed.

Suddenly I didn't care for the lights and the music, the amphetamine that still coursed through my veins, and then I felt another hand on my arm. I went to shake it off.

'Get off.' I spun round. I was surprised to see it was Kiefer.

'What are you doing?' I shouted over the music.

'You need to get out of here now!'

'Why?'

'The police. They are on their way.'

'What? Really?' I said.

'Yes!' Kiefer shouted and was nodding his head enthusiastically. 'We need to go now.'

I looked back at Todd. 'Todd, what are you doing? Let's go.' Soames and Lofty had already disappeared.

'Chill out. It will be fine.' Todd went to put his arm around me and draw me closer. I shook him off.

'Frankie, stay. Please.'

'Kiefer said the cops are on their way!'

Todd shook his head. 'He hates me.' He pointed at Kiefer with his beer bottle.

'No, he doesn't.' I tried to reassure him.

'No, he does, he wants you to go 'cos he hates me. He's been trying to get between us for weeks.'

'He said the police are coming. He drove all the way out here to tell me that,' I said.

Todd shook his head, I fumbled into his pocket so I could grab what he had shoved in there and throw it down the toilet or empty it into a bush. He realised, too late, what I was doing.

Kiefer looked at me and grabbed my arm.

'Frankie. We have to—'

But before he could finish his sentence there was a huge commotion at the front of the warehouse. People were being pushed out of the way. Huge bright torches were being shone into the building, almost completely illuminating it. The police were here.

'Shit, Frankie!' Kiefer said and grabbed my arm. He pulled me and I jerked away from Todd who didn't seem to notice what was going on. Kiefer pulled me towards the DJ's booth where there was a back door. We pushed it open and there a policewoman in body armour stood in front of us. We both shot past her, Kiefer must have bashed his body against hers as she stumbled backwards. There were three other policemen heading our way but we shot past them and veered to the left where there was the old abandoned coach park, now brimming with cars. We weaved our way in and out of the cars until we found ourselves next to a small brook. We jumped across some rocks, with Kiefer leading the way all the time until we were on the other side and then we were on a small towpath next to a canal. Opposite us was a bridge which took us to the other side of the towpath where some steps lead up to a small dark street.

'How the hell do you know where we are?' I said, out of breath.

'I know these streets, Frankie, more than you know. I parked the car up there, look.'

He pointed to his green Mini a few feet away.

'Okay,' I said, barely able to speak, I was so out of breath.

We got into Kiefer's car and immediately heard the sound of sirens.

Kiefer started the engine and I went to put my seatbelt on when I realised I was still holding the drugs that Todd had been given.

'Kiefer, look.' I held out the plastic bag in my hand which contained some brown powder.

We were both startled by a loud rapping on the window. I turned in the darkness to see a figure outside but even with no lights in the street I could see it was a copper.

'Shit,' Kiefer said again and accelerated really hard so the wheels spun. I watched as the policeman stepped back in alarm and started hurrying in the other direction.

'Fuck, fuck, fuck, what do I do with this gear?' I said.

'In five minutes open the window and throw it out.' Kiefer instructed.

'Okay.' I sat tight. I could hear Kiefer breathing hard as he manoeuvred the car, changing gear and turning. He was still driving carefully but he was going faster than I had ever seen him drive before. We drove round some small village streets for a few more minutes until we reached a junction which would lead us onto a country road that would take us back into town. We sat at the junction as Kiefer looked left and right and then we heard the siren.

'Go!' I screamed and Kiefer accelerated out into the road.

'How did you know?' I said quietly once we were safely on a straight bit of country road.

'I just knew, Frankie, when will you ever learn to trust me?'

I looked down at my white boots which now had splodges of mud all over them. I thought about how I had put them on a few hours earlier all ready to enjoy a night out. Now here I was being driven away from chaos and potentially with a police car on our tail.

'Is it bad?' I asked.

'Yes, Frankie, it's bad. All those lot are bad. Todd has fallen in with a bad crowd, he has been for a long time, Soames and Lofty are dodgy as anything. You need to stay away from all of them, do you understand?'

I was beginning to but the thought of never being able to speak to Todd again was heart-breaking.

We drove along the country road for what felt like a long time. I didn't speak and neither did Kiefer. I looked over at him, I was worried about him having not really driven on these country roads much before, even though he said he knew them; he had only been driving for a few months. I could feel the car clinging to the road as we hurtled around the corners. Kiefer looked focused, not tearing his eyes from the road for a second. I needed to trust him. He took a sudden swerve to the left as we hit a corner that Kiefer hadn't seen coming.

'Shit,' Kiefer mumbled under his breath. I could feel the tension rising in the car. We couldn't hear any sirens any more.

'Can I throw the gear?' I asked with a wobble to my voice.

'Yes,' came Keifer's tight reply. I wound the window down two inches and posted the bag out of it.

Kiefer took another hard corner and I clung to my seat. We were still five miles from the town.

He was staring hard at the road and wouldn't take his eyes away from it. I felt him hit the brakes for a second and my body was flung to the side of the car as he took another corner. Once we had rounded that one we were still travelling at some speed and then I saw it, the mass of trees and bushes and then I knew it was too late. I was thrown forward. I felt the seatbelt cut itself across my neck as the car slammed into something and the windshield imploded. And then... nothing.

I sat in the house cradling a cup of coffee and considered swapping it for something stronger when my phone rang. It was Damian.

'What the bloody hell is going on? Harriet has just rung to tell me there are two police cars outside the house.'

'We had a scare; I witnessed a crime and they needed to come and get a statement,' I said off the top of my head.

'This is bollocks, Frankie. I'm coming over.'

'No, Damian. You can't. I don't want to see you,' I hissed. 'I know what you've been up to, leaving spliffs around for Maddox to pick up and play with, putting dead mice in the coffee cupboard, loosening all the screws on Pixie's bed so she nearly broke her neck the other night!'

'What? What happened? Is she okay? Frankie, you have lost the plot. Okay, I admit the spliff was mine. Harriet has been giving me some for free to help me while I try and figure stuff out.'

Then coming down the receiver at Damian's end I hear a, 'Hiiiii, I'm back!' really loud and Damian's muffled voice as he tried to talk to the person who just announced their entrance.

But it was too late, I already knew there's only one person who walks into a room and announces their entrance as loudly and as boldly as that. Damian came back on the line, trying to continue the conversation.

'Is that Nancy with you?' I asked, already knowing it was.

'What? No.'

'Damian, shut up, you're lying. I know my best friend's voice anywhere.'

Damian let out a sigh and started talking in a hushed tone.

'Fine. I've been staying here. Rob's place wasn't available. Harry has been away, and Nancy said it was fine to stay. I can go to Rob's next week. It's just temporary.'

'But you've been at Nancy's all this time?'

'Yes and she said she was going to tell you and she obviously hasn't so that's not my—'

'But you hate her?' I interrupted Damian.

'I don't hate her, Frankie, I just found her to be a bit over the top, but she's been really helpful and a real listening ear since you and I, well, since you started this job and you have barely been here.'

'Has she, now.'

'Listen, Frankie, don't think anything of this, it's just—'

'Was she in our house? In our bedroom?'

'What? I don't know – maybe? I was showing her where you keep your diaries. We've both been worried about you. I have wanted to try and help you and I just don't know how to any more.'

'I knew there was something dodgy going on when Nancy knew all the details of Mason's dinner party and I hadn't told her anything. Then she was cagey on the phone and when she came here she could barely look at me. The pair of you deserve each other.'

'Oh, come on, Frankie, this is a massive issue between us that has been going on for far too long and we needed to find a way to sort it out. Nancy was just stepping in to help.'

'I know exactly what she was doing. I found her earring in the bedroom. I know what you got up to when I was away. Well she can have you, Damian, 'cos I'm done with the pair of you.'

'I—' Damian tried to interrupt.

'Oh, and I've changed the locks on the doors, Damian, so don't try coming back here 'cos if you do I'll call the police and tell them you tried to murder our daughter.'

'Frankie, what the – you've lost your mind, you need help!'

'No, Damian, I do not. Now leave us alone.'

I pressed the red button to end the call, longing for the days of the landline so I could smash the receiver down as hard as I could.

* * *

That night, once I had the kids in bed, I went to the fridge and poured myself a glass of wine. My head was spinning. There were text messages all over my phone from Damian asking me to call him because we needed to talk this through and then some from Nancy apologising for not saying Damian was staying there and that they were both worried about me. It was such tripe. I turned my phone off but not before a text came through from Mason.

Hope you feel better. Let me know if you need anything. I want to help
M x

I looked at the text for a good minute or so, my finger hovering over the reply bar, a thousand thoughts racing though my head about what I could say to him, without making my life sound like the total disaster that it was right now.

I'm feeling better. See you on Monday x

Ok, if you're sure. Thinking of you. Take care M x

I put the phone down and went upstairs to take a shower. The day had run away with me and I had been sweating non-stop. I stopped by the spare room I had made up for Todd, and I stared at how he had made the bed neatly, then my eyes were drawn to some bits of debris on the duvet. I wondered where they could have come from. I looked up at the ceiling. To the left of the bed was the hatch to the attic. I couldn't tell if it was slightly on an angle as though it had been opened recently or if I was imagining it. Perhaps Damian had been up there when he came over to collect things, but thinking back, Damian wouldn't have had much time to do anything if he had spent so long dismantling Pixie's bed. Maybe Todd had looked up there for a nose around. I didn't like attics. I found them to be such sad places. I had only poked my head into ours once when we moved in to agree with Damian that indeed it was very roomy and could one day make a very nice conversion. I looked at the neat bed again. I didn't need to worry any more. Todd wasn't here and the locks had been changed.

* * *

I hadn't slept in my room last night and when I went in I looked at the floor where I had left the notebooks, one open on the page where I had written in it. I looked at the words and how they were such a contrast to my diary entries from twenty years ago. I was angry then. I felt a terrible sense of injustice about what happened on that night and I thought bringing Todd into my house would help repair what I had been feeling and would try to bring some balance back to all the chaos, but it hadn't. I should have known Todd still held a grudge against me for what happened that night, for Kiefer and I running away and leaving him there to get arrested. Was I then to blame for his rapid decline and for why he was on the streets? Yes, I felt some responsibility, but who was the biggest loser of all from that night? Not Todd. But Kiefer.

Kiefer, who lost his life trying to rescue me.

52

OCTOBER 1998

I lay crumpled on one side. I touched my lip, it was bleeding. I looked over at Kiefer, his head tilted to one side, blood coming from his mouth. His eyes were slightly open. I reached out, I tried to touch him. I didn't dare touch him. I couldn't move. I couldn't speak.

I could hear a siren coming closer and closer and then the shattering sound of glass and metal hitting metal. Then silence.

I tried to lie in bed in the dark and sleep, but my mind was whirring with a million thoughts about Todd and where he was now. I knew it was past midnight but I couldn't help but wonder about him; I didn't know him at all any more. I was a fool to let him in after so long.

I heard a loud thump and my heart leapt into my mouth. Perhaps one of the kids had fallen out of bed, but they hadn't done so for so long. I sat silently for a minute, waiting to hear one of them cry out. But they didn't.

All I could think of was Todd. Of course, he was going to come back. I should have called Mason; I should have brought someone round. I could still alert the police. I looked to my bedside table and my phone wasn't there. I remembered my anger from earlier when Damian was trying to contact me, and I realised I had switched it off and left it downstairs.

Eventually, after another minute, I slipped out of bed and took the baseball bat from Damian's side of the bed.

I went out into the hallway and peeked around the door of each child's bedroom and saw them sleeping.

I stood at the top of the stairs, staring down into the darkness. Something I felt I had been doing for so long and I was starting to tire of it. I had been a sitting duck all this time. I should have taken more precautions to keep me and the kids safe, not just changed the stupid locks, but involved people, brought in backup. I had been denying what had been happening, my senses hadn't been alert enough to the fact that someone had been bothering me, stalking me even. Why hadn't I reached out and taken the help Mason had offered? Because I felt silly? Because I felt I could manage on my own the way I had been doing for twenty years? I realised it was too late. I was stranded at the top of the stairs; my phone was downstairs. I was alone with my kids and there was someone in the house.

54

I unclipped my seat belt and pushed open the passenger door. The car was at an angle so I clung to the roof to pull myself out. I clambered through bracken that cut through my trousers. Sharp pain resonated through my legs, adding to the dull aches and tenderness I could feel in other parts of my body, my neck, my right arm. I found myself on an empty road; silence penetrated my ears. I shivered in my jumpsuit. I looked backwards. I could see Kiefer's car, smoke billowing around it as one headlamp remained alight, casting a misty glow. I was unable to decipher if I had just come from there or I was never there at all. Maybe I was dead and this was me, my spirit walking away from the wreckage. Was I in a dream? I needed to go to sleep. Then I could wake up from this nightmare. I turned round fully and saw, just beyond the wreckage, the woods. They looked so inviting, so warm. I stumbled across a ditch I had just scrambled up, past the car, fell down into the soft springy moss and leant back against a tree. I couldn't stop shivering, but I would be okay. I just needed to close my eyes and then it would all be over.

Suddenly there was a bright light shining at my face and I heard muffled words. It sounded as though someone was talking into a tin can. But it was just a dream so I kept my eyes closed and waited to wake up.

'Yes, the ambulance that was sent to the scene has been in a collision with another vehicle on the same road. Please send another ambulance,' came a loud female voice and then, 'Hello there, are you okay?'

I heard a few grunts and the torch light wavered as someone made their way closer to me.

I felt a hand on my arm. 'It's okay, love, just hang on in there, darling. Another ambulance will be along soon.'

I prised my eyes open and all I could see, illuminated by the torch light, just inches away from my eyes were four numbers, bright and white on the shoulder of a faceless woman. I couldn't take my eyes off them as her soothing words came at me. I started repeating the four numbers over and over: 2461, 2461, 2461, 2461, 2461... until eventually I heard a siren. This time it got louder and closer until I was being slowly lifted and carried. Suddenly weightless.

55

NOW

I walked down the stairs. I expected to see a broken pane of glass, but nothing. The kitchen light streamed bright, but I saw no evidence of anything.

I looked round the kitchen and then saw my phone on the island where I had left it. I grabbed it, turned it on and within a few seconds I was alerted to several text messages from Damian telling me to damn well pick up and reply to him.

Then there was another text, this time from an unrecognised sender. It wasn't from the same number I had been used to seeing messages from.

All it said was the same 4 digits over and over again.

2461, 2461, 2461, 2461...

56

OCTOBER 1998

I spent three days in hospital. Minor injuries really. But I was mostly in shock. I had seen doctors, nurses, psychologists, police, they had all been through to speak to me, but I had barely said a word. Then, on the final day before I left, a lady from a charity arrived; it was a charity for people who had lost loved ones in a road accident. She handed me a stack of coloured notepads.

'Take these. Write in them every day. Anything that comes to your head. Don't worry if it doesn't make sense, you just need to document your feelings. These are your diaries. Keep them to yourself. But this is part of your healing process. It will take some time, but these will help and you can look back on them some day and see how far you have come.'

I took them from her, tears welling up that hadn't left my eyes for three days. Just before she went, she handed me a pen.

I opened the first notebook and stared at the blank page for a long time before I finally took the lid off the pen and wrote the date: 28 October 1998.

Then I wrote the first and only thing I would write in those diaries for the next three weeks until they were almost full.

I took the pen, pressed it onto the paper and wrote 2, 4, 6, 1 over and over.

57

NOW

I took my phone and clutched it to my chest, walking slowly back up the stairs and into my bedroom. I put it down on the bedside table and then stood for a moment, my mind reaching for something it couldn't quite get to. Something wasn't right downstairs. I walked back the front door. To the left of the door was a small alcove where we put post. On top of the letters, placed clearly and obviously where I could see it, but where I had definitely not left it, was the toy Mini Cooper.

I lay on top of the hospital bed on the final day, waiting for Mum and Dad to come and collect me. They had had so many other practicalities to deal with over Kiefer's death that they weren't able to stay with me all the time. They were there for most of the visiting hours and Nancy was also there when she could be.

As I lay there I recognised the voice of the lady who had given me the notebooks, I knew it was her because I will always remember it as the kindest voice I had ever heard.

I sat up and looked at her as she walked past.

'Oh, hi,' she stopped at the end of my bed, 'You're still here?'

'Yes. Going home today.'

'How are you getting on with your notebooks?'

'Good,' I lied. Thinking of the number I had written over and over. Hoping she wouldn't make me open them and show her.

The woman was clutching more notebooks.

'Who are they for?' I asked.

'A woman in the next ward. She has a lot of feelings bottled up. She's already filled one book. Maybe you two could talk?'

'Maybe.'

'She lost someone too.' She said solemnly and walked away.

There were twenty more minutes until my mum and dad would arrive to collect me and take me home to our empty house without my brother, so I got up and walked to the next ward. I peered round the door and saw the woman from the charity sat in a chair with her back to me handing over the notebooks to a young woman lying in a bed. Her face was covered in a sort of thin mesh, with bits cut out for her eyes, nose and mouth. Her short dark hair was messy and greasy. I watched them from the doorway for a moment then skulked away.

I hurried back upstairs, then went back into my bedroom and gasped when I saw that every single one of the diaries were back on my bed and open. Did I leave them like that before I fell asleep? I was sure I had put them on the bedside table. Perhaps I hadn't? Perhaps I had left them on the end of the bed like I did sometimes with the kids' books or a magazine. Come to think of it, I was sure I had put them back in the safe and locked it.

I could feel a scream building up inside me. I tried to swallow it down but I felt as though I was going to choke. I scanned the room, looking for the children, looking for Damian, trying to find a plausible explanation.

I looked back down at the open pages. The numbers went on for five diaries, all except the final page of the last diary which back then I had left blank for some unknown reason. But I had written in it just the other day. And I could see from where I was standing; I had written just six words with bold print in capitals.

IT IS TIME TO FORGIVE YOURSELF.

I heard a rustle from the walk-in wardrobe. I thought it was one of the kids and expected to see Pixie or Maddox step forward, but instead it was someone else and I almost keeled over backwards. The wall saved my fall as I saw who stepped out of the shadows and into the room.

Mum and Dad came to pick me up. They barely spoke a word, there was a small gesture of a hug from Mum, and Dad shakily nodded at me a lot; a tight sympathetic smile etched across his lips. Dad picked up my overnight bag and we walked through wards and corridors towards the exit.

'What's that you got there?' Mum said slowly. I knew she had already started taking some tablets for the shock and her speech sounded slurred as she gestured to the pile of notebooks in my hand. I looked at them and did a quick count. I realised there were only five in my hand. The red one I had written in first was missing. I must have left it back in the ward. I turned and looked back along the long corridor we had just come down.

Mum stopped and looked at me. The walk back to the ward was too far. I began walking again and so did Mum.

'A lady from a charity gave them to me, she told me write in them, to help me deal with the shock and grief,' I said, looking down at the five remaining notebooks.

Mum nodded.

'There's a girl in the other ward, too, she's a bit older than me, she had burns on her face. She got some notebooks too.' I carried on giving my mum seemingly insignificant information.

'That's the girl from the other crash,' Mum said, no emotion to her tone.

'What other crash?' I asked.

'There were two accidents that night. Yours and Kiefer's. Then when the ambulance came to get you it crashed into a car, damaged that girl's face and killed her twin sister.' Mum stopped walking and looked ahead of her at nothing. 'Such a lot of death, so many young lives ruined.'

I thought she might cry but she just carried on walking.

I wasn't sure if it was the tablets or if she had seen something beyond that but as she looked into the distance, her stare was as cold as ice.

61

'What the hell!' I screamed, and before I knew what had happened, she was next to me with a knife held near to my throat. She closed the door and told me to move over to my dressing table chair and sit down.

I went to grab my phone but she stuck her leg out. I tripped and fell, hitting my head on the dressing table. I was stunned for a few seconds but then I realised my hands were being tied. I tried to struggle but it was too late, her leg was in the back of my knees. She was too fast. I lay on my side, thinking of the kids. What would happen to them.

I knew, as I lay there hearing her panting, the exertion of what had just happened had tired her and she was taking a moment to regain her strength, maybe suss her next move. But surely she had it all worked out? This had already all been so calculated. Little bits of information filtered through and I tried to piece them together like a jigsaw. Everything that had happened in the last few weeks, none of it had made any sense. I had doubted so many people. But this person was here for me.

I lay on my side, too terrified to try to turn my head. I could hear her breathing. She reached an arm over me to pull me more onto my back so she could see me, and more importantly, so that I could see her. And as she did I saw the scars on her arms.

I squeezed my eyes tight as she moved me to an upright position, leaning against the dressing table leg. Then I slowly opened one eye and then the other until she was framed fully in front of me.

'Hello, Frankie,' Penelope said.

62

NOW

'Was it you?' I asked her as she stood over me, beads of sweat clinging to her forehead. Her black hair was scraped back into a tight high ponytail. She was wearing a pale pink sweatshirt, the sleeves rolled up, and grey sweatpants. The knife in her hand hung by her side. A strange rational part of my brain was trying to work out where she got it from and whether it was one of mine from the kitchen.

'It depends what you are referring to, Frankie.' Penelope was shaking, she looked weak. I noticed she wasn't wearing any shoes. So many thoughts were rushing through my head. Mainly I needed to know the children would be safe. I needed to get to them.

'How did you get in my house? I had the locks changed, I locked all the doors and windows.'

'You left your keys at reception, Frankie, it isn't hard to get one copied.'

I shook my head in bewilderment. 'But I had the locks changed!' I said, my voice high with anxiety.

'Well, it's a good job I got my copy done and made use of your spare facilities before your locksmith showed up.'

'Meaning?'

'You have a very nice attic.'

I felt my blood run cold as I took in what Penelope was saying and then it all made some sense. That short gap after dropping off the key at reception had obviously been enough time for her to take it and then replace it before Damian collected it.

'I managed to get it cut, get in your house and, let's say... ummm, meddle a little, before I left again.'

'You! You did that to my daughter's bed?'

'Just a little preview of what was to come,' Penelope sneered at me. Beads of sweat clung to her face. There was a pungent smell coming from her. Was it possible she was in the attic all this time?

My heart pounded in my chest.

'You don't get to touch my kids, you hear me?' I shouted. I didn't care what she did to me.

'But I never even got the chance to have kids, did I? There was never going to be any kids. These,' Penelope pointed to the scars, 'these are the visible scars from that night, but my insides were crushed when that ambulance, the one sent out for you, hit my sister's car and killed her.'

I looked blankly at Penelope and realised they weren't self-inflicted wounds. They were wounds from shards of glass that splintered from the windscreen when her sister's car collided with an ambulance.

I wanted to know everything. If this was it, if Penelope was going to kill me for what happened to her, then I needed to somehow make sense of the last few weeks.

'There was never a man, was there? In the pub after work that night.'

'As soon as I saw you following Mason's Instagram account, I knew it was you. When I looked you up properly, I saw you had plenty of marketing experience. So I made sure you saw the job for New Product Developer. I too, was preparing for the twentieth anniversary of my sister's death. It wouldn't have mattered how drunk you were at the pub. I already knew.'

'I didn't kill your sister, Penelope. It was an accident. My brother wasn't drunk. He crashed the car on a dodgy road. Why were *you* out at that time of night?' I asked with contempt.

Penelope paced up and down the bedroom like a caged animal.

'I shouldn't have been in that car. I shouldn't have called my sister out. I had gone back to someone's house, I didn't know his name. I had been trying to become independent from her. People always thought we were supposed to be together all the time because we were twins. I only wanted one night out away from her. Just one! But I couldn't do it! She was always the wiser one, older by three minutes, for fuck's sake. When things turned sour with the guy, I knew I didn't have anyone else to turn to. I made my sister drive out and get me.'

Penelope stopped pacing and turned to face me. 'And she should have been able to drive safely there to come and get me without that ambulance that was there because of your stupid brother, running her off the road! It was your fault, Frankie. He drove out to collect you because it was an illegal rave. It was all over the papers. I sat in the goddamn inquest and watched you churn out all your sorrow. Pathetic! You didn't care about anyone but yourself!'

'I was sixteen,' I said as the tears fell down my cheeks. Fear penetrated my every fibre. She was a woman possessed. I now knew what she had been capable of. 'I was a child. I didn't know what I was doing.'

Penelope launched herself at me and stopped right in front of my face. The knife hung precariously close to my leg as it dangled from her hand.

'You had a choice. You could have not gone to that party!'

She rubbed her hand over her face.

'And you had a choice not to get drunk and go back to that guy's house. Alone!' I sobbed and Penelope stared through me as the weight of my words rang true.

We stayed there for a few minutes, me sitting on the floor and Penelope pacing. I started to think about all the ways I could coax Penelope out of her mindset. I had to keep the kids safe.

'It seems you've been a little busy entertaining, these last few days,' Penelope said spitefully. 'Quite the hostess, aren't you?'

I thought back to when Todd was here. I had bought myself a few extra days by having someone in the house, but why hadn't she struck last night? Why wait until now?

'You could have done this last night, surely? Why wait?'

'It was quite nice to have the peace and quiet, if I'm honest.' Penelope looked wide-eyed and wired as though she hadn't slept properly for days. 'I had a chance to write a few things down in my diary. I hadn't written in it for years. It was a good bit of reflection time.'

I suddenly thought of Todd, who I had blamed for all of this.

'And that phone, it was in Todd's belongings?'

'Planting a phone on an unconscious hobo isn't as difficult as you might think, Frankie.' I saw a small smirk appear across Penelope's face. 'I followed you out of the office many times. You would never have seen me, you were always so focused on your own dilemmas. He had been lying there for ages, unconscious. How could you just think that chucking some money at him would solve the problem?'

'I had to think about it before I brought him here. I have my kids to think about.' I paused.

'And my hotel room,' I said flatly as it all seemed so obvious. 'You knew about the number.'

Penelope stopped pacing and looked at me. 'I came to see you after the accident, at your bed, because that interfering woman from the charity told me I should. She told me you were in an accident and we might get on.'

Penelope stopped and did a loud snort, the same as I had heard her do in the office. 'What a joke that was! Of course, she didn't know who you were. That you and your stupid brother had killed my sister. She was just trying to be nice. But I heard the nurses discussing it one night as I passed their office. So I passed your bed on the way back to mine, saw you were sleeping and you had left your notebook open. It was just like mine only you had filled it up already with the same number over and over: 2461. And I knew the number must have some significance, otherwise why would you write it down so many times?

'When you were discharged, you left one behind. I kept it as a reminder to myself that one day I would find you and I would make you pay for what happened to my sister.'

'What was your sister's name?' My question was met with silence. Penelope sat down on the end of the bed, the knife dangling next to her leg. She seemed to be somewhere else in her mind.

I stayed quiet. I listened for the children.

'And it was you who booked the hotel rooms, and made sure I got that room number.'

'Yes, and it took a huge amount of my time up as well. Do you know how many hotels there are with rooms that have four numbers? Turns out not as many as you would think.'

I was listening to everything that Penelope was telling me, but I was also trying to think quickly and to shift ever so slightly, half an inch at a time. I wanted to aim to get my legs out to the side; I could lift myself to standing without the use of my arms. I tensed the muscles in my stomach and tried to subtly pull my legs towards my chest, all the while my ears pricked for the slightest sound from the children. I needed to get to them before all of this commotion woke one of them. And I knew it would be Pixie. She was the lighter sleeper. Maddox would sleep through every thunderstorm. I stole a glance at Penelope; her eyes were wide as though she were looking at something that wasn't there. I nudged my legs up a little more but the noise of my feet against the carpet brought Penelope's attention back into the room.

She jumped up and she was next to me. Her sour breath on my skin.

'What would you do, Frankie? Tell me? If you were me, what would you do?'

I thought quickly. This was my opportunity to say something that might have an impact on Penelope. I could change things; I could make this stop. All I could visualise were Pixie and Maddox in the next rooms and that either of them could wake at any moment.

'I would talk to someone, maybe get some help, maybe we could go together? Counselling?'

'I've had counselling,' Penelope snapped and stepped backwards. 'Loads of it and it hasn't changed anything. I still feel all this...' Penelope stopped and gestured up and down her body, 'this raging anger, it's there every day. It will never go away. I think the only way I can deal with it is by dealing with you! You were the one who did it. For years I wanted to hurt someone, your brother, but I knew he was dead. I knew your name but I would have thought after what happened you would have left town? But you stayed, all this time you were here and finally we are brought together by Mason Valentine. As soon as I saw you follow him on Instagram I knew it was you. I contacted the recruitment agency and gave them your details, and then you just came running. It was too easy really.' Penelope laughed loudly.

'Mummy,' came a voice from the doorway and my heart leapt into my throat. No, no, no. Penelope stood between me and Pixie in the doorway, her head darted towards me and then Pixie. She didn't know what to do.

'Go back to bed, sweetheart,' I said, my voice wobbling but it was too late, Penelope was at the doorway and had grabbed Pixie and was dragging her into the room.

'Owww, Mummy,' Pixie moaned.

'Sweetheart, it's okay, Mummy is okay,' I said weakly.

'You stand there.' Penelope pointed towards the wardrobe and Pixie, the ever-diligent child, complied and walked to the wardrobe. I could see she was tired, that her eyes were half closed.

'Did Mummy wake you up, darling?' I whispered as Pixie stood in her pyjamas, rubbing her eyes.

'I heard voices, loud voices—' Pixie said.

'That's enough!' Penelope shouted. 'Now, this has got a whole lot more complicated, hasn't it?'

'Mummy?' Pixie whined.

'Sweetheart, it's okay,' I said through tears.

Penelope paced the room, looking visibly stressed. She wouldn't hurt a child, surely?

Suddenly Penelope stopped pacing. She stood stock still.

'Look, Penelope—' I began.

'Shhh!' Penelope spat. 'I'm listening.'

I looked at Pixie, who had started to silently weep by this point.

Then I heard a sound so familiar, yet this morning I would have been happy to have never heard it again. The heavy clumping sound on the stairs meant Penelope was aware that someone was coming and so she headed for the door as though she might be able to stop them with her weight. At that point Pixie launched herself over to me.

'Try to untie me, baby,' I whispered and Pixie looked down at my hands behind my back and started to cry again.

'Get away from her,' Penelope shouted but the footsteps were coming closer and louder. Penelope was at the door, the knife poised in her hand, ready to stab who ever came through it.

I opened my mouth and screamed, 'Damian! Watch out!'

The door opened and Penelope launched herself towards it, shoving it closed. I heard a thud and Damian cried out. The door opened again, and this time Penelope wasn't quick enough, Damian was in the room, his nose bloodied but he quickly assessed what was going on. He headed towards Pixie but Penelope was at his side, the knife raised.

I tried to wriggle my arms to encourage Pixie to work faster and as she did I saw Damian had his hand on Penelope's arm. Penelope made a high-pitched squealing noise, then I heard a thud and saw Damian had managed to push her to the floor. Finally, I felt the rope slacken on my wrists.

Damian was at my side, taking over from Pixie. Questions flew from his mouth, questions I couldn't answer. He tugged at the rope as Pixie stood by, her hands shook as she tried to hold onto to my arm.

I screamed as I saw Penelope appear behind Damian, her arms raised above her head, the knife was gripped in her right hand and she was ready to plunge it into anything.

At the same time as my wrists became free, I pushed my hands to the floor and launched myself forward into Damian. The combination of both of our weights catapulted Penelope backwards towards the door. All the while I was aware that Pixie was there, that I couldn't let Pixie see anything that would traumatise her. I couldn't let her see death the way I did.

Damian scrambled to Penelope and lay on top of her, restraining her with one hand while he pulled his phone out of his pocket with the other. Penelope was dazed but still tried to fight back and managed to knock the phone out of Damian's hand. I lunged forward and grabbed it from the floor where it landed. I looked at Damian, who now had both hands firmly on Penelope.

'Call the police, now. Who the hell is this mad woman?' Damian half turned to look at me. I could see Penelope's legs kicking out from under him as she wailed like an animal in pain.

I punched three nines into Damian's phone and crouched on the floor as Pixie clung to my side. I spoke breathlessly into the phone.

'Please help us, there's an intruder in our house.'

I lay in bed, the duvet pulled up tight to my chest. I was shivering from the adrenaline, I couldn't seem to gain control over my legs. Pixie lay curled up next to me, her soft breath indicating she was finally asleep.

Damian opened the door and walked over to the bed.

'Maddox is asleep now.'

'Finally,' I said, my teeth chattering.

'He went back off fine.' Damian rubbed his head. He looked exhausted.

Maddox had woken as the police arrived and Penelope's screams and protests came to a deafening climax. Maddox, who slept though most things, woke sweaty and terrified.

Damian walked round to his side of our bed and sat down, his back to me. His head was in his hands.

'She could have killed you. She could have killed you all,' Damian whispered. Even though the kids were both asleep we didn't want to risk them ever hearing anything they didn't need to. Luckily, Maddox would have forgotten about it by the morning and we could fob him off with a nightmare as he had remained in a half asleep state. But Pixie, my darling Pixie, had seen too much. I would need to spend a lot of time with her over the next few days to try and help her make sense of it all.

Damian stood up and began to remove his jeans. He climbed into bed wearing his t-shirt and boxers. Even with Pixie between us I could feel him shivering.

I took my hand off the duvet where I had been clutching it and reached over Pixie's body and took his hand in mine. We both lay there, holding each other's hands for what felt like a long time. I had so much to say to Damian, so many words were hanging on the edge of my tongue, but I didn't know where to start.

We had grown so far apart recently but as we lay and held hands, it felt as though the gap that had opened up between us could be slowly closing. I knew Damian was a good man. I had been so lost. I had carried the false memory of my diaries for so long and told Damian over and over that I had done my therapy. But I had barely begun to scratch the surface of dealing with my grief. I had been carrying it with me for two decades, hiding behind alcohol and seeking protection from my feelings in my place of work. I had even sought comfort from Mason.

Then there was the blame for all the inexplicable incidents. I had suspected everyone at some point, even my own husband and best friend. And then, of course, there was Todd. I couldn't bear to think where he could possibly be now and what I had put him through these last few days; being there for him one minute and turfing him out the next.

I vowed I would do everything to try to make it right for him. If I could find him. As much as the idea of him sheltering in his usual alleyway filled me with dread and fear for his safety, it was the only place I could begin to look for him.

I gave Damian's hand a gentle squeeze.

'I'm sorry,' I whispered and my voice broke as the tears fell from my eyes.

Damian squeezed my hand back, then he sat up, leant over Pixie and kissed my head and I felt, for the first time in a long while, that I was safe.

* * *

The next morning I snuggled the kids up in the snug with hot chocolate and a happy family film.

Later that day a text came through. It was from Mason and I realised the police must have been in touch with him.

Frankie, I am in shock. I cannot believe what has happened. Please accept my sincere condolences to you and your family for what you went through last night and these last few weeks. Take as long as you need. We can talk again when you are ready. Mason x

'I've called the guy to come out and repair the window,' Damian said as he came back into the room, having just checked on the kids.

'It was quite an adventure just getting in through that last night,' Damian scoffed, and I looked at the small bandage on his arm where one of the police had kindly wrapped it up for him, instructing him to get to the doctor if it showed any signs of infection. But it was a small cut. The fact I had refused to answer his calls and texts had driven Damion to distraction. He said he couldn't stay away and so came over to check on us. When he realised that I had indeed changed the locks he decided to smash the window.

I sat on the sofa in the kitchen, a thick cardigan wrapped around myself. Damian made us some coffee and came and sat next to me.

'I'm going to get some help now,' I said as Damian took his first sip. He just nodded.

'I'm sorry that I told you I was over Kiefer when I wasn't.'

'It's okay, Frankie.' Damian sat back and stroked my hair. 'You've been stuck in limbo. I get it. Just take your time. We'll find the right person to talk to.' He cleared his throat, 'And um, well, you know, I haven't been feeling at my best lately. I've been really stressed and getting down about everything, work, us. I didn't know what to do any more. Hence the spliff.'

'And the running,' I said with a small smile in my voice.

Damian laughed. 'Yeah, and the running.'

I had one question that had been lingering and I hadn't wanted to ask it but I knew I couldn't wait any longer.

'Why did you stay with Nancy?' I asked, taking a sip of my coffee.

'I told you, she just offered.' Then he cleared his throat. 'I think… she's lonely. Her and Harry, I'm not so sure it's going well.'

I absorbed Damian's words. 'Do you think she saw an opportunity, what with us separated?'

Damian took his hand off my head. And cradled his coffee. 'I don't know, Frank. That's a conversation you need to have with her.'

I thought about Nancy and how that conversation would go. I wasn't worried. I knew now I had barely been myself for twenty years. What kind of a friend had I been to her if I couldn't see what was going on in her life?

* * *

Three days later I felt ready to leave the house. I was going to meet Mason for coffee around the corner from the Bliss offices.

He pulled me into a tight embrace and I inhaled that scent of his that had been distracting me and sending confusing signals for so long.

But I knew now what I had been feeling towards Mason was not love or lust, but a longing. A need to escape from my own mind that I had not had any control over for so long.

'I'm not sure I can come back, you know,' I said to Mason. 'After everything, that office. Plus, us, you know…'

'Frankie, there was no us. I know that.' Mason smiled at me and then sipped his coffee and placed it gently down on the table between us. 'Don't you worry, Keegan. We'll work it out – if I have to find new offices and start again somewhere, I will. And you can work any hours you like. I just like having you on my team.' Mason gave a rueful smile. 'Just let me know if there is anything I can do for you. I mean it, anything.'

I wasn't ready to make any decisions yet about my job, but I knew where I needed to go and where the help that Mason was so determined to give me could be utilised.

* * *

I left Mason at the coffee shop and took a slow walk back up the road, knowing where I was headed. I reached the alleyway and peered in. It was still early so I could see a few figures curled up along the side of the wall. It was cold. The unforgiving November wind had set in and there was talk of snow soon.

I walked into the gloom of the alley and looked at the three piles of sleeping bags and blankets with bits of cardboard sticking out underneath. I tentatively went over to each one and lifted the blankets until I found him. I saw a flash of straw-like hair and I breathed a sigh of relief. I bent down and tugged at the blankets to rouse the body. He moved slightly and I leant into whisper.

'Todd. It's me, Frankie.'

'Huuuugh,' came a noise but no movement.

'I'm sorry for what happened. I know now it wasn't you. I'm so sorry.'

Todd's body shifted under the weight of all the blankets. I lifted the one so I could see his face. I sucked in my breath as I saw how terrible he looked. Red eyes and sore chapped lips. His eyes looked hollow but somewhere, underneath the darkness, I could see a tiny glimmer as he tried to smile.

'I will help you,' I said.

Todd blinked slowly and then closed his eyes.

I stayed with him for the rest of the morning, just reiterating to him that I would help him and that everything was going to be okay.

As the morning turned to afternoon a bright stream of light shone down the alleyway and I rose up and walked towards it. As I arrived out on the street the whole path was illuminated by the midday sun. I had been hiding in the shadows for so long, waiting for the darkness to find me and hold me captive. It was cold still and so I wrapped my coat tightly around me, took in a long deep breath and walked towards the light.

EPILOGUE

I looked around the room and took in the minimal décor. The walls were a sandy beige; they matched the two seater sofa I sat on. There was a coffee table to my right with the obligatory box of tissues and above that, on the wall, was a picture that had been separated into three. The broken pieces of the image hung next to one another with a two inch gap between them, looking like a half finished puzzle. I wondered if that was supposed to represent the clients who sat here daily, all of us little puzzle pieces that needed to be put back together.

I looked at Helen opposite me. She set aside her paperwork, crossed one leg over the other and leant in towards me with a warm smile.

'So, Frankie, can you tell me why you sought therapy and what particular issue led you to seek counselling?'

I took a deep breath and began to talk.

ACKNOWLEDGMENTS

Wow. What a year it's been. I can't actually believe I'm writing the acknowledgements for my second book.

Firstly, thank you to all the readers who bought and read my first book, *The Daughter In Law* and for continuing to support me on my writing journey.

The literary world is still so new to me and I'm learning all the time, so a huge thank you to my agent, Lina Langlee, for your all your advice and calm responses.

Thank you, Nia Beynon, for your input during the structural edits and for yet again making the second book a better version of what it was.

Thanks to the Boldwood team for all their dedication and hard work in 2019 into 2020. To be the first author launched in August last year was such an honour and I'm thrilled to bits to be here with my second book and now writing my third!

Thanks to fellow author, Rachael Lucas, who hosted the most perfect writing retreat in Yorkshire last year and where I was able to get a huge chunk of this novel written and polished.

Thanks, Chris, for being there for our beautiful babies whilst I make stuff up. They are all so young still and I know it's hard, but this time next year, Rodney...

Thanks again, Mum, for all you do and the unconditional love and support you give Chris and I.

Finally, I want to acknowledge every single person who was there with me throughout the nineties. Friends, boyfriends, club buddies. It was an era that shaped me. I still feel so much nostalgia for those special days. To all of you who are still here, and to those who are in another place... I love you all.

BOOK CLUB QUESTIONS

1. Which narrative did you prefer: 1998 or present day?
2. Do you think Frankie was imagining the tension and odd looks from colleagues in the office? Is this something you have ever experienced in an office environment before?
3. What is it about Mason that Frankie is most attracted to?
4. Can you empathise with 16-year-old Frankie and how much she cared for Todd?
5. Do agree with how present day Frankie took Todd in? Would you have done something similar?
6. Why do you think Frankie found it so hard to open up to Damion about her past and how she was feeling in the present day?
7. Do you think Nancy was a good friend to Frankie?
8. Why were 16-year-old Frankie's friends so important to her and how much do you feel we are shaped by our childhood friendships?

MORE FROM NINA MANNING

We hope you enjoyed reading *The Guilty Wife*. If you did, please leave a review.

If you'd like to gift a copy, this book is also available as an ebook, digital audio download and audiobook CD.

Sign up to Nina Manning's mailing list for news, competitions and updates on future books.

http://bit.ly/NinaManningNewsletter

The Daughter In Law, another gripping psychological thriller from Nina Manning, is available to order now.

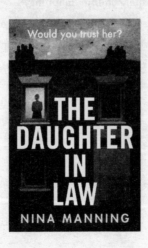

ABOUT THE AUTHOR

Nina Manning studied psychology and was a restaurant-owner and private chef (including to members of the royal family). She is the founder and co-host of Sniffing The Pages, a book review podcast. She lives in Dorset.

Visit Nina's website: https://www.ninamanningauthor.com/

Follow Nina on social media:

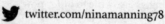 twitter.com/ninamanning78
instagram.com/ninamanning_author
facebook.com/ninamanningauthor1
bookbub.com/authors/nina-manning

ABOUT BOLDWOOD BOOKS

Boldwood Books is a fiction publishing company seeking out the best stories from around the world.

Find out more at www.boldwoodbooks.com

Sign up to the Book and Tonic newsletter for news, offers and competitions from Boldwood Books!

http://www.bit.ly/bookandtonic

We'd love to hear from you, follow us on social media:

facebook.com/BookandTonic

twitter.com/BoldwoodBooks

instagram.com/BookandTonic